A Sheaf of Corn by Mary E. Mann

"I WENT A PILGRIM THROUGH THE UNIVERSE,
AND COMMUNED OFT WITH STRANGERS AS I STRAYED,
IN EVERY CORNER SOME ADVANTAGE FOUND,
AND FROM EACH SHEAF OF CORN I DREW A BLADE"

Mary Rackham was born in Norwich, Norfolk on August 14th 1848.

After her marriage to a farmer, Fairman J. Mann, they moved to Shropham village. In her later writings this would become 'Dulditch'.

Her husband was a churchwarden and parish guardian. Mary was involved with the Union Workhouse, and was committed to visiting the sick and the less privileged of the parish. Much of these experiences would later be used in her literary works.

Mary took up writing during the early 1880s and published her first novel, 'The Parish of Hilby' in 1883. It was the beginning of a long and productive career spanning 35 years during which she wrote forty works with the majority concerning the Norfolk yeoman farmers during the late 19th century as they endured agricultural and economic upheaval. Her stories are true and authentic accounts of the local poverty, deprivation and of rural English life.

With the death of her husband in 1913, she moved to Sheringham, where she died, aged 80, on May 19th 1929.

She was buried in Shropham churchyard.

She has been admired by writers of the stature of A. S. Byatt and D. H. Lawrence. Some critics her called her Norfolk's Thomas Hardy.

Index of Contents

A SHEAF OF CORN

WOMEN O' DULDITCH

Dinah Brome stood in the village shop, watching, with eyes keen to detect the slightest discrepancy in the operation, the weighing of her weekly parcels of grocery.

She was a strong, wholesome-looking woman of three-or four-and-forty, with a clean, red skin, clear eyes, dark hair, crinkling crisply beneath her sober, respectable hat. All her clothes were sober and respectable, and her whole mien. No one would have guessed from it that she had not a shred of character to her back.

The knowledge of this incontrovertible fact did not influence the demeanour of the shop-woman towards her. There was not better pay in the village, nor a more constant customer than Dinah Brome. In such circumstances, Mrs Littleproud was not the woman to throw stones.

"They tell me as how Depper's wife ain't a-goin' to get over this here sickness she've got," she said, tucking in the edges of the whitey-brown paper upon the half-pound of moist sugar taken from the scales. "The doctor, he ha'n't put a name to her illness, but 'tis one as'll carry her off, he say."

"A quarter pound o' butter," Dinah unmovedly said. "The best, please. I don't fancy none o' that that ha' got the taste o' the shop in it."

"Doctor, he put his hid in at the door this afternoon," Mrs Littleproud went on; "he'd got his monkey up, the old doctor had! 'Tis a rank shame,' he say, 'there ain't none o' these here lazy women o' Dulditch with heart enough to go to help that poor critter in her necessity,' he say."

"Ler'm help her hisself," said Mrs Brome, strong in her indifference. "A couple o' boxes o' matches, Mrs Littleproud; and you can gi' me the odd ha'penny in clo' balls for the disgestion."

"You should ha' heered 'm run on! 'Where be that Dinah Brome?' he say, 'that ha' showed herself helpful in other folks' houses. Wha's she a-doin' of, that she can't do a neighbour's part here?'"

"And you telled 'm she was a-mindin' of 'er own business, I hope?" Mrs Brome suggested, in calmest unconcern.

"I'll tell you what I did say, Dinah, bor," the shop-woman said, transferring the sticky clove-balls from their bottle to her own greasy palm. "'Dinah Brome, sir,' I say, 'is the most industrousest woman in Dulditch; arly and late,' I say, 'she's at wark; and as for her floors—you might eat off of 'em.'" She screwed the half-dozen hard red balls in their bit of paper, and stowed them lightly in the customer's basket. "That the lot this week, Dinah?"

Dinah removed her basket from counter to arm. "What'd he got to say for hisself, then?" she asked.

"'A woman like that can allust make time,' the old doctor he say. 'Tell her to make time to help this here pore sufferin' woman.' I'm a-sayin' it as he said it, Dinah. I ain't a-hintin' of it myself, bor."

"Ler'm tell me, hisself, an old interfarin' old fule, and he'll ha' the rough side o' my tongue," the customer said; and nodded an unsmiling good-afternoon, and went on her way.

Her way led her past the cottage of the woman of whom they had spoken. Depper's cottage, indeed, was the first in the row of which Dinah's was the last—a half-dozen two-roomed tenements, living-room below, bedroom above, standing with their backs to the road, from which they were divided by no garden, nor even so much as a narrow path. The lower window of the two allotted to each house was about four or five feet from the ground, and was of course the window of the living-room. Mrs Brome, as she passed that of the first house in the row, suddenly yielded to the impulse to stop and look within.

A small interior, with furniture much too big for it; a huge chest of drawers, of oak with brass fittings; a broken-down couch as big as a bed, covered with a dingy shawl, a man's greatcoat, a red flannel petticoat; a table cumbered with the remains of wretched meals never cleared away, and the poor cooking utensils of impoverished, shifty housekeeping.

The woman of whom they had been speaking stood with her back to the window. A stooping, drooping skeleton of a woman, who, with weak, shaking hands, kneaded some dough in which a few currants were stuck, before laying it on a black-looking baking tin.

"A fine time o' day to bake his fourses cake!" the woman outside commented, reaching on tiptoe, the better to look in at the window.

The tin having its complement of cakes, the sick woman essayed to carry it to the oven. But its weight was too much for her; it hung limply in her weak grasp; before the oven was reached the cakes were on the ragged carpet of the hearth.

"God in heaven!" ejaculated the woman looking in.

She watched while the poor woman within dropped on all-fours, feebly trying to gather up the cakes spreading themselves slowly over the dirty floor.

"If that don't make me sick!" said Dinah Brome to herself as she turned and went on her way.

The cottage of Dinah Brome, distant from that of Depper's wife by a score or so of yards, was, in its domestic economy, as removed from it as the North Pole from the South. Small wonder that Depper—his name was William Kittle, a fact of which the neighbourhood made no practical use, which he himself only recalled with an effort—preferred to the dirt, untidiness and squalor of his own abode the spick-and-span cleanliness of Dinah Brome's. Small wonder that in this atmosphere of wholesomeness and comfort, he chose to spend the hours of the Sabbath during which the public-house was closed; and other hours. Small wonder, looking at the fine, capable figure of the woman, now bustling about with teapot and cups, he should esteem Mrs Brome personally above the slatternly skeleton at his own hearth.

Having made a cup of tea and cut a couple of slices of bread-and-butter, the owner of the fresh-scrubbed bricks, the fresh polished furniture, the dazzlingly white hearth, turned her back on her household gods, and, plate and cup in hands, betook herself, by way of the uneven bricked passage separating the row of houses from their rows of gardens at the back, to the house of the wife of Depper.

"I swore I wouldn't," she said to herself as she went along; "but I'm dinged if the sight o' Depper's old woman a-crawlin' arter them mamucked up bits o' dough ha'n't tarned my stomach!"

She knocked at the door with the toe of her boot, her hands being full, and receiving no answer, opened it and went in.

Depper's old woman had fallen, a miserable heap of bones and dingy clothing, upon the broken-down couch, and had fainted there.

"I'd suner 'twas anyone in the warld than you a-waitin' on me like this," she said, when, consciousness having returned during the ministrations of the other woman, her weary eyes opened upon the healthy face above her.

"And the las' time you told me to walk out o' your house, I swore I'd never set fut in it again," Mrs Brome made answer. "But I ha' swallered worse things in my time than my own wards, I make no doubt; and you ha' come to a pass, Car'line Kittle, when you ha' got to take what you can git and be thankful."

"Pass? I ha' come to a pass, indeed!" the sick woman moaned. "You're wholly right there, bor; wholly right."

"So now you ha' got to drink this here cup o' hot tea I ha' brought ye; and let me help ye upstairs to yer bed as quick as may be."

"When I ha' baked Depper's fourses cake, and sent it off by 'Meelyer's little gal—she ha' lent her to me to go back and forth to the harvest-field, 'Meelyer have—I kin go," the wife said; "not afore," hiccoughing loudly over the tea she tried to drink; "not afore—not afore! Oh, how I wish I could, bor; how I wish I could!"

"You're a-goin', this instant minute," the masterful Dinah declared.

The other had not the strength to resist. "I'm wholly done," she murmured, helplessly, "wholly done at last."

"My! How ha' you got up these here stairs alone?" Dinah, having half-dragged, half-carried the feeble creature to the top, demanded of her, wiping her own brow.

"Crawled, all-fours." Depper's wife panted out the explanation. "And to git down 'em i' the mornin's—oh, the Lord alone knows how I ha' got down 'em i' th' mornin's. Thankful I'd be to know I'd never ha' to come down 'em agin."

"You never will," said Mrs Brome.

"I don't want to trouble you, no fudder. I can fend for myself now," the poor woman said, when at length she lay at peace between the sheets; her face bathed, and the limp grimy fingers; the scant dry hair smoothed decently down the fallen temples. "I'd rather it'd ha' been another woman that had done me the sarvice, but I ain't above bein' thankful to you, for all that. All I'll ask of ye now,

Dinah Brome, is that ye'll have an eye to Depper's fourses cake in th' oven, and see that 'Meelyer's gal take it and his home-brew, comf'table, to th' field for 'm."

Dinah, having folded the woman's clothes, spread them for additional warmth upon the poor bed-covering. "Don't you worrit no more about Depper," she said, "Strike me, you're the one that want seem' to now, Car'line."

The slow tears oozed beneath Car'line's closed lids. "I kin fend for myself if Depper ain't put about," she said.

When Depper returned, with the shades of night, from the harvest-field, he might hardly have known his own living-room. The dirty rags of carpet had disappeared, the bricks were scrubbed, the dangerous-looking heap of clothing had been removed from the sofa, and a support added to its broken leg; the fireside chairs, the big chest of drawers, redolent of the turpentine with which they had been rubbed, shone in the candlelight; the kettle sang on the bars by the side of a saucepan of potatoes boiling for the meal. It was the sight of Dinah Brome at the head of affairs, however, which drew his attention from these details.

"Well, I'm jiggered!" Depper said, and paused, door in hand, on his own freshly-washed step.

"You wipe your feet, afore you come in," said Mrs Brome, masterful as ever. "Here's yer supper ready. I ain't a-goin' to ate it along of you, Depper; but I ha' got a ward or two to say to you afore I go."

Depper entered, closed the door behind him, sat down, hat on head, in the freshly-polished chair by the hearth; he fixed his eyes, his mouth fallen open, on the fine form of Dinah standing before him, with hands on hips, arms akimbo, and the masterful gleam in her eyes.

"Depper, yer old woman's a-dyin'" Dinah said.

"Marcy on us! Ye don't tell me that! Kind o' piney, like, fer the las' six months, my missus ha' bin', but—"

"Now she's a-dyin'. D'ye think I ha'n't got the right use o' my senses, arter all these years? Wheer ha' yer own eyes been? Look at 'er! No better'n a skeercrow of a woman, under yer very nose! She's a-dyin', I tell ye. And, Depper, what du I come here to find? I find a bare cupboard and a bare board. Not a mite o' nouragement i' th' house, sech as a pore suff'rin' woman like Car'line's in need of."

"Car'line's a pore manager, as right well you know, Dinah. Ha'n't I telled ye—?"

"You ha' telled me—yes. But have you played th' husban's part? You ha' telled me—and I ha' put the fault o' yer poverty home on ter yer pore missus's shoulders. But since I been here, I ha' seen 'er crawlin' on 'er han's and knees to wait on you, wi' yer fourses i' th' harvest-field. I ha' heered her manderin' on, 'let things be comf'table for Depper,' and let her fend for herself. And I can see with half an eye the bute is on t'other fut, Depper. And this here is what I'm a-goin' ter say to you, and don't you make no mistake about it: I'm yer wife's woman while she want me, and none o' yours."

Depper was a small, well-made man, with a curling, grizzled head, and a well-featured face. It is possible that in his youth the word 'dapper' may have applied to him; a forgotten fact which perhaps accounted for his nickname. He gazed with an open mouth and puzzled, blear eyes at the woman before him.

"You and me," he said slowly, with an utterance suspiciously slow and thick—"you and me ha' kep' comp'ny, so to speak, fer a sight o' years, Dinah. We never had no fallin's out, this mander, afore, as I can call ter mind. I don't rightly onderstan' what you ha' got agin me—come ter put it into wards."

"I ha' got this agin ye," the valiant Dinah said: "that you ha' nouraged yer own inside and let your missus's go empty. You ha' got too much drink aboard ye, now, an' her fit ter die for the want of a drop o' sperrits. And I ha' got this ter say: that we ha' come to a pass when I ha' got to make ch'ice twixt you and yer old woman. Arter wha's come and gone, we t'ree can't hob an' nob, as ye may say, together. My ch'ice is made, then, and this is how I ha' fixed it up. When yer day's wark is done, and you come home, I go out o' your house. Sune as yer up an' away i' th' mornin', I come in and ridd up yer missus and wait on 'er, while the woman's in need of me."

Whether this plan met with Depper's approval or not, Dinah Brome did not wait to see. "For Car'line's peace o' mind, arter wha's come and gone, 'tis th' only way," she said to herself and to him; and by it he had to abide.

It was not for many weeks. The poor unlovely wife, lying in the dismantled four-poster in the only bedroom, was too far gone to benefit by the 'nouragement' Mrs Brome contrived to administer. The sixpenn'orths of brandy Depper, too late relenting, spared from the sum he had hitherto expended on his own beer—public-house brandy, poisonous stuff, but accredited by the labouring population of Dulditch with all but magical restorative powers—for once failed in its effect. Daily more of a skeleton, hourly feebler and feebler, grew Depper's old woman; clinging, for all that, desperately to life and the hope of recovery for the sake of Depper himself.

"Let go the things of this life, lay hold on those of Eternity," the clergyman said, solemnly reproving her for her worldly state of mind. "Remember that there is no one in this world whose life is indispensable to the scheme of it. Try to think more humbly of yourself, my poor friend, less regretfully of the world you are hurrying from. Fix your eyes on the heavenly prospect. Try to join with me more heartily in the prayers for the dying."

She listened to them, making no response, with slow tears falling from shut lids to the pillow. "'Tain't for myself I'm a-pinin', 'tis for Depper," she said, the parson being gone.

"All the same, Car'line," Mrs Brome said, sharply admonishing, "I'd marmar a ward now and agin for myself, as the reverend ha' been advisin' of ye, if I was you. Depper he can look arter hisself; his time for prayin' ain't, so ter say, come yet. Yours is. I should like to hear a 'Lord help me,' now and agin from yer lips, when I tarn ye in the bed. I don't think but what yu'd be the better for it, pore critter. Your time's a-gettin' short, and 'tis best ter go resigned."

"I cud go resigned if 'tweren't for Depper," the dying woman made her moan.

"I can't think what he'll du all alone in th' house and me gone!" she often whimpered. "A man can't fend for 'isself, like a woman can. They ha'n't the know ter du it. Depper, he ain't no better'n a child about makin' the kettle bile, and sechlike. It'll go hard, me bein' put out o' th' way, wi' Depper."

"Sarve 'm right," Mrs Brome always stoically said. "He ha' been a bad man to you, Car'line. I don' know whu should speak to that if you and me don't, bor."

"He ha'n't so much as laid a finger on me since I was ill," Car'line said, making what defence for the absent man she could.

"All the same, when you're a-feelin' wholly low agin, jes' you say to yourself, 'Th' Lord help me!' 'Tis only dacent, you a dyin' woman, to do it. When ye ha'n't got the strength ter say it, I'll go on my knees and say it for ye, come to that, Car'line," the notorious wrongdoer promised.

They sent for Depper to the White Hart to come home and see his wife die.

"I ain't, so ter say, narvish, bein' alone with 'er, and would as lief see the pore sufferin' critter draw her las' breath as not, but I hold 'tis dacent for man and wife to be together, come to th' finish; an' so I ha' sent for ye," Mrs Brome told him.

Depper shed as many tears over his old woman as would have been expected from the best husband in the world; and Car'line let her dying gaze rest on him with as much affection, perhaps, as if he had indeed been that ideal person.

"There'll be money a-comin' in fro' th' club," were almost her last words to him. She was speaking of the burial-club, into which she had always contrived to pay the necessary weekly pence; she knew it to be the surest consolation she could offer him.

Depper had made arrangements already for the payment of the eleven pounds from the burial-club; he had drunk a pint or two extra, daily, for the last week, the innkeeper being willing to trust him, in consideration of the expected windfall. The excitement of this handling of sudden wealth, and the dying of his wife, and the extra drink combined, completely upset his mental equilibrium. In the first moments of his widower-hood he was prostrate with emotion.

Dragged downstairs by the strong arm of Dinah Brome, he subsided into the chair on the hearth, opposite that for ever empty one of his old woman's; and with elbows on knees and head on hand he hiccoughed and moaned and wept aloud.

Above, Dinah Brome and that old woman who had a reputation in Dulditch for the laying-out of corpses, decked the poor cold body in such warmth of white flannelette, and such garniture of snipped-out frilling as, alive, Car'line Kittle could never have hoped to attain to.

These last duties achieved, Dinah descended, her arms full of blankets and pillows, no longer necessary above. These, with much banging and shaking, she spread upon the downstairs couch, indicating to the still weeping Depper it was there he was expected to pass the night.

"Bor, you may well blubber!" she said to him, with a kind of comfortable scorn of him and his sorrow. "You 'ont ketch me a-dryin' yer tears for ye, and so I tell ye flat. A crule husban' yu ha' been as any woman ever had. If ever there was a wife who was kep' short, and used hard, that was yer wife, Depper, my man! Bad you ha' been to her that's gone to 'er account, in all ways; who should know that better'n me, I'll ask ye? An' if at las' 'tis come home to ye, sarve ye wholly right. Tha's all the comfort ye'll get from me, bor."

"Stop along of me!" Depper cried, as, her work being finished, she moved to the door. "'Taint right as I should be left here alone; and me feelin' that low, and a'most dazed with affliction."

"Tha's how you've a right to feel," the stern woman said, unmoved by his tears.

"I keep a-thinkin' of wha's layin' up above theer, Dinah."

"Pity you di'n't think on 'er more in 'er lifetime."

"'Taint nat'ral as I should be left wholly alone with a dead woman. 'Taint a nat'ral thing, I'm a-sayin', for me to du, Dinah, ter pass the night alone along o' my old missus's corp."

"Bor, 'taint the fust onnat'ral thing you ha' done i' your life," Mrs Brome said; and went out and shut the door.

An hour or so later Depper opened it, and going hurriedly past the intervening cottages, knocked stealthily upon the door of Dinah Brome.

She looked out upon him presently from her bedroom window, her dark, crinkled hair rough from the pillow, a shawl pulled over her nightgown.

"Whu's that a-distarbin' o' me, as ha'n't had a night's rest for a week, at this time o' night?" she demanded sharply.

"It's me; Depper," the man's voice answered, whisperingly. "Le' me in, Dinah. I daren't be alone along of 'er no longer. I ha' only got you, Dinah, now my old woman's gone! Le' me in!"

"You're a rum un ter call yerself a man and a husban'—you are!" Dinah Brome ejaculated; but she came downstairs and opened her door.

CLOMAYNE'S CLERK

Into the stinging sleet and rain-laden winds of the March morning there emerged from the door of a physician in Harley Street a boy of seventeen. He was slightly built, with stooping shoulders, and, meagre of proportions as he was, was protected from the cruel weather by an overcoat much too small. As he faced the biting wind, and "all the vapoury turbulence of heaven," the dusky pallor of his skin took on a bluey tinge, he shivered and trembled in the grim grasp of the storm.

A few yards from the door a child, dressed in a long, cheap mackintosh, and carrying within a strap slung over her shoulder a collection of school books and papers, awaited him.

Into the lustrous dark eyes of the youth she looked, asking with her anxious blue ones a question she did not put in words; for a minute he did not answer.

"Come under my umbrella," she said, as they walked on together. "And turn up the collar of your coat, Peter. Didn't he have a fire for you?" she asked, with a distrustful glance in the direction of that great physician whose portals the youth had just quitted.

"There was a roaring fire," Peter said. "It isn't the cold so much—it's the inside of me that's shivering. Cicely, it's going to be no use. He doesn't mean to pass me."

Cicely, a fairly well-grown girl of fourteen, with straight thin legs, straight, thick-hanging, dark hair, a straight, serious face, came to a stop on the wet pavement. Answering to a tug upon his coat-sleeve, the youth stopped too.

"He must!" she said. "You shouldn't have left him. You should have made him, Peter." The tears came into her eyes and her lip shook. "Oh, Peter, he will—he will!"

"He spotted that place on my throat," Peter said, with dejection.

"I told you to tie a handkerchief over it!"

"Handkerchief? I should think I did! He told me three times before I took it off. He wouldn't have so much as a rag on me. 'What's this?' says he. 'A little trouble I had a year or so ago, with a gland that swelled,' says I. 'It had to be cut, and has been as right as rain ever since.' Just in that offhand way, Cicely. Quite brisk and cheerful. 'Tubercular, eh?' says he, very soft and thoughtful-like. And I knew it was all up with me."

"You should have told him it wasn't!" Cicely said, tearfully impatient of him. "Oh, if I'd been there—!"

"Don't you be afraid! I told him fast enough, or tried to, but he stopped me. 'That'll do, thank you,' says he. 'I form my own opinion.' He wouldn't listen."

"Did you stand like that?" Cicely demanded, with a condemning glance at the stooping, shivering figure beneath the umbrella; "or did you hold your head up and throw your shoulders back, and push out your chest as I told you?"

"I stood up as brave as a lion," the young man assured her, his teeth chattering. "I yarned to him about how fond I was of athletics and swimming, how many miles I could walk at a stretch. Oh, I wasn't going to lose the berth for the want of a little gas. Only—" he stopped and sadly shook his head; "he'd made up his mind," he went on in a drooping tone. "He'd made it up as soon as he looked at me. 'Keep on with your walking; live in the open air,' he said. 'You're not fitted for the office-stool. Stooping all day over a desk would be about the worst thing you could do. Thank you. That's all. Good-morning.'"

"And you came away? You shouldn't have come away! You should have told him what it is to you. What you will have to put up with if you can't get the berth. You should have said, 'You're taking the bread out of my mouth, you're stealing the coat off my back. It's life and death to me.' You should have said that, and made him hear. And you came away!"

Peter looked back upon that action, sorrowfully considering it. "I thought it very affable of him to shake hands," he said, "but he had a very final way of doing it. And, besides, I didn't care to make a tale of my private affairs, and seem to cringe. I didn't want him to think—"

"What does it matter about him?" Cicely demanded, with scorn. "Do we care what he thinks? Oh, Peter, go back to him, dear; do—do go back. Tell him he must pass you. Tell him it's your chance, your only—only one. And how you've tried and tried—and this is the only one; and how cruel everyone is at home—just as if it was your fault that no one—no one will give you work to do. And tell him you'd rather be dead than go home and say you'd lost it. Oh, Peter, say that; it is true—it is true—!"

She was crying. The rain blown on her cheek by the angry wind mingled with the tears there. She held his wrist—that bony, flat wrist, which had had its own tale to tell to the examining physician—protruding from the shabby coat-sleeve, and led him, he nearly unresisting, back to the door. On the door-step he hesitated, looking at the child with beseeching dark eyes.

"He's awfully busy—his room's full—he isn't the sort to take liberties with—I don't want to bother him again."

But she kept a relentless hold upon the wrist, and herself rang the bell, and when the door opened, pushed him within with remorseless urgency. "Never mind cringing," she whispered. "Tell him everything. Tell him how they treat you at home. Don't mind what he thinks."

So, in Peter went, and Cicely, her school-books tucked away under her arm for the protection afforded by her mackintosh, the rain coming on faster and faster, walked the pavement, or waited on the doorstep, and now and again crossed the road in the baseless hope that she might not find the other side so wet, for a miserable two hours.

"Why, I thought I had finished with you, sir, more than an hour ago," the physician said, looking up, not too well pleased, when Peter, nervously smiling, his dark-curled head with its pale Jewish features pushed well forward, appeared in the consulting-room again.

The doctor, a fine-looking, red-faced man with keen blue eyes, looked a giant of health and strength and well-being beside the slight and meagre form. He was physician to the great firm of Clomayne, Company, Limited, who never appointed a clerk to their offices without a favourable report from him. Peter had already passed the educational test by which they weeded out the applicants to fill their vacancies. As a typist he had proved himself expert; in shorthand he had attained the highest speed. Nothing but the medical examination stood between him and the office-stool, which to him was as much an object of desire as is a throne to a prince.

"I think, sir," he said, his eyes, very dark and softly luminous, on the doctor's face,—"I'm afraid you didn't form a very high opinion of my physique. I wanted to ask you—I wanted to beg you, sir, to pass me. It would be the making of me, sir, to get to Clomayne's. I've been trying for more than a year to get a clerkship. The market is so very full, and I've been unfortunate. This is a great chance for me. I hope very much, sir, you won't let me lose it."

The doctor looked down from his goodly height upon the stooping shoulders of the suppliant. "I've got my duty to Clomayne's to perform, you know," he said. "They send their clerks abroad into all sorts of climates—very unhealthy, some of them. Climates where you, my poor fellow, could not live a month."

"I could take my chance," Peter said quickly. "I'm not afraid, sir. I shouldn't ask any favour. If I died, it would make no difference to Clomayne's. I mean the inconvenience would be mine."

"My dear fellow, you're a phthisical subject—not to mince matters. You told me your family history—"

"You asked me, sir," Peter interrupted, with a note of reproach in his softly thick voice.

"It was my duty to ask. Your father died a year ago of pneumonia, your mother ten years ago in a decline. Do you ask me to conceal these facts from Clomayne's?—to say that I consider you in strong health? Then, you ask what is absolutely impossible. I am sorry, but it is impossible. I think that is all I have to say on the subject, and—my time is very short."

"I am going almost at once, sir," Peter said, speaking with an effort of cheerfulness, but with a load of sorrow and disappointment lying, a physical weight, upon his heart. "I came because Cicely thought if I told you 'twas a matter of life and death, sir—. It is that to me, almost—it is. I'm very good at shorthand—hundred and twenty a minute; my arithmetic and book-keeping, too, are more than fair. My hand-writing's good, I might say. My hands don't always shake like this—"

"My dear boy," the doctor said, with an impatience at once angry and pitiful, "all that has less than nothing to do with me!"

"But if you'd give me a chance, sir!" His eyes were extraordinarily bright and pleading, his slight frame shook with eagerness; he made as though he swallowed something with difficulty. "After all, I shall have to cringe," he said to himself. "Since my father died, I have had to depend on my uncle, sir," he went on. "I owe everything to him. He's very good—but there are a lot of his own children; and there's my aunt—and she thinks—. My uncle doesn't grudge me anything, he often says so, but he naturally wants me to be getting my own living—and so does my aunt; and she doesn't quite understand how difficult it is, nowadays, to get in to anything—and my cousins don't understand it either, except Cicely, she's different. Of course, I can't at present contribute anything for my board and lodging and my clothes." He stopped, a minute, and looked down at his shabby overcoat, then lifted his eyes, alight with their soft, irresistible appeal, to the physician's face; his voice dropped in a kind of awe. "This berth carries a pound a week, sir. It would be all the world to me to get it."

"You want me to perjure myself?"

Peter did not shrink from the stern tone, nor blush at the imputation. "I want you not to take away my chance," he said.

He did not leave for some fifteen minutes longer, and when he did leave, it was with eyes lit almost to rapture, a glow of happiness on his pale face, and words of thanks bubbling forth from trembling lips. The doctor had consented not to conceal the state of the young man's predisposition to tubercular mischief, but to make the best of his chance of escaping the family taint. He had promised, too, to explain matters to one of the managers with whom he was on very friendly terms. Peter's position at Clomayne's was assured.

"I will never forget it, sir, never!" the boy said, stopping again at the door of the consulting-room to reiterate the fact. "It will be the making of me. I shall get on—you'll see I will. There's men that don't make the most of their chances—but I will. I've got a splendid one—thanks to your goodness—and I will. I feel it in me. You'll never regret it."

"Oh, that'll do—that'll do," the doctor said. He was a little ashamed of his weakness in the matter, knew it was a bad precedent, didn't wish to hear any more about it. "Haven't you got something warmer to put on?" he asked. "You're not going out into this pouring rain in that thin coat?"

"This is my great-coat, sir," Peter explained, with a glance at the sleeve that exposed the flat red wrist. "And Cicely is waiting outside for me with an umbrella."

The doctor was sufficiently interested to walk to that window in his consulting-room which looked upon the street in order to watch the youth who had taken what was in his experience the very unusual course of questioning his fiat. He saw the stooping figure of the lad join the upright one of the child, hurrying to meet him. He almost saw the glad words of the reversal of his doom upon the young man's lips; he saw the change on the straight-featured serious face of the child from an expression of unchildlike anxiety to one of almost womanly joy. The pair stood for three minutes in the drenching rain before the window, and even at that crisis Cicely did not forget to hoist her dripping umbrella over the head so eagerly thrust forward. Then Peter put a thin wrist through a mackintoshed arm, and looking in each other's faces, and eagerly talking, unconscious of the eyes that watched them, the wet impatient people pushing past, the boy and girl walked slowly away.

The doctor touched the bell that would bring his next patient for inspection, then took one more look through the window. The pair had taken hands and were running now, running over the clean-washed, shiny pavement. Cicely turned her face so that he saw it once again, and it was a laughing face.

"It's something to be young," the doctor said to himself as he turned away. "Young—and to have the thing you wish for! Yes, even if you're never to know a day's health while you live, and have got to die a lingering, painful death in a year or so."

He only saw Peter once after he obtained his heart's desire and the proud position of a post as a junior clerk in Clomayne's office. It was on a platform of Liverpool Street Suburban line. He was going down to Enfield in his professional capacity, and while he waited for his train, walking up and down, his attention was caught by a figure which appeared in some way familiar to him standing at the book-stall. A minute, and he had recognised it as that of the youth who had been so bent on becoming Clomayne's clerk.

He was better dressed now, and wore a warmer over-coat (for the summer was over, by now, and winter coming on again), and a more fashionably shaped bowler. Cicely, in her waterproof still, although there was no rain, and with her straight, heavy hair upon her shoulders, was by his side.

The physician, having established in his own mind the identity of the pair, resumed his pacing to and fro of the platform, and forgot them. In a minute, a voice at his elbow spoke his name, and glancing down, he saw, taking off his hat to him, and accosting him with a very eager look on the duskily pale face, the youth whose name, even, he had forgotten. A light of triumphant gladness was in the mild darkness of the eyes.

"Excuse my speaking to you, sir," Peter said, "Cicely would have me come. She thought you'd be pleased to hear our very good news."

"I'm always glad to hear anyone's good news," the big doctor said. "Let's see—it's Mr—?"

"I'm the young man at Clomayne's," Peter explained. "You were so good—"

"I remember perfectly. And how are you getting on?"

"First class, sir. That's what I wanted to tell you. Cicely wanted it too."

"You like your work?"

"I enjoy my work, sir. I don't have a dull moment. And—" here his voice sank with the immensity of the tidings with which it was charged—"you'll be very glad to hear, sir, I'm promoted."

"I am indeed glad. Doubled your pay, have they?"

Peter smiled. "It doesn't affect my pay, sir. But pay isn't everything, I take it."

"Certainly not," the physician hastened to say. "To be chosen for an honourable position, for instance—"

"It's like this," Peter said, anxious to proclaim the good fortune which had befallen him. "Clomayne & Co. are starting another branch—you may have heard—and there's heavy work entailed. Clomayne's have had to put on several of their clerks to stop at the office over-hours. I'm one of those selected."

"I see," the doctor said, meeting with his penetrating blue eyes the mildly exultant gaze of the black ones.

"I've been at it now for a month," Peter went on. "Instead of getting home at seven, I'm at the office till nine, and sometimes ten o'clock. I enjoy it very much. The firm allows us something for our teas. My fellow-clerks and I have a rattling good time. If it hadn't been for your kindness, sir, I should never have got to Clomayne's; and I thought you'd be glad to hear how splendidly I'm doing there."

"And how's the health? Extra hours spent in bending over your desk aren't very good for you. You haven't yet lost your cough?"

Peter looked away, evidently not caring to be questioned on that theme. "I've been very fit, thank you, sir," he said. "The mist—it's been a bit misty in the evenings lately—has got on my chest rather. This, being Saturday," he further explained, "is a holiday. Cicely and I always have the Saturday afternoons."

Ah! And how did they spend them, he was asked. In the air, it was hoped.

Not always, it seemed. For Cicely was fond of pictures, and sometimes they went to the National Gallery. Cicely was fond of reading too; and once or twice they had been to Westminster Abbey because she had a fancy for Poets' Corner. But this afternoon they were going to their home at Edmonton, and if they could get away again, and if it didn't rain, they were going to the Chingford hills, for Cicely, of all things, loved a glorious walk.

"Cicely's a dear kiddie. She's my friend. I'm awfully fond of her," Peter said. He made the avowal without the slightest embarrassment—from his infancy, probably, he had not known what it was to feel shy. "Before I got that berth at Clomayne's, I should have had a rough time at home if it hadn't been for Cicely. My aunt and my cousins didn't believe in me, you see, sir. Cicely always did."

The physician looked across to the bookstall where the child still stood, watchful of him and Peter beneath the shadowing brim of her hat. Obeying a good-natured impulse, he crossed to her and laid a hand on her shoulder, and called her "Cicely," and said he had been hearing she was fond of reading.

"We both are," Cicely said, with a calm, middle-aged self-possession. "It is the thing Peter and I like best in the world."

"And what sort of reading?" the doctor asked; and learnt that Peter liked books of adventure and happy stories, but that Cicely loved poetry, and liked best stories that were sad.

"They make her cry, sir," Peter explained. "She cries, and cries—don't you, Cicely?—but she likes them too."

So a kind doctor, looking over the wares displayed, bought a volume of Longfellow's poems, which he gave the girl—he knew nothing of poetry, but was sure Longfellow must be safe, as his mother had liked him—and he got for the boy, Wells's Sea Lady.

"I don't read such things, myself," he said, "but I've gathered from the newspapers the man has a quite creditable acquaintance with science, and does not write sentimental rubbish."

Cicely, regarding the donor with an unsmiling face, said—"Thank you very much," in her staid, middle-aged way; but Peter, using his tongue volubly, overwhelmed him with thanks.

"It is kind of you!" he said fervently. "I shall always treasure the book, and so will Cicely hers. We go to the Library—we've got a splendid one, you know, in Edmonton, Passmore Edwards gave us. Before I got to Clomayne's—they didn't want me at home, and I had nowhere else to go—I spent most of my days in the Library. Of course I've read H. G. Wells, and I learnt a lot of him by heart to tell Cicely, but I love to have him for my own. I have very much to be grateful to you for, sir, and I shall be grateful while I live."

"For how long will that be, poor fellow, I wonder!" the doctor said to himself as he walked away. He had done the poor boy a kindness, and he let his mind dwell on him with a pitying pleasure. It was hard that Fate should grudge to this unfortunate that humble place in the world of men which he held with such a boyish pride, those poor pleasures in which he took such innocent delight! He thought of his own son, as the train bore him away to his consultation, good and fairly satisfactory, but guarded on every side, petted, pampered. How much would it cost to bring into his own boy's handsome face the glow of surprised delight which had overspread the pale features of this poor lad at the gift of the four-and-sixpenny book.

But even as the thought passed through his mind, his lips curved with a smile of proud tenderness. The absurdity of the comparison! His own handsome, well-grown lad, with his fair, frank face and proudly carried head, and the poor little city clerk—the pallor of ill-health and confinement on the dusky face; the meagre figure; the head, over-heavy with its brown curls, thrust forwards, as if in eagerness to reach the goal before his feet could carry him there.

"Ah, happiness is found in unexpected places, and is a matter of temperament only, and not of circumstance at all," the doctor told himself, when Clomayne's clerk and the girl he called Cicely, passed the door of his first-class carriage, their destination reached. Peter was holding the girl's sleeve and hurrying her along, his head pushed forward, and on his face that look of eager joyousness which to the eyes that watched and that knew was so full of pathos. The voluble tongue was wagging as the pair trotted past. He heard his own name mentioned. And so Clomayne's clerk passed from the eyes that watched, for ever.

"I'll keep an eye on that poor fellow. I'll speak about him to Ladell; and when he begins to go down-hill, I'll lend a helping hand," the doctor said, making one of those resolutions that testify surely to the spiritual part of us, and do honour to the hearts that record them, even when, as now, they are not kept.

The doctor fully meant to keep his when he made it, but he forgot.

He forgot it, until one sunshiny morning in the spring of the next year, when, as he sat at his solitary lunch, there was brought to him a letter. It was in a careful and childish hand, and he read it almost at a glance as he ate the biscuit and drank the glass of Burgundy which he allowed himself for his midday meal.

"Dear Sir," the letter ran—"Peter was coming to tell you he had been promoted again. A junior was wanted to help with some work through the Easter holidays. Peter offered and was accepted. He was coming to tell you, but he was drowned last night in the River Lea. So I thought I would let you know.—Yours affectly., Cicely.

"P.S. He was not to have had more pay, but it was the honour."

The physician, who had never time for anything but his profession, made time to go to the funeral of Clomayne's clerk, paying his poor remains a compliment he had refused to those of many a man of distinguished name and high estate whose fees he had taken. On a Saturday afternoon in the sweetest month of the spring-time, he travelled down to Finchley with Ladell, that manager of Clomayne's who was his friend.

"We asked his people to hurry the funeral by a couple of days, so that the clerks could come," the official said.

Peter had looked up to this man as to a king among men. A "good-morning" from him, and a nod in the street in response to an eagerly snatched-off bowler, left the junior clerk elated in spirits for the day.

"Mr Ladell asked me if I wouldn't like to change places with Jones who sits nearer the fire," he said once to Cicely, his eyes humid with gratification. "He'd noticed how cold my hands were when I passed him a pen. They shake, you know; I can't stop them. It's something to be noticed like this by him, Cicely! I shall do now!"

"He was only one of the youngsters, of course, and not of much account, but he'd made a lot of friends. They've got a wreath as big as a haystack for the poor little man. They've made him into a hero; and they're all here—good fellows!" Thus the manager to the physician, as the train bore them along.

"It was simply silly, chucking away a life like that, of course," he went on. "A little fellow that could barely swim, to fling himself in, after a casual suicide! A hulking, great beggar who had good reason, no doubt, for wanting to be rid of his life. He probably wouldn't have thanked the boy, even if he had saved him—which he didn't."

He had a goodly following, poor Peter! How his eyes would have glistened, could he have known! Quite a regiment of clerks from Clomayne's were there, walking two and two; to say nothing of the uncle who had grudgingly fed him, and the goodly array of cousins who "had not believed in him." He had been put in a burial-club by his not too-loving relations; so, although he had gone so long in shabby clothing, and had known the sorrow of broken boots and wrist-bands that must be hidden away, he rode in state to his resting-place, drawn by four horses, in a silver hearse, his coffin covered with flowers.

But his grave was a humble one—the money from the burial-club not being sufficient to secure him a decent privacy in decay—and very, very deep. The clerks, crowding forward when the service was over, could hardly read his name and the account of his few years, on the silver plate of his coffin, so deep in the bowels of the earth they laid him—poor Peter! "the joys of all whose life were said and sung!" His was the first coffin in the grave destined to hold seven more.

The physician, waiting until the rest had turned away, stood for a few minutes alone, gazing into that profundity.

"Such a chucking away of life!" the admired gentleman who had been Peter's chief had said. But the physician had his own thought on that matter.

The poor boy—the foolish, enthusiastic, perhaps hysterical boy—enjoying the poor blessings that were his with the prophetic eagerness those doomed to an early death so often exhibit, had taken his seat upon his office-stool as upon a throne; had blessed God for his career of junior clerk as for a high imperial lot; then had flung away, his short race hardly begun, the life he prized. True; but in a blind belief in his own strength; and for the high purpose, suggested by the poetry and the books he and Cicely loved and talked over, of giving himself for another! The physician knew that in giving all he had but exchanged a year or two of failing power, of the pain and weakness of daily dying, the grief of finding himself a burden again upon unwilling shoulders for—what? For the moment of exultation when into the dark waters of greedy Lea he had flung his poor little body, clothed as it was in the new coat and trousers of which Cicely and he had been so proud; the moment of absolute belief in himself and his strength; the moment more, perhaps, of recognition that he had failed, but in a great cause. Peter had exhibited an effusive gratitude for the few favours Life had bestowed upon him; for this last favour of Death's according the physician knew he might well have been thankful.

That beautiful "floral tribute" for which Clomayne's clerks had contributed their shillings, had been lowered upon the coffin, together with one or two humbler, and obviously home-made, wreaths. As the physician turned away he noticed, lying almost at his feet, a little bunch of violets, dropped as the flowers had been removed from the coffin. Attached by a bit of white ribbon to their stalks was a tiny square of notepaper, and on this was written in the careful but unformed hand the doctor recognised, "From Cicely."

Holding them thoughtfully for a minute, the physician slowly opened his fingers; and through all that dismal space, soon to be filled with other coffins, Cicely's violets fell upon that which bore Peter's name. Upon the coffin of Clomayne's fortunate junior clerk; in luck's way still; promoted to the blessed company of those who die in what they believe to be a good cause.

IN A TEA-SHOP

The duties of the tea-shop were not particularly hard, but to Lucilla, whose head was filled with memories of a perfect holiday just over, a little irksome. The church clock, in the market-place upon which the windows looked, chimed the half-hour past five. The tea-room closed at six-thirty.

"At last it ringeth to evensong," Lucilla said.

At least, these were the words which repeated themselves in her brain; what she really said was— "Hot toast for two—sixpence; a pot of tea—sixpence; how many pieces of cake, sir? Thank you; cake—fourpence. One shilling and fourpence, if you please."

It had been a busy afternoon, but the couple who paid the one-and-fourpence, pushing some coppers towards the waitress, who, with a dignified motion and an aloof-voiced "We do not receive gratuities," pushed them back, would in all probability be the last customers. Lucilla having discovered the man's hat for him, restored to the woman the wrist-bag and pocket-handkerchief and parcel she would have left behind her, and watched the pair from the room, yawned aloud as she piled the soiled teacups, plates, and saucers on the little brown Japanese tray, and carried them to that screened-off angle of the room where china was washed and bread and butter cut all the day long.

She returned, yawning still, to dust the crumbs from the little bamboo table. Half-past five! What, in those delightful fourteen days which had composed her yearly holiday, had she been doing at that hour? So precious the memory of that fortnight, so treasured every incident, almost she could have accounted for each minute of the time.

As she set the chairs straight before the dozen bamboo tables, put each illustrated paper in its allotted place, her inward gaze was turned upon scenes she had left behind with the delightful luxuriousness of a life which, for that small, allotted space, she had been permitted to live.

She had driven, she had motored, she had paid visits, had danced. Yes—danced! She paused on that word, and her lips trembled to a smile.

She had read of such an existence, dreamed of it, perhaps; at last, she had lived it. Would it make her days in the tea-shop—and out of it—easier?

For one thing, she had returned a little ashamed of her work. "Don't mention about the tea-shop, even before your cousins, dear," her aunt had admonished her. Her aunt, being an old-fashioned person who did not realise that a lady can get her living by any honourable means, in the present day, and remain a lady still. Lucilla had, of course, obeyed her aunt's injunction, but had felt, for her own part, not the slightest repugnance to mention the means by which she gained her livelihood, until a couple of evenings before she had returned. That evening of the dance, whose memory brought the quiver of a smile to Lucilla's lips.

"Suppose I had told him!" she said to herself as she moved from table to table, mechanically putting all in order. "He asked me how I passed my time. What would have happened? Would he have gone on dancing with me, and gone on sitting out with me when I couldn't dance? I'm glad I didn't tell, even if it did deceive him—even if I am a snob. I'm glad I had my hour."

She looked out of one of the windows into the market square, around which the lamps were lighted now, and a pleasing vision rose before her eyes of herself in her cousin Alice's last year's ball-dress, looking so supremely happy, and as pretty—he had said that—as a dream. Yes; she was thankful he would never have to know. What would he think of her if he could see her now in her full-skirted brown merino frock, her brown muslin apron, the big white chrysanthemum, which was the emblem of the tea-shop, embroidered in its corner and on its bib, her high muslin cap with the stiff strings tied beneath her chin?

"He would never recognise me; but I'm glad he will never see me," Lucilla said.

Then she turned from the window at the sound of a step upon the stairs, and saw him coming into the room.

He was accompanied by a lady, young and pretty.

"Such a crush, and so badly managed, and so under-waited!" she was volubly declaring as she came in. "Half a cup of cold tea, and a quarter of an inch of fishy sandwich was all I got hold of. It was a splendid thought of yours to turn in here for a feed, Captain Finch. I couldn't possibly get along on that till dinner-time. Bread and butter, please, for two, and a good lot of it. Two hungry people. And—oh, where is the young lady who usually waits?"

It was the attendant from behind the screen who was taking the order, a girl with a fine figure, a sharp-featured, high-coloured, alert face, and wearing the brown uniform of the establishment. The other young lady was engaged elsewhere, she said.

"Oh!" said the customer on a falling note, and repeated in a flatter tone her order. "I wanted you to see this other girl," she said to Captain Finch as the waitress moved away. "She is called a beauty. One or two men rave about her. Women can't judge of these things. I wanted to hear what you thought of her."

"My word—on such a subject—would be final," the man said.

Lucilla, cutting bread and butter behind the screen, quivered at the voice, the rather hesitating utterance which was characteristic, the little laugh at the finish. Ah, what a mercy she had had that minute in which to dash into the corner and to drive Miss Dawson forth to take her place! She remembered how beautifully, intoxicatingly deferential he had been to her in her charming ball-dress, niece to the lady who was wife of the most influential man in Workingham. Words could not express how he must despise her if he saw her now.

"They make you judge at all the beauty shows in India, I suppose?" the lively lady was saying.

"They'd like to. I couldn't stand the fag."

"Poor dear! You appear to be very much exhausted."

"That beastly wedding! I never was so bored in my life."

"That doesn't excuse your yawning in my face."

"Oh, I say! Did I do that, now? I beg your pardon."

"If only this pretty girl I was telling you about had been here!"

"Oh, come! Good-looking women aren't so rare, I know a dozen I can see any day, Mrs Eaton. But as we're here, can't she be produced?"

The lady tinkled the little bell with which her table was supplied. "Some walnut cake, please." As it was set on the table, "I hope the other young lady has not left?" she inquired.

"Oh no, madam."

"A little more hot water."

"An officer, I'll bet my eyes! And a fine-looking fellow! Did you say he was a pal of yours, miss?" Miss Dawson whispered to Lucilla as she replenished the jug.

"If they mention me again, say Miss Browne—you can call me that—is gone home, and isn't coming back any more for a month."

The bell tinkled again.

"I thought perhaps you had forgotten the hot water," the lady said sweetly.

"No, madam," replied Miss Dawson as she placed the jug on the tray; "Miss Browne, our other young lady, being gone home, we're a little short-handed, like. The young person who is taking her place is rather awkward at the work, and puts us backward," she raised her voice here that Lucilla might enjoy the joke.

"Ah. I thought things were not quite so nice," the customer said.

"No, madam," acquiesced Miss Dawson, and giggled, and pinched Lucilla as she retired behind the screen.

The lady at the tea-table was a vivacious creature; she rattled on with hardly a break in her stream of chatter through the half-hour, during which she ate all the bread and butter and drank nearly all the tea. Lucilla, behind her screen, listening for the pleasant tones of the man's halting speech, grew weary of the high-pitched, untiring voice.

"It is getting late," Captain Finch said at last. "I had better put you in a cab."

"You aren't going to take me back?"

"Sorry. I've got to buy some things."

When they had left the room and were going downstairs, the woman's tongue still volubly running, Lucilla came with a soft rush from behind the screen and looked from the window. The shops round the market place were brilliantly lighted now; the elegant backs of the couple emerging from the confectioner's beneath the tea-room were easily visible. The man raised his stick and hailed a hansom.

"How wonderfully things happen!" mused Lucilla. "He said, I remember, that he was going to the wedding of a friend; to think that it should have been here!"

"If you and him are friends, I can't think why you didn't show yourself," Miss Dawson called from behind her screen.

"I daresay you can't," said Lucilla to herself.

"Where'd you see him first?" Miss Dawson asked. "Did he come up and speak to you?"

The withering glance which Lucilla cast in the direction of the screen. "Come up and speak to me!" she repeated.

"And why not, pray? Rubbish!" laughed Miss Dawson, rattling the teacups she was washing. "What does it matter in the end? Comes to the same thing when you do know them."

"You and I look at such things from a different point of view."

"Heap of nonsense!" Miss Dawson shrilled. "Your father was a lawyer that failed and couldn't pay his debts; mine was a bankrupt greengrocer. Both of 'em's dead now, and one as good as another; and us, too."

It was not the first time Lucilla had heard the argument; she listened to it now with compressed lips, in silence. Then she went to the mantelpiece, made an entry in a memorandum book lying there, tore out the page, counted the money in the bag which hung at her side, piled it upon the loose leaf, which she folded around it, preparatory to carrying it to the desk in the shop below.

"If you don't want to know the man, say you've never met him before, and bounce it," Miss Dawson called after her in contemptuous tones as she disappeared.

Two short flights of stairs led from shop to tearoom, and these were divided by a small landing, where spare cups and saucers and teapots were stacked. From the upper flight the lower was invisible. Lucilla, descending, was unaware therefore of the gentleman coming up until she met him on the square of landing beneath the unshaded gaslight. He held a great, loose bunch of long-stalked violets in his hand; and he was, of course, Lucilla's partner at the heavenly dance, Captain Finch.

Lucilla's heart beat tumultuously, her face turned white. "Bounce it," said the practical Miss Dawson's voice in her ears. She kept her head up, therefore did not notice the proffered hand, would have passed the gentleman by.

"Miss Mavis, I have brought you some violets," he said.

"You are mistaken. My name is Miss Browne," said Lucilla. "I do not accept flowers from men I do not know."

He stared at her, his lips fallen apart beneath his moustache. "I—was under the impression we had met at the dance at Workingham Town Hall," he said.

She took courage from his hesitating manner, and smiled with great self-possession. "You are unfortunately mistaken. Will you allow me to pass?" she said.

Lifting his hat, he moved aside; then turned to watch her make her deliberate descent. The soft folds of her full brown skirt dropped from stair to stair; the light from the flaring gas-jet fell on the knot of brown hair massed between the high, stiff cap and the high, stiff collar.

"Is that you, miss?"

It was a voice from above which called the superfluous question; he turned from the contemplation of the young lady in brown, who had now reached the bottom stair, to that of the young lady in brown who stood at the top. Towards the latter he mounted with a lingering step, as if not quite aware that he did so, and followed her into the tea-room.

"That young lady who has just gone down—?" he said.

"Miss Browne, sir."

"Er—is that so—really?" He lost himself, apparently; for the moment had nothing more to say; until, with a happy inspiration, "and—your name?" he asked.

"I'm Miss Dawson, sir. Miss Nellie Dawson."

"Really? Pleased to have made your acquaintance. Er—I've—er—brought you some violets, Miss Nellie Dawson," he said.

He appeared again the next morning, and had lunch at the tea-shop; the only man among a bevy of women lunching off scones and tea. He was shy of his isolated position, perhaps, for he held the illustrated paper he took up rather persistently before his face. At that hour a servant stood behind the screen and washed the china; both the girls waited. Above the top of his paper and round its edges he watched the more elegant of the two moving with noiseless tread among the tables, standing with bent head in the attitude of dignified attentiveness to receive orders, carrying her light burden of brown tea tray and Satsuma china. It was Lucilla he watched, but it was Miss Dawson who waited on him.

He ordered two poached eggs—the most substantial item on the menu card. He had to wait a long while for them, and when they were eaten, and he had given himself time to read his Punch two or three times through, he apparently discovered himself to be still hungry, for he ordered two more. By the time these were consumed, and he had conscientiously looked through The Ladies' Field, with which Miss Dawson had thoughtfully supplied him, the room began to empty.

A couple of ladies, evidently from the country, strayed in. One, in a low and secret voice demanded stout, which could not be supplied. Lucilla, with her head at a charming incline, suggested as a substitute tea, coffee, or chocolate; finally took the order for chocolate, supplied it; then, there being no one else to wait on, sat down by the fire, drew a strip of knitting from her apron pocket, began to work on it.

Captain Finch, rising from his table, pulled down his waistcoat, picked up his hat and stick, crossed the room, and placed himself before her. In the hand held in the fall of his back he carried a book.

"I—er—will you allow me—to—pay?" he asked. "Four eggs—er—coffee—er."

Lucilla, without raising her eyes from the brown silk she was knitting into a narrow strip, slightly waved a hand in the direction of Miss Dawson. "The other young lady," she said.

But Miss Dawson, at that moment, was in spirited controversy with an elderly, handsomely-dressed customer, whose carriage and pair of horses awaited her at the pastry-cook's door, who could only remember to have eaten one slice of walnut cake, while Miss Dawson was of opinion that she had eaten two.

"Am I not permitted to pay Miss—er—Browne—if I prefer to do so?"

"It is the rule for each customer to pay the young lady who waits on him."

"Thank you. Miss—er—Browne, when I had the happiness to meet you at the Workingham Town Hall—at that delightful dance—"

"Pardon me. You did not meet me there. I do not dance."

"You spoke of a wish to read one of—er—Bernard Shaw's plays. I've got this for you." He produced the hand from the small of his back and tendered her the book.

She laid down her knitting and rose; a belated customer had appeared. "I am sorry," she said, without looking at man or book. "The lady you speak of would doubtless think it very kind of you. I have no wish to read the plays, and could not possibly take the book."

With the slightest inclination of the head she passed him, and, the menu card in hand, leant over the newcomer.

Left with the book, Captain Finch poised it in his hand, looking rather stupidly at it for a few minutes; then tossed it to the mantelpiece, and went from the room.

The clock had struck six when he came in for tea, that evening, and all the little tables were empty. Miss Dawson, who was second in command, was, as usual at that hour, behind the screen; he had come in so quietly that Lucilla had no chance to rush and take her place. Her face paled as she saw him. The man was persistent, her strength at the moment small; there was only her pride to carry her through.

The day had been a busy one, she was fagged, and read in his face that he saw her to be so. His face, although not a clever one, was so heavenly kind!

"I won't trouble you to fetch any tea," he said. "If I might be allowed to—er—stay here and talk to you for a few minutes—"

"Tea or coffee, sir?"

"Oh, well, tea, then—confound the stuff!"

He threw down his hat and stick, and stood while she placed the brown tray, the tiny teapot, the minute muffin-dish before him. "If you know how I hate to have you—er—wait on me—" he said; but she gave him no chance to enlarge on the theme.

He sat for a few minutes over the tea-tray, not touching its contents, and with his eyes on Lucilla's back as she stood at the mantelpiece making her entries, counting the money in her bag. When she moved to the door he got up and intercepted her.

"You are Miss Browne while you are in the—er—shop, I understand?" he said. "I don't care for her—for Miss—er—Browne. It is the girl I met at the dance I care for, and want to see again. I can't find her here. Can I—er—find her outside? If I wait at the door for an hour, say, will you—will she be there?"

Lucilla drew back, with hurt eyes and a reddening face. As if she were any Miss Dawson, with the pavement for a rendezvous!

"I can't possibly say where you may meet your friends," she told him. "I, for my part, do not make appointments to meet men who are strangers to me—in the streets."

She passed him then, and went downstairs, her head held high, although her heart was sore. She watched, hidden in the shop, for his departure. It seemed to her impatience a long time before he left.

Miss Dawson was warbling to herself, with rather shrill-throated gaiety, whisking her full skirt among the bamboo tables, when Lucilla returned to the tea-room.

"I like your friend, miss," she said. "He hung about for a good time, waiting for you; but as you didn't choose to come back he's gone."

Lucilla had come in with her arms full of great, bronze-coloured chrysanthemums, which had been sent in from the flower shop to deck the tables for the morrow. In silence she went about the work of replenishing the vases. Miss Dawson quavered some high notes of her song.

"Did he say that he wanted to see me again?" Lucilla, in spite of herself, was obliged to ask.

"Dear me, no, miss. He said he stayed to thank me for wearing his flowers."

Lucilla viciously snapped off the stalk of a giant chrysanthemum. The Princess violets in the other girl's bosom had been as thorns in her own, all the day. She glanced at the mantelpiece where she had seen him toss the book of plays.

"You've got his book as well, I suppose?" she asked.

Miss Dawson gave her high laugh. "Oh yes!" she acknowledged. "I know it's your leavings; I'm not proud."

She sang in her florid style for a minute or two, then descended to speech again.

"You wouldn't let your friend wait for you outside, miss," she said. "You're so mighty particular. I ain't. I told him I had no one to walk home with me to-night; so he's waiting for me."

Captain Finch brought his erect, handsome form, his kind, foolish face no more to the tea-room. Lucilla, longing as much as she dreaded to see him, felt her heart throb at the sound of each manly footstep on the stair, paled at the sight of coat and trousers of a certain shade, trembled at the sound of a voice that recalled his hesitating tones. But he came never again. The "bounce" which Miss Dawson had counselled had had its effect. Either he now disbelieved the evidence of his own eyes, or, more probably, he bowed, as a gentleman would, to her desire to disavow the acquaintanceship.

"A man in his position could not meet on equal ground a girl in mine; and—and I won't meet him on any other level," she said to herself. Aloud, she would not speak of him again. Neither did Miss Dawson any more allude to the gentleman who had presented the violets and the volume of plays, and with whom she had gone for a walk on the first evening of their acquaintanceship. Relations between the young women, never very friendly, had become strained since that evening.

"A girl who could do such a thing!" said Lucilla to herself; and held her head disdainfully, and curled her lip at the other girl.

But Miss Dawson, if she noticed that scornful attitude, was not at all impressed by it. She switched her brown skirt with more than her usual air of jaunty alertness around the chairs and tables, looked in the little glass behind the screen at which the pair adjusted their caps and aprons with a smirk of self-satisfaction, and always wore a bunch of Princess violets in the bosom of her dress. Soon, the string of amber beads at her throat was discarded in favour of a gold chain and pearl and turquoise pendant, which Lucilla despised as imitation, of course, but which, nevertheless, looked real.

Then, one day, at an hour when the tea-room was empty, arrived a letter, from her influential aunt at Workingham, for Lucilla.

A certain portion of this letter she read again and again; then, the need to a bursting heart of the outlet of speech being imperative, spake with her tongue.

"Your advice to me to—bounce it—wasn't very happy advice, Miss Dawson," she said, with bitterness. "Captain Finch knew all the time. He knew when he came to this place. He came to see me. He knew I served in a tea-shop. It made no difference. He went to my uncle the day after the dance, and spoke—spoke about me—" Her voice was not under control; she turned away.

Miss Dawson, energetically rubbing a bamboo table on which some coffee had been spilt, made no answer.

"I wish—I wish—" said Lucilla, with her back turned, a world of regret in her eyes, "I wish I had not been so silly."

Miss Dawson looked up momentarily from her occupation. "You can put it all right with him, you know," she said; "Captain Finch is still hanging round."

"Here?" Lucilla cried. "He went three weeks ago!"

"Not he. Every night of the three weeks he's waited outside to walk home with me. For the first week he went to talk about you. For a fortnight he hasn't mentioned your name."

She ceased to rub the table, shook the cloth, folded it with nicety, the other girl speechlessly regarding her.

"He gives me these every day," Miss Dawson went on, and dashed a hand towards the violets in her breast. "He gave me this," she lightly fingered the turquoise and pearl pendant. "I don't wear his ring yet, our rules not allowing it."

She whisked off with her cloth to the screen, deposited it, reappeared. "His leave's up in six weeks," she said. "Him and me are to be married in a month; have a fortnight's fling, and off to India. I chuck this, at the end of the week. They know, downstairs. I hope you'll like your new pal when she turns up, miss."

Only once, during the few days that remained, did Lucilla and Miss Dawson speak of matters not strictly concerned with teas, scones, and girdle-cakes. It was on the last day of her service in the tea-shop that the latter brought with her, and flung upon the mantelpiece, the book of plays which Captain Finch, on his second visit, had deposited there for Lucilla.

"This was meant for you," she said, "and you may as well have it. Such stuff isn't in my line, thank goodness! and I can't make head or tail of it. But there's a word in it I happened upon, first time I opened the book; and it's stuck in my memory, for it happens to be holy sense, and not tommy-rot. This is it—or something like it—

"'If you want a thing very badly, go straight for it, and—GRAB it!'"

She put her common face close to Lucilla's disdainful one as, with an insolent emphasis, she made the quotation, then laughed as she turned away.

"That is what you should have done—you idiot!" she said.

PART I

She was junior music-mistress at the high school for girls, and he mathematical master at the boys' college hard by. On most afternoons of the week it happened that, their day's work being done, they encountered as they left the scene of their respective duties, and, their homes lying within a few doors of each other, walked there together.

He was a tall man, loosely put together, with iron-grey hair, stooping shoulders, and a look on his long-featured face at once dreary and gentle. She was small and dark, alert and pretty, and, from the crown of her neatly-dressed head, in its plain straw hat, to the soles of her sensibly shod feet, wholesome-looking.

The day that was soon to melt into evening had been sultry, the class-rooms airless, their tasks fatiguing. The pavement beneath their feet was hot; both were glad to breathe what tiny breeze was astir; both were tired. They walked side by side in that best of all companionships which demands no effort at sprightliness, nor the utterance of one word not spontaneously spoken.

"Shall we see you down by the river to-night?" she asked him, at length.

If he could get away he would go there, he said.

"Do come!" she gently urged him. "It does you good to get away."

Then the man's house was reached. It was one in a street of £30-a-year houses, with large bow-windows, small gardens, red-and-white striped curtains to protect green-painted front doors. He made a motion of his hand, half-heartedly inviting her to enter.

She shook her head.

"I've been in once to-day," she said. "Mrs Kilbourne asked me to get her something in the town, and I took it in."

"So long as you remember the caution I gave you—"

"You may be quite sure I remember."

As she would have passed on he stopped her.

"One minute," he said. "The rose I told you of is out, to-day."

The tiny garden was fashioned into a square of grass-plot, a bed full of rose-trees in its midst. The Frau Karl Druschki, recently acquired, had only one half-unfolded bloom. He gathered it and gave to her as she stood beyond the iron rails.

"Only one! How could you pull it for me!" she reproached him.

"Absolutely pure white—quite flawless, you see," he said.

His touch lingered on the flower, for he loved roses; then he put it into her hand, and she went on her way.

In the bow-windowed front room of Horace Kilbourne's house his wife was lying on the sofa—semi-paralysed, a drunkard.

"That you, Horry dear?" she said, as, with a gloomy, hopeless face he looked in upon the unlovely sight.

She raised a frowsy head from its pillow, put a dirty hand to her eyes to shade them from the sun entering the darkened room by the open door, smiled fatuously upon her husband.

"Come and haul wifey up, and make me comfy, and give me a cup of tea," she invited him.

One side of her was helpless. She was a tall and broadly-made woman, enormously fat. It required the exertion of all his strength to get her into the desired position. One leg was like a log, and was lifted as if it did not belong to her. All the cushions had to be shaken up and replaced, the coverlet respread on her ice-cold feet.

But Kilbourne was used to such services; if his face was lowering as he performed them, his fingers were deft.

Tea was set forth with no daintiness upon the untidy, coloured cloth of the centre-table. He poured out a cup and took it to her. She received it with a coaxing leer in her eyes, looking up at him.

"Just a drop!" she whispered, in a thickened whine. "Just a teeny drop, Horry!"

He turned his back on her, without a word in reply, and went to his own tea. Two of the three rounds set forth of unappetising bread-and-butter he ate, swallowed a great cup of lukewarm tea. His eyes were fixed drearily upon the dish of biscuits which also graced the meal. He counted them idly, wondering for how many afternoons the same six had done duty for the like occasion.

"One leetle, teeny drop!" his wife said again. "You know tea gives me indigestion without, Horry. One teeny, weeny one!"

She was allowed by the doctor a certain modicum of whisky in the day, and the dose, for safety's sake, Kilbourne always administered himself.

"You can have it half now and half when you go to bed at night, if you like," he said at length, and got up and poured the portion from a bottle, which he locked away again in the sideboard.

She sighed heavily with anticipation as he held it to her, and he felt her breath upon his face.

"You've been having brandy?" he said.

"No, Horry, no!"

She shook her head, which was already heavily tremulous, and, seeing fear lest the precious beverage with which she was now supplied should be filched from her, buried her face in the cup and gulped it down.

"Where'd you get the brandy?" he persisted; and she began feebly to cry.

"Naughty Horry, to speak to wifey so! Didn't I promise you and the doctor I wouldn't touch it? And me left without a penny to buy it with! And only water the whole day long has passed my lips. I'll take an oath! I wish I may die to-night, Horry, if I've had a drop!"

He turned from her and rang the bell.

"Where did your mistress get the brandy she has had to-day?" he asked of the pert, untidy-looking maid-of-all-work who appeared.

"Where'd she get it? Out of the bottle, of course. I fetched it for her away from the grocer's, right enough," the servant said, with an impudent face and a tossed-up head.

"I thought I had given you orders never to fetch your mistress anything of the sort?"

"An' the missus she give me orders to fetch it," the girl said. "'Ow do I know which I'm to mind, between ye? An' me shut up with 'er all the day, an' 'er a-badgerin'—"

"Take the tea-things. That will do for the present. Go!" he said.

He walked to the foot of the sofa, and looked long at the huge, unlovely bulk, once the admired form of his handsome wife, that lay there.

"You disgrace!" he said.

She whimpered afresh, her mouth shaking, the tears running down her cheeks unrestrained, like those of a child.

"There's a way to speak to a poor, suffering wife!" she whined. "And my head like splitting open! You might feel for me a little, Horry. Look at my poor arm!" With her able hand she moved the disabled one towards him. "It's quite numb. Rub it, Horry," she pleaded, looking weepingly up at him. "It's numb, yet it aches right up into my throat. And my poor tongue—poor wifey's tongue—is like fire! Look at it, hubby."

She opened the tremulous mouth, the great, parched tongue lolled out.

He looked at her, not stirring, with hard eyes.

"You disgrace!" he said again.

"Aren't you a disgrace to say so, then?" she whimpered. "Who'd believe you were my husband, calling me disgraces, and things? No one would think there was any affection between us, going on like that. And me with one side of me useless, and a fatty heart, as the doctor told me plainly, and said I was to take the greatest care. And who should take care of me if my own husband doesn't? And you stand there glaring at me, and not a kind word to throw at me! And haven't I always been a true and loving wife to you?"

He looked at her deliberately, with loathing in his eyes.

"You have been the curse of my life!" he said.

Then he left her.

In half an hour the pert maid-of-all-work came in. She was in walking costume, a string of pearls about her bare throat, a hat-box in her hand.

"This 'ere's my luggige," she explained. "You can go through it, if you like, to make sure I 'aven't took none of your rubbige away with me! I'm a-going, I am! The master he come and give me notice to leave at the end o' the month, but I don't choose to stay in no sech a place so long. I've 'ad enough of a tipsy missus, and an' ouse without an atim o' comfit! I'm a-goin!"

The woman on the sofa, with the inflamed, red face, the bloodshot, painful-looking eyes, the loose mouth, looked helplessly upon the maid-of-all-work.

"A little drop of something to quench my thirst before you go!" she implored. "I can't get up to fetch it for myself, as you know, Maria; and my throat's swelled up with being so parched."

"And if you die of it, so much the better!" Maria said frankly. But she went and pumped some water, all the same, and brought it to her, the glass dimmed in her red, bare hand. "For all I've had to demean myself to wait on sich as you, I'm a Christian!" she said.

"A leetle drop of the brandy left, Maria?" the woman asked.

"Trust you for that! Not a drop!"

"Drain the bottle and see, Maria."

"You are a one, you are!" the emancipated servant said. "I ha' seen a sight o' bad 'uns, but never one like you. And if I was th' master, I'd up and chuck you inter th' street, see if I wouldn't, and git a little peace in 'is 'ome with a diff'runt woman than you! 'E wouldn't have to go far, neither, before 'e found one to 'is mind, master wouldn't, an' so I tell you! An' as for me, I'm done with you, so there!"

The woman looked after her as she bounced to the door, hiccoughing, holding the now empty glass in her shaking hand. Her brows were knit; she seemed in her muddled brain to be considering something.

"The girl Grantley promised she'd come to-day," she said. "She promised she'd bring me something."

"And did so, right enough. But you 'aven't got no memory nor nothin'!"

"Where is it, then, Maria dear? For my poor head's splitting—"

"Why, in th' basket as stan' agin your sofy, where you put it yourself, for I see ye do it."

Left to herself, the woman put the glass to her lips, sucked from it the few drops that hung upon its sides, lay with it in her hand, alternately looking into it and looking into space, lifting it to her lips again and again.

The machinery of her mind was too far destroyed for it to work in any suggested groove. It strayed off the line continually into all sorts of hazy, dim byways.

A disgrace!

She had broken her word to him, often enough, but he had never before called her that. It was very cruel of him, and not like a husband to use such a word to his wife, that had ever a loving word for him when he came home, and was always waiting for him, so obliging and kind. Her mother would vouch for that—she had often said she had a loving nature.

Once she had walked unexpectedly into the little sitting-room at home, and she had heard her mother saying to Horace—"Julia has a very loving nature." Why didn't her mother come and say kind things to her now? She was all alone. If her mother came and sat by her side—

She would like, if she could walk there, to get off the sofa and go to look for her in that little sitting-room, at home. It was so cool in there always, with the window open to the garden. There was a basket of violets on the table. She wondered if they were there now. She would like to put her lips, that were so hot and uncomfortable, down upon them—

With difficulty she half turned on the sofa with the idea of reaching them; but remembered as she did so that her mother had been dead for years and years, and that there were no violets now.

She cried afresh, and held the empty glass to her lips in the hope a forgotten drop might trickle down upon them.

Her mother had once scolded her—once when Horace had told tales—and had said that she had broken her heart. But, for all that, she would not have liked to hear her called a disgrace.

She wished her husband would come in and put her to bed. He would have to do it alone to-night, as Maria was gone. Or perhaps old Susan would come and help. Old Susan had carried her up to bed quite easily, last night—when she was a child. No sticks, nor bother of people pushing and dragging—had carried her up as light as a feather, and popped her into her cool, soft bed, and tucked her up—

"Susan!" she called. "Susan!" And opened her aching eyes to look for her; and cried again when she remembered why the old servant could not come, and that she was not a child again any more.

A disgrace!

It wasn't a nice thing to say to such a good wife, and she so afflicted! He had another name for her when she used to walk about like other people—like the girl Grantley, for instance, that her husband always came home from school with. She used to go to meet Horry, herself, in those days, and go down to the river in the evening with him, and sit on one of the chairs beneath the trees to watch the boats. To watch the boats! How they glided along—gently, gently! It made you sleepy to look at them. She was in one herself now, rocking, rocking; and the sun was going down behind the trees; and a lot more boats, more and more, all rocking; and the sound of the oars, and the water lapping at the sides. She would like to put her hand in the river. It looked so cool—so cool!

The hand dropped heavily at her side, the glass broke; and she was on her sofa still, not in a boat at all; and it was the girl Grantley who sat by the river with Horry.

The girl Grantley! Where was that she had brought? The basket into which she had dropped it was easily within her reach. Here was the parcel, fastened as chemists' parcels are fastened. She shook it, and a gleam came into her eyes. Liquid! Something to drink, to moisten her burning tongue and swollen throat. No matter what—

Down by the river, on the broad path beneath the trees, where half the population of the place repaired in the summer evenings, the girl Grantley walked with her brother, and by their side walked Horace Kilbourne.

Presently the brother stopped to speak to a friend, and the girl and the other man walked on—walked through the crowds of people to where the crowds grew less, and on still, till there was comparative solitude.

Only the girl talked, telling him of her day's work—of what it had brought her of pleasure, of what had gone amiss. She had the habit of talking out her heart to him, bringing him all her difficulties and distresses.

"It rests me as nothing else does," she told him, when he had listened to the end, and said what had to be said. "And you? Have you nothing to tell me?" she asked him.

"Nothing," he said.

She glanced sideways and upwards at him as he towered above her, walking with drooping head.

"Something has happened," she said softly. "Can't you tell me? It helps, to tell a friend."

"It is nothing to which I am not well used," he said. "The same old wretched story. I have never told it in so many words. I am too ashamed to tell. You know it, well enough. Who is there that does not know?"

She turned on him a face that startled him, who knew it well, and had learnt by heart, he thought, its many changes.

"Why do you not kill her?" she said.

"Sh-sh-sh!" he whispered, surprised and reproving.

Her vivid face was aflame with passion; almost, it seemed, with hate.

"It would be no crime," she said. "Do you think God wants His world so cumbered? Why should your life, other people's lives, be destroyed? Are you to bear a burden like that for ever?"

"Sh-sh-sh!" he whispered again.

He put a hand upon her arm, and gently turned her with him. They began to retrace their steps.

"I was right never to speak to you about it before," he said presently. "Mutual confidences are for happy people, Kate. Men burthened with great sorrows know them to be incommunicable. Forgive me that I for a moment forgot."

Her passion had died away as quickly as it had blazed forth. She heard him in silence, a sob in her throat.

Soon they were back in the perambulating crowd, chattering, laughing, listening to the band upon the river. The broad stream was filled with boats, in which charmingly-dressed women indolently reclined on bright-hued cushions. The occupants propelled themselves by means of lazy hands laid upon the sides of neighbouring boats. Be-flannelled men, and boys in their slim canoes, slipped here and there among them. The music mingled harmoniously with the light dip of the paddles, the soft lapping of the water, the murmuring voices. The sweet scent of hay, freshly cut in the meadows across the river, was in the air, the peace of the midsummer evening over all.

Such a happy, prosperous throng; such a concord of sweet sounds and scents and sights! One man and woman, at least, looked on, sorrowful-eyed, bitterness within their hearts.

"I am sorry if I shocked you," Kate Grantley said at length. "I thought if we two spoke together—even of that—face to face—"

"It is impossible," he said. "There are troubles in which no friend can help, Kate. The friend that is dearest to me in life cannot help me in mine."

He looked at her steadily, holding her eyes with his own, for a space; then left her and went on his way.

He went into his house, the door of which stood open to the night.

In the airless, bow-windowed room, upon the untidy sofa where he had left her, his wife was lying dead.

PART II

No inquest was held on Horace Kilbourne's wife. The doctor had attended her almost daily. For years her husband had been warned her heart was in such a condition that she might die suddenly, at any moment. She had so died. Except that it was a happy release for herself, and for her husband—that over-tired, good, and patient man—one of Heaven's mercies, there was nothing to be said. Unless Kilbourne himself, in remembrance of other days, and in the tenderness of his heart, shed a tear for her, there was not a soul to weep for drunken Julia Kilbourne.

Although, to the best of his ability, he had lived retired from all society, and in his sensitiveness to his wife's shame had kept, as well as he could, her history to himself, it was well known in the town. There was none who knew who did not respect and pity him. Kind hands were eagerly put out to him. At last he, who had shrunk from going to other men's houses because he could not ask them to his own, was free to do so.

It was a little disappointing that he repulsed all such advances.

The only adverse criticism which had been passed on him had been that, a heavily burthened man, he had not known how to conceal his misfortune, but had carried about with him a face as miserable as his history. That his face would now bear witness to his new-found delight of liberty was confidently expected.

It was strange that, instead of the looked-for lightening of gloom, there was, if possible, in his bearing, his wife being safely dead and buried, an increase of melancholy.

Kate Grantley, who thought she knew him better than the rest, was not surprised that the little letter she wrote him on the first news of Mrs Kilbourne's death remained unanswered. The words her pen had written had come warm from a heart realising the shock, the bewilderment, from which it was inevitable that he must suffer. But it was a letter which it would have been painful to him to answer, perhaps. He had known that she would understand.

She would not be hurt that he ceased to linger for her at the hour they both came out of school. Often she walked to the street which held her home and his, with his tall figure a dozen yards in front of her. She would not hurry a step to overtake him. All in good time. She no more doubted him—she no more doubted that in due time he would ask her to be his wife—than she doubted what her answer would be when he did so. Between them there had been no vulgar philandering; no word of what might have been, what yet might be, had passed their lips. Yet, deep in their hearts was guarded an unspoken compact which—she would have staked her life on it—neither would betray.

But she was unpleasantly startled, coming face to face with him one day, he walking down his garden path, which she was passing, to find that he did not even purpose to speak to her. Pretending to fumble at the lock of the gate, he hung back until she was well in front.

Later on, the pair had encountered in a shop. She had put out a hand to him, and he had taken it. But there had been hesitation, almost reluctance, on his part, and it seemed to her that he had looked at her with intolerable reproach in his eyes.

She was haunted by the remembrance. Was it possible that his wife's death could have been really a grief to him? Such a grief as that? Or was the lonely life he was leading, coming upon the shock of finding the woman dead, telling upon him physically and mentally?

"Go and ask Mr Kilbourne in to supper to-night!" she commanded her brother. She lived with him in another little bow-windowed house, with a purple clematis over the bow-window, a crimson rambler over the door, and about it the same air of sweetness, of neatness, of wholesomeness its mistress wore. "He is looking ill and wretched. Try to bring him in."

"I have asked him every day of my life. He won't come," the brother said. "He gets out of my way when he can," he added. "He does not seem to wish to be friendly any more."

She looked at him in silence, considering the statement. Kilbourne's punctiliousness was exaggerated, but she thought she understood it. It was delicacy carried to an extreme, perhaps, but she was proud to think it was characteristic of him.

"I don't see why he need be afraid of being civil to me, for all that," the brother said, almost as if she had spoken.

The next time Kate Grantley had an opportunity of looking in Kilbourne's face she was painfully struck by his appearance. The man was thinner, more worn, years older. His head seemed to droop beneath a heavier burthen than of yore; he walked as if his feet were shod with lead.

Several months, in which she had had no word with him, had gone by since his wife's death. At this rate, before he dared to stretch out a hand to gather for himself the happiness ready to bloom for him, he would be dead! She thought she saw that the man, lonely, sensitive, to a fault, was passing his days in brooding melancholy, in unmerited self-reproach. He had had more than enough of sadness in his life. For an idea, a stupid convention of other folks' manufacture, and not worth respecting, he should have no more. He should not be allowed to take his own path, to push her on one side again.

Once resolved on any course, she was a very practical young person, alert to take the opportunity the moment gave.

She overtook him determinedly, one afternoon, as he walked ahead of her from school, as usual. The holidays, during which neither had left home, were over; the summer was over, the winter term well begun.

"Mr Kilbourne, will you come into No. 6 for one minute to-day?" she said. "I particularly wish to speak to you."

He had been ready enough to go there in the old days, with or without pretext; now he had the look of a man called on to do a thing at which his soul sickened.

"If you will excuse me—" he said.

But Kate was resolute.

"I cannot excuse you. You must come at once," she said.

She had assumed the little air of authority over him which in her he had found to be so pleasant. With a look upon his face as if he were going to his execution, he obeyed.

For many weeks she had gone about, the words she meant to speak to him, of encouragement, of comradeship, upon her lips; the chance to use them had never come. Now she would not use them, but would speak to him as if there had been no hiatus in their communion, as if no tragedy had come between.

She faced him as they entered the bright little sitting-room, of exquisite neatness, and sweet with flowers, which had ever seemed such a haven of rest to him.

"Have you seen Alick?" she began. "Have you heard that they have promoted him, and that he is to be sent to the Paris branch?" (Alick was a clerk in one of the banks.)

He had not heard.

"He'll be pleased. It's what he wished for, isn't it?" he asked, not looking at her, gazing before him with lack-lustre eyes.

Her heart sank as, seeing him close at hand, she noted the change in him. Although, with his slouching gait and loose-hung limbs and hanging head, he had never been a smart-looking man, he had yet been one possessed of great personal nicety; in that matter—in the shipwreck of his life—being careful not to let himself go. But now there was about him a look of neglect, making to ache with pity the heart of the woman who observed it.

Alick was pleased, she admitted, with sinking spirit. "But it is about myself I want to ask your advice," she went on.

He glanced at her quickly with his deep, sad eyes, and glanced away again.

"Shall I throw up what I am doing here, and go with Alick? It is this I want to ask you. My brother could share lodgings with a friend he has there. He does not really want me; but I used to wish for Paris—long ago, before we met, you and I. I might meet with a good appointment there. It is a chance for me. Help me to make up my mind. Shall I go?"

There fell a complete silence between them.

She sat on the music-stool, her back to the open piano, a pretty, slight girl, with a dark and resolute little face. It confronted the gloomy one before it now with an expression progressing from expectation to surprise, to irritation, in its gaze. On her part, she determined not to say another word to bridge the pause; but it seemed that the silence would never be broken.

At length he slowly lifted his eyes to hers.

"I think, perhaps, it would be better for you to go," he said.

She sprang up from the stool, turned to the piano, began sorting, with quick, nervous fingers, the music there.

"You think so? Very well; I'll go, then," she said. "I only wanted to hear what you would think of it."

He had risen with an air of relief and picked up his hat. He looked in silence for a minute at her straight back in its trim Norfolk jacket, at her thick braids of black hair beneath the plain straw hat.

"Of course you know best what you wish," he said hesitatingly.

She placed the freshly arranged music with an air of decision on the piano.

"I know very well what I wish, thank you," she said.

There was another silence.

"Is that all?" he asked her.

"Quite all. Except"—she turned round upon him and showed him that the dark skin of her face had whitened, that her eyes were hurt and angry—"except that Alick has to go next week. I suppose I ought to give a term's notice; but also, if I don't, I suppose they'll do without it—I shall be ready to go with him. We shall be busy till we start. I may not see you to speak to again—this will be our good-bye."

"Is that so?" he said.

She could hardly believe her ears; she held her breath in the cruelty of the surprise, and set her teeth to help her to bear the pain.

"Ours has been a long friendship," she said, striving to steady her voice. "Two years—seeing each other every day. Strange, isn't it, how things come to an end?"

"Except some things which are endless," he said.

She took heart of grace at that.

"You mean Faith?" she asked; "Love?" She looked at him eagerly.

"I mean Pain," he corrected her, and held out his hand.

She would not put hers within it.

"If, after these long two years, you can go like that, your friendship is not what I thought it. It is not worth a hand-clasp. Good-bye," she said, and turned her back upon him, not deigning to watch him go.

"Do you go or stay?" her brother asked, when he came in from the bank that afternoon.

"I—go!" she said, but not with her usual bright promptness; and, looking at her face across their little tea-table, he saw that it had lost something of its usual serenity.

"Seen Kilbourne?" he asked.

She told him yes, with an air of careful unconcern; that he had come in that morning; that she had told him of their contemplated departure, and had said good-bye to him.

"I used to think—" the brother began, but she cut him short.

"I know. You often said so; don't say it any more," she said. "All that was a mistake—and absurd."

"You know what they are saying of him, Kate? They are saying he killed his wife."

Her dark face whitened, her dark eyes opened wide.

"They cannot!"

"They do. They say he couldn't look such a miserable, hangdog wretch for nothing. The worst is, the boys at the college have got hold of it. One of the little wretches wrote up on the white wall of his class-room the other day, 'Who killed his wife?' Bryant, the science master, told me Kilbourne took no notice, but his face was sea-green for the rest of the morning."

"He should have thrashed the whole class—thrashed them within an inch of their lives!"

"Well, he didn't. He did nothing." Alick dropped his voice. "Bryant told me he looked as if he were afraid," he said.

"What beasts people are to say such things!" she burst out. "And of such a man! The gentlest, the kindest—"

"I know, my dear. I'm sorry for poor old Kilbourne. I daresay he didn't kill his wife; but something's happened to him, and she did die uncommonly sudden. Anyhow, from what Bryant said, it's evident he's lost his nerve and his courage. At that rate, he'll precious soon lose his post."

Kate Grantley and Kilbourne, arriving from opposite directions, reached his gate at the same moment, the next morning. Rudely chalked upon the stone post was the question which had confronted Kilbourne on his class-room walls.

He pointed to the words with his stick which shook in his hand; his face was ashen white.

"Isn't it fitting that you and I should be confronted by that question?" he asked her.

She stared from the writing to him.

"I don't think it at all fitting!" she said. "Why don't you send for a policeman, and stop it?"

He pushed open the gate, and, taking no further notice of her, walked up the little path to his door. Reaching it, he found her behind him.

With that air of girlish authority he had once found so pleasant, "I am coming in," she said.

He led the way into that bow-windowed room in which Mrs Kilbourne had died. The pervading aroma of alcohol had left it; airiness and a certain formal tidiness now reigned in place of stuffiness and neglect; but the room was perhaps more depressing than before to a sensitive mind.

The sofa was in the same place; the basket, which had held the things she liked to have at hand, still stood beside it. The over-large table at which the unfortunate Julia had so often watched her husband eat his unappetising meals, and where he still made a pretence of eating them in sight of the empty sofa, still occupied too much of the available space.

Kilbourne turned and confronted the girl, who had followed him in. His eyes shone now, and there was the working of excitement in his face.

"I thought we had said our last words," he began; "I thought that that, at least, was done with—and you were going away. You have no right to follow me, Kate, to overthrow me in this fashion. My strength is almost exhausted; I have tried too much—too much—and all alone—"

"I know," she said, with her fine air of decision. "That is why I have come. You mustn't be alone any more. You must come with us."

He had tossed away his hat, and thrust his hands which were shaking, into his coat-pockets. He turned with excitement upon her, but she went firmly on.

"With Alick and me. You are too good for the post you hold; with your degrees you can easily get a better one. Come to Paris. Turn your back upon all that has been depressing and worrying you; upon this melancholy room"—she gazed round upon the unlovely space—"upon this"—she waved a peremptory, small hand towards the vacant sofa.

He looked at her with his accusing eyes, with a scarcely controlled emotion; but she stopped him when he tried to speak.

"We have been good friends," she said. "If I have not helped you through these two years we have walked as comrades together, you, at least, have helped me. Helped me so much"—she paused a moment, and the level tone of her voice quavered musically—"that I cannot lose you; that I need you terribly still."

"And I!" he burst forth then. "And I! Can you ever picture to yourself the magnitude of my need of you?"

He clenched the hands in his coat-pockets, and turned his back on her, and she saw his shoulders heave.

"It is killing me," he said—"killing me—just that."

His voice, which had been raised, sank brokenly. She listened, when it was silent, to the beating of her heart.

In a minute she went to him and laid a hand upon his arm.

"Then, why?" she asked him, whisperingly. "Why?"

He flung round upon her, and she fell back from the vehement accusing of his eyes.

"Why?" he repeated. "Why?" He threw a hand at the empty sofa. "There!" he said. "There—where you ask me to turn my back—my dead wife lies there—always for me. And she is between you and me for ever."

It sounded to her but the utterance of morbidity. The strange words were only a token of that from which she had come to save him. She had the courage to be unmaidenly, to persist.

"I, at any rate, do not see it so," she said. "To have me for your friend is to do no wrong to your dead wife."

"How can we be friends—you and I?" he asked her; and she, who knew they could not now be merely that, did not speak.

"I, who for your sake cursed her in my heart," he went on, his shaken voice hushed to an awe-struck whisper. "You, who put into her hands the poison which killed her."

"I?" she breathed, and drew back, staring at him, wondering, for one dreadful moment, had his unhealthy brooding turned his brain. "Killed her? I?"

"You!" he said, wildly. He went across the room, and shut the door behind her they had left ajar. "If it had been I myself I could have borne it; but you—you—! I found the empty bottle, that night, dropped from her hand; the label—'Poison'—and your name—"

"The chloral bottle?" she asked him; and the cloud of fear and dismay lifted from her eyes, and they were alight with understanding and with hope. She went swiftly to him and caught his arm. "Horace, do you remember that you warned me never to give her any narcotic, however earnestly she might beg for it—that it would not be safe—that she would kill herself? Do you remember?"

"But you gave it, all the same. Your name was on the bottle—"

"On the bottle—of water," she said. "It never held anything else. I used to take it home and fill it every day. The doctor told me to do it—it was a harmless fraud we played on her. She used to drink it, never doubting, and fall asleep—"

"Kate!"

She held him tightly by his arm, and looked with eyes that were dimmed with tears of most blessed relief upon the working of his face.

As, later, they went together through the little garden, and passed again the rudely-chalked question upon the gate—"Shall I stay here with you, and face the music," Kate Grantley asked, "or will you come away with me to Paris?"

"AS 'TWAS TOLD TO ME"

Her husband had died suddenly in the third year of their marriage, and she had been left a young widow with their only child.

The husband had been dead a year—a year passed in close seclusion in her country home—when she went out on a bright morning of the early spring, taking her little daughter with her, to gather primroses in the plantation bordering one extremity of the park around her house.

She had remembered when she arose in the morning that the day was the anniversary of her husband's death.

A year only! It had seemed like twenty years. For she was very young, and fairly rich and much admired, and the life she had hitherto led had not prepared her to support loneliness and retirement profitably. The shock of the sudden death had been terrible. She had thought that she should die of it; but she did not even fall ill. And there was the child, whom she adored. And later there had arisen a new interest.

The new interest, in the form of Major Harold Walsh, was at her elbow on this kind morning of sweetest spring. He was a middle-aged man, with a handsome, hard face and a very tender manner, and he chose, as some may think inopportunely, the anniversary of the husband's death to make the widow an offer of marriage.

The widow reminded him of what had happened on that day a year ago, pointed out that she could not possibly entertain such a proposition so soon, even cried a little when she spoke of her husband. But in no other way did she discourage the tender-mannered major with the hard face.

It would have been well-nigh impossible for a man to make an offer of marriage with a child of three years old clinging to her mother's skirts and incessantly babbling in her mother's ear; so the child with her nurse was sent into the interior of the plantation, in search of the lovely primroses said to flourish there, while the two elders wandered with slow steps and down-bent eyes upon the outskirts of the coppice.

So they would have been content to wander for hours, perhaps—he begging for assurances that she with an only half-feigned, pretty reluctance gave—but that their agreeable dalliance was cut short by a sufficiently alarming interruption.

She did not absolutely dislike him? Liked him—very much, even? That was well. Years hence, if he waited patiently—and he would try, he would try to wait—she might even get to love him a little?

Was that asking too much? Well, not just yet, then; he would wait. But he was not to go away unhappy? Not utterly discouraged? He need not, for what had taken place between them, debar himself entirely of the delight of her society, he might—?

It was at that instant of the major's soft-voiced pleading and of the widow's low, monosyllabic replies, that a voice from out the plantation on their left smote sharply upon their ears. It called affrightedly upon Mrs Eddington's name.

The mother, whose mother-love was, and would always be, the strongest passion of her life, fled into the wood. Following the direction of the voice, in two minutes she came upon the kneeling form of the nurse; and the nurse's white and terrified face looked up at her across the unconscious form of the little child.

"I found her so," the woman got out through chattering teeth. "I sat reading, and she ran to the other side of the tree. She was talking to me, and then she didn't talk, and I went round and found—this!"

With shaking fingers the mother tore asunder the broad muslin strings of the hat upon which the child lay, rent open the dainty dress at the throat—"Look at mother! Milly! Milly! Look at mother!" she called wildly, impatiently, fiercely even.

As if in answer to the passionate appeal, the child's dark lashes stirred for a moment on the transparent cheek; were still; stirred again; then the dark eyes, so like the dark eyes of the dead father, opened upon the mother's face.

"Only fainted," the gentleman who had been proposing to officiate as Milly's stepfather said. He was much relieved that the scene, at which he had looked on awkwardly enough, was over. That for a three-year-old child to faint was an unusual, an alarming occurrence, he did not, of course, understand. Certainly, if Mrs Eddington thought it necessary, he would go for the doctor. He could probably bring him quicker than a groom. Should he carry the little Milly home first?

But the mother must carry Milly herself. No; nurse should certainly not touch her. Never again should nurse, who had let the child for a minute out of her sight, touch Milly.

Nurse, surreptitiously grasping a frill of the child's muslin frock, wept, silent and remorseful, as she walked alongside.

Once, the child, who lay for the better part of the half-mile to her home in a kind of stupor, opened her eyes again beneath her mother's frightened gaze and was heard to mutter something about some flowers.

"She is asking for the primroses she had gathered!" Mrs Eddington whispered, in a tone of intensest relief. "Did you bring them, nurse?"

The unfortunate nurse, of course, had not brought them.

"Milly's po'r flo'rs is dead," Milly grieved in the little weak voice they heard then for the first time. "Milly's daddy took Milly's flo'rs, and they died."

To that astonishing statement the child adhered during the first days of her long illness, till she forgot, and spoke of it no more. For any questioning, she gave no explanation of her words. She never enlarged upon the first declaration in any way, nor did she even alter the form of the words in which she gave it expression. Always she alluded to the curious delusion with a grieving voice, often with tears.

"Dear daddy is dead, darling," the mother said to her in an awed whisper, kneeling at her side. "He could not come to Milly."

"Milly's daddy took Milly's flo'rs, and they died," the sad little voice protested; and the child softly whimpered upon the pillow.

"The child can't, of course, even remember her father," Major Walsh said, with impatience, being sick of the subject and the importance attached to it. "She was only two when he died."

"How can you tell what a child of two remembers?" Mrs Eddington asked. "She was very fond of Harry. I think she does remember."

Persistently, in her mind recurred an episode of the last day of her husband's life. He had carried his little daughter, laughing and prattling to him, down from the nursery, and had put her in her mother's arms. The child, when he turned to go, had clung to him. "Don't leave Milly, daddy. Take Milly too," she cried. Laughing, he had kissed her. "Not now—not now," he had said—"but later I will come and take Milly."

Then he had gone out, with a smile still on his face, and had fallen dead as he walked across the park.

It was inevitable that in these days the memory of her husband should more fully occupy the young widow's mind. He had died of heart disease; his child, it was now discovered, had a certain weakness of the heart. A superstitious feeling that she had not remembered him enough, and that this was her punishment, took possession of Mrs Eddington's brain. She remembered with remorse what had been occurring at the moment her child had fallen insensible among the primroses. On the very anniversary of her poor Harry's death she had forgotten him so far! Never would she forget him again.

The words the child spoke had recorded a mere delusion, the doctor told her, of the little dazed brain in the moment preceding unconsciousness; but for all that rational view, they awed the mother, haunted her.

"Milly's p'or flo'rs is dead. Milly's daddy took Milly's flo'rs and they died," Milly had said.

Never would Mrs Eddington leave her child, or forget Milly's daddy again.

Yet, when the anniversary of poor Harry Eddington's death came round again, Milly had been for three-quarters of a year running about as of old; her mother had been for two months the wife of Major Walsh.

They had spent their honeymoon at Major Walsh's own place in Wiltshire, had stayed for another month in his London house, and they at last turned their steps in the direction of the home which had been Harry Eddington's, where his child had been left under the guardianship of the new Mrs Walsh's mother.

"You used to complain of the dulness of the place and of how buried alive you were there. You have been away for eight weeks, and you are mad to get back to it," the husband said, with a jealous eye upon his bride.

She subdued, judiciously, the joy which had been in her voice. "I am glad to see the old place again—yes," she said. "Won't it be delightful for us to be together there, where we first knew each other?"

"It is the child you want—not me," he said, with grudging reproach. She found it necessary to make some quite exaggerated statements to reassure him.

Her mother was in the carriage which met them at the station. "Milly is staying up, till you come," she told them. "I left her capering wildly about the nursery with delight."

"I hope she won't over-excite herself," the mother said, and the grandmother laughed at that anxiety. No child of hers had ever had a weakness of the heart, and she was inclined to ridicule the idea that Milly required more care than had been given to her own children.

Full of longing to see her child, Mrs Walsh sprang from the carriage, and ran up the broad steps to the wide-open doors of her home. Then, with a happy after-thought, turned on the mat, and held out her hands to the new husband.

"Welcome—welcome to our home, dear," she said.

He grasped the hands tightly. "After all, I suppose I am a little more to you than the child?" he asked.

She smiled a flattering affirmative; and at the instant there came a scream in a child's voice from a room above, followed by an ominous silence.

When the others reached the nursery from which as they knew, the sound had come, the mother was already standing there, holding in her arms the unconscious form of her little girl. From a tiny wound in the child's white forehead drops of blood were oozing.

"I left her for one minute to fetch the water for her bath," the nurse was saying, hurriedly excusing herself. "She was running up and down and round about, calling, 'Daddy, come to Milly! Come, daddy, come!'"

"She fell and struck her head against the sharp corner of this stool," Major Walsh said. "Look, it has sharp corners."

The child was only unconscious for a minute. She opened her eyes, smiled upon her mother, hid her face in her neck, and presently was whispering a question again and again in her ear.

Mrs Walsh looked up in a bewildered fashion from the little hidden face. "What does she say?" the grandmother asked.

"She says, 'Where is my daddy gone?'" the mother repeated, faltering a little over the words, and with scared eyes.

"He is here," said the practical grandmother, and took Major Walsh by the arm. "We have told her her daddy was coming with her mother," she explained. "She was more excited about him even than about you, Millicent. Look up! Here is your daddy, darling."

Slowly the child lifted her head from the mother's shoulder, and looked at the big man with the hard face now stooping over her—looked for half a second, shut her eyes again, and again hid her face.

"It isn't my daddy," she said, with a baby whimper, "Milly wants my daddy that came and danced with Milly. Where's my daddy gone?"

Later, when the child had been put to bed, the mother, having hurriedly dressed for dinner, knelt by the side of the crib to hold her daughter in her arms; kissing the tiny wound upon her forehead, she asked how it was she had managed so to hurt herself.

"My daddy came and danced. He whirled Milly round and round," the little one said, grievingly. She knew nothing more of the occurrence; it was the only explanation she ever gave.

The look of awe which had been there once before came back to Mrs Walsh's eyes. Only to the doctor did she ever repeat the child's words. He, being a man of good common sense, refused of course to be impressed with the coincidence.

"She made herself giddy by, as she says, whirling round and round. In the moment of losing consciousness—who can tell by what unintelligible mental process?—the figure of her dead father, undoubtedly impressed with unusual clearness on the child's memory, was present with her. A vision? yes, if you like to call it so; say, rather, a dream in the instant before unconsciousness. Such a babe as this knows no distinction between dreams and realities—between the momentarily disordered mental vision and the ordinary objects of optical seeing."

For the rest, the unsatisfactory condition of the heart was still existent. Nothing that with care might not be obviated. With the absence of all excitement, with entire rest of mind and body, the child would outgrow the evil.

Yet, in spite of this cheerful view of the case, it was long before Mrs Walsh could successfully conceal the uneasiness and unhappiness she felt. Her punishment again, she told herself with morbid iteration. She had turned her back on her child, had forgotten her dead husband; nay, even in the moment of the child's accident, had she not been in the act of welcoming another man to that dead husband's home?

So, with a new life just begun for her, and new interests arising on all hands she found her mind continually dwelling on the days of her earlier married life. Often, when bent on any expedition with Major Walsh, dining with their neighbours, receiving them in her home, walking, driving with him, talking over the details of the business of the little estate, she was thinking, thinking how she and that other man had gone here and there, said this and that to each other. How he had looked, the words he had said; his gestures, his laugh, came curiously back to her; and her heart sank beneath a constant sense of self-reproach. How could she not have remembered all this before, and been true to the claims he had on her—that poor young husband who was the father of her child?

Once, but that was months later, and she was weak in body as well as depressed in mind, she sat alone over her bedroom fire as the dark came on, too tired to dress, and longed for her husband to come in and cheer her. Then the memory came to her of how once before, a few weeks before Milly was born, she had so sat in that very room, and had longed inexpressibly for that other husband; of how she had felt that she would die of fright and of longing for his comforting presence if he did not come; of how he had come at last, bringing warmth and love and courage to her failing heart; of how he had laughed, and said he had felt she was wanting him, and so had put what he was doing on one side and hurried to her. And as she thought of this, lying with shut eyes in her armchair, a curious feeling that he was there again with her in the room, took possession of her. She was not afraid; she lay quite still, hardly breathing, feeling "Harry is here! If I open my eyes I shall see him."

And often, in the weeks that followed, she was haunted by that strange consciousness of her first husband's presence; the curious, forcible impression that there was between her and him but a slight veil she lacked the resolution to rend, but that, rending it one day, she should see him.

Then Harold Walsh's child was born, and these unhealthy fancies were naturally vanquished.

It was a son, and there was much rejoicing. Poor little Milly's nose, it was said, must indeed be put out of joint by this advent of an heir to his father's large estates.

The child was born at Royle, his father's place, and christened there, while Milly had stayed on in her own home with her grandmother; the home where she had been born, where her father and mother had passed their brief married life together. When the son and heir was two months old, he came with his father and mother to stay in that house also. Then her mother and the neighbours who had known her through all her experiences of joy and of sorrow were glad to see that the Major's wife had got back her health and spirits and happiness.

The boy was a fine boy, and his mother idolised him; the father, contrary to general expectation, continued to be very much in love. They were a prosperous and happy trio, seeming to suffice to themselves. Little Milly, who had longed for her mother and the new brother, found herself of comparatively small importance, and decidedly on the outside of the completed circle.

Who can measure the bitterness, the desolation, which no after-experience of the unkind tricks of destiny can ever equal, of the little heart which feels it is not wanted where it longs to cling?

Then Milly's birthday came, and she was six years old; a delicately lovely child with dark, straight hair, dark eyes, and a complexion which was as a finger-post to her father's history and her own, and should have said "Beware!" Milly had always a birthday-party; this year also she must have one.

But it was not a party such as Milly had been promised; with the small drawing-room turned into a cave of delights, where a real, white-robed fairy with silver wings and a wand presided over presents to be given to Milly and all her little guests. The promise, in the pleasurable excitement of the Walshs' arrival, had been forgotten by all but Milly. When Milly demanded its fulfilment it was too late.

So the little guests could only dance—those that were big enough—or assisted by their elders, in the form of governess or elder sister, play at forfeits and twilight, and blindman's buff. These innocent gambols they carried on in the wide entrance hall. Some flags had been hung, to please Milly, against the heavy beams of the ceiling, and the gardener had filled every niche and corner with hothouse plants.

Bent, apparently, on spoiling his sister's pleasure, the heir of the house of Walsh must be taken with a colic on that day. His mother was anxious about him, fancying him feverish, and insisting on the doctor's presence. So it came to pass she was oftener sitting in the nursery, seeing her son jogged, howling lustily, on the nurse's lap, than making merry with Milly and her friends in the hall.

As the afternoon drew to a close, and carriages began to arrive for the children and their guardians, Mrs Walsh came out of the nursery, and standing in the comparative darkness of the corridor, looked down upon the bright and pretty scene. The children in their dainty white dresses, with their flushed faces and tossed curls, were as lovely as the flowers everywhere surrounding them; the music of the chattering voices, of the clear laughter, was more agreeable to the ear than that of the piano Milly's governess was playing.

The fun, as is apt to be the case when such a gathering is nearly over, waxed livelier as the time came for the children to part. "Just one more game!" Milly's little excited voice was heard pleading— "only one more!"

It was Kiss in the Ring, the old world favourite they chose, and they formed themselves into a circle, putting the littlest boy—boys were scarce among them, and very small—in the centre.

It was in the midst of much laughing and chatter and noise that the two little girls on either side of Milly Eddington felt her hands turn ice-cold in theirs, and slowly slip from their grasp. The next instant she had fallen to the floor between them.

The doctor, luckily on the spot, attending to the baby-brother, was with her in two minutes. There was nothing to be done. She was dead.

She had been the loveliest and the gayest there, laughing her pretty, happy laugh, babbling with the rest. Several of the elder guests, it was afterwards found, had been looking at the child and listening to her, when all at once she had become silent, had sunk backwards, and died.

So much they who looked on had seen, but nothing more.

Her mother, standing above, in the shadow of the corridor, and looking down upon the brightly-lit hall below, had seen this—

She had seen the figure of her first husband—the smile upon his face with which he had left her and her little daughter on the last day of his life—come silently into the hall. She had seen him, moving softly, attracting no notice from them, pass the groups of ladies standing near the walls, and noiselessly thread his way through the ring of playing children, till he stood at the back of his own little girl. She had seen him, smiling still, and clasping his hands tenderly beneath the child's chin, pull her softly backwards, and lay her dead upon the floor.

FREDDY'S SHIP

"A day or two, and I must return these people's call," Mrs Macmichel said to herself as she passed the Rectory gate. "What a bore!"

Two or three days ago the rector and his wife, calling on their new parishioner at the Court, had found her just returned from lunch with the shooting party in the field.

"Bad luck, wasn't it?" she asked, later, of the half-dozen men to whom she was giving tea in the billiard-room. "If I'd stayed to watch you shoot for another five minutes, I should have escaped them! Not a bad, dowdy little woman—the man a worse stick in the drawing-room than the pulpit, if possible. Subjects: his—parish room he wants to build; hers—son at sea, or going to sea, or has been to sea, or something. What is it to me? If he is drowned fifty fathoms deep at the bottom of the sea, do I care?"

"Now, if I only have the good luck to pick on a day when they're out!" she said as she stepped briskly along; a tall, and handsome, and fashionable-looking woman, in her hat with the green twisted veil and the green cock's feathers, her short, workman-like skirt and belted coat.

Down the short path from the Rectory door to the gate the rector himself was coming. Mrs Macmichel bowed a condescending head as she passed on, receiving no form of salutation but a stare from a pair of vacant eyes in return.

"Well, really! Such people!" the lady said to herself, as she walked disdainfully on. "Even here you would expect a man would know he is always expected to take off his hat when a woman bows to him!"

"Mrs Macmichel!" a voice said at her back. A hand was laid upon her arm. She turned a look of astonished questioning upon the man who had ventured to touch her.

"Stop, please," he said; his voice was breathless as of one in great agitation. "Mrs Macmichel, I think you owe my wife a call? I want you to pay it now—at once—"

"It is very kind of you; I—"

"You mustn't make excuses. You mustn't deny me. You must go; and you must—stay."

The thought that he might be mad was succeeded as she looked in his face by the thought that he must be ill. The healthy colour natural to them had left his large cheeks, their fatness was only flabbiness, the small eyes were filled with a strange, pleading, protesting misery as of a man in terrible bodily discomfort.

"Mr Jones, I am afraid you are not well?"

He stopped her with an impatiently thrown-up hand. "It's not that—I'm all right. It's worse—it's my son—"

"The sailor?"

"News has come that the Doughty has gone down. All lost."

"Your son was in that ship?"

He did not answer, but pressed his lips, which were piteously quivering, together, and looked at her in staring misery.

"I am going into the village to wire for—confirmation. Till I return you must keep with my wife."

"But, Mr Jones! I am deeply, deeply sorry; but you must let me telegraph, and you, yourself, stay with Mrs Jones."

"No. She would know as soon as she saw my face. I stole away—I dare not see her." He stayed a minute, biting at lips drawn inward over his teeth. "Our only one!" he said. "No other! When I know—when there is no hope—no hope—I must tell her. I could wish that she might die before— that we might both die."

Tears had gushed upon the flabby cheeks; he mumbled his lips for a minute, unable to speak.

"If there was anything else I could do—anything!" Mrs Macmichel said. "But this—!"

"You will watch over her till I come back," he said, not even noticing her remonstrance. "It is a service I ask of you by right of our common humanity. Go in to her at once, please."

With his hand on her arm he turned her to the gate, and opened it for her. "Let no one else come near her," he said. "The butcher delivering our meat gave me the news. He saw it on the newspaper board at the village shop. Everyone in the village who reads it will come up at once to tell my wife. Keep them away. She has a weak heart; told suddenly, she might—Don't let her stir out. Don't let her hold communication with anyone till I return."

He put up a trembling hand in the direction of his clerical hat, but lacked the spirit to lift it, and turned hurriedly away.

"But, Mr Jones!" she called. She made a step or two after him. "It will be so awkward—for her, I mean. She won't understand. You see, I hardly know your wife."

He raised his strengthless hand for a few inches, and let it fall with a gesture of hopeless wretchedness. "Oh, what do such things matter?" he groaned.

She was ashamed to persist. "I thought perhaps someone in the village—someone she knew—"

"They could do nothing with her," he explained. "If she wanted them to go, she would tell them to go; she can't tell you. If she wanted to go into the village, she would go—"

"How soon will you be back?"

"An hour. Two hours. I must wire to Portsmouth, and wait a reply." He began to walk on again. "When I come back I shall—know," he said, and shuffled forward, with drooping back, and legs that shook beneath him, on his way.

Once he turned, and, seeing her still at the gate, pointed a weakly imperative finger at the house without stopping in his progress.

Hardly crediting that it could be upon her, Flora Macmichel, accustomed to move in paths so carefully smoothed, to have all ugly things hidden from her sight, that this task of matchless unpleasantness had been thrust, she turned and walked slowly towards the Rectory door. There are so many women in the world, shrieking, gesticulating, ready to rush into any fray a-brewing; so many quiet and strong and helpful, aching to take other people's burdens upon their shoulders; she had never sought to identify herself with one or the other species, holding the comfortable doctrine that we cannot all be servers, that in the general scheme those who only stand to be waited on also hold a useful place.

Why need she do this thing? Three weeks ago she had not known these people existed; three days ago had not set eyes on them. For humanity's sake, he had said. Well!

But she thought of the mumbling lips, the look of anguish in the poor eyes, went on, and rang the bell.

Mrs Jones was in, of course. She was sitting over the dining-room fire, writing a letter. A short, rather fat, rather dumpy woman, with plain features, an ominous flush on her sallow cheeks, iron-grey hair, and very large, very luminous dark eyes.

"How very good of you to call so soon!" she said, and got up to welcome, rather effusively, the rich woman who had come to be a parishioner. "Let your master know at once that Mrs Macmichel is here, Mabel," she said to the servant, and gave Mabel a look which indicated tea was to make its appearance with as little delay as possible. "Are you walking or driving? Walking? Really? Now, would you rather sit near the fire or the open window? It is the kind of day—isn't it?—when either is agreeable."

She had a slightly nervous manner, or she was not quite at ease with the strange caller. She altered the position of the chairs, rattled the poker in the fire, pushed away the little table which held the writing things.

"I was just writing to my son," she said, and smiled, as if sure of her interest in the subject, at the woman, who, chill to the marrow with the discomfort of her errand, had taken a chair by the side of the fire. "I think I told you he is in the navy? He is commanding the Doughty, the new destroyer. Going trips in her every day or so. I suppose these destroyers are terrible-looking things? Ah! I have never seen one, but I imagined so. What a comfort to me to know they are, after all, so safe as Freddy tells me they are."

"Such a mild day for the time of year, isn't it? And such a pretty stretch of road from the Court here!"

"We often say so!"

"And just the right length for a walk!"

"Exactly a mile and a quarter."

"Really?"

"Exactly! We always called it a mile; but the last time he was home on leave Freddy measured it with his new cyclometer. 'Now, mother,' he said, 'please to remember it's a mile and a quarter, and, don't let's have any dispute about it in future?'"

"It's so nice to know—to an inch or two!"

"Well, Freddy has a very accurate mind. He can't bear anything slipshod in the way of a statement. Now, you are sure, after your walk, you do not feel the fire too much? Then move into this chair. You have really taken the least comfortable in the room. Now, isn't that better?"

Mrs Macmichel said that it was delightfully cosy. She was inwardly shivering; the tips of her fingers felt like ice. She pulled off her loose gloves, and held a pair of white hands blazing with jewels to the flame. She must force herself to talk, and to keep the poor woman off the topic of her son; but she, who was considered ready-tongued and ready-witted, sat dumb, she had not a word to say.

"There is so much difference in chairs," she said, at length.

The banality did not affect Mrs Jones to laughter, as the speaker had a fear it might have done. She seized eagerly on the remark.

"Isn't there? Some are straight in the back, and some slope too much for comfort; some are too high in the seat for short legs, and some quite ridiculously low."

"But this is perfect."

"I am so glad you find it so! It is Freddy's. It was one he bought when he was in barracks. But he sent it to me. It was much too comfortable to be anywhere but in his own home, he said. Isn't it delightful that young men are so much attached to their homes, nowadays?"

It was indeed delightful, Mrs Macmichel answered; and added with an effort the original remark that home was a delightful place.

She supposed it was, the other lady agreed. "I never go away from mine, my health does not allow me," she said; "and so, perhaps, I can hardly judge."

She looked round the rather dismal, rather shabby room with a something critical in her gaze. Perhaps the presence of the fashionably-dressed woman seated there—a person so evidently out of harmony with her surroundings—helped her to see the familiar dowdiness with other eyes. She gave a quick sigh as she looked, then turned to her visitor with her nervous smile—

"It is a mercy Freddy does not see the old fashion, the shabbiness. He only sees—home," she said.

Always Freddy! Poor Freddy, who would never see home again!

Searching wildly in her, at this crisis, stagnant mind for anything to turn the poor woman from her subject, Mrs Macmichel remembered the Parish Room. Here should be a mine of conversational wealth. She would work it for all it was worth.

"My husband is so—interested in the scheme," she said, and gulped a little at the lie. "Tell me over again, please, all those details you gave me before. He would like to know how much you have in hand; what you want to complete the room; what the bazaar brought in, and how much you expect from the concert."

Mrs Jones rose easily to the bait. She rose, too, talking all the time, to fetch from her writing-case the type-written circular where the parish's need for such a room was stated, and the paper, in her husband's handwriting, on which the sums already collected, and their source, were set forth. A hundred and thirty pounds were still wanted. What was a sum like that to this millionaire at the Court? And what a lot of begging, writing, giving of jumble sales, supposing they were moved to give that sum, would be saved to the Joneses!

Mrs Macmichel took the papers, glanced at them, laid them on her lap, tried to say yes and no in the right places to the information now eagerly poured forth to her; tried to keep her eyes from that letter which the clergyman's wife had been interrupted in writing. It had fluttered to the floor as she had looked through her writing-case, and now lay, unheeded by her, at the visitor's feet.

"My own darling boy," it began.

"Such a poor parish." "So much indifference." "So disheartening," fell on Flora Macmichel's unreceptive ear.

"My own darling boy."

Something other than curiosity, stronger than her will, glued her eyes to the page.

"Your last dear letter reached me—"

Last! Yes, last indeed!

"Only five shillings and twopence in the bag; and of that, two shillings were contributed by Mr Jones and myself. Discouraging, is it not?"

"—This subject we will discuss more fully when you come home again," in spite of herself she read the words.

Come home again! Come home again! When the sea gives up its dead!

The servant came in, bringing tea; picked up the letter, returned it to the table.

"If you please, ma'am, Mrs Pyman have called, and wish to speak with you."

"Ask her to wait," the mistress said; then glanced at her visitor to deprecate the anticipated polite protest on her part. "Anne Pyman will like very much to sit down in the kitchen for a while," she said. But as the maid withdrew she apparently altered her mind. "This good woman is the biggest gossip in the village," she explained. "She is always running up here to tell me this or that which she picks up. I think, after all, if you would excuse me for one minute—?"

"Of course!" the visitor said, mechanically; then awoke to the remembrance that she had undertaken to keep Mrs Jones from all outside intercourse. She turned an anxious look upon her hostess—"I think if we could have tea—?" she said.

Then she strangled a laugh in her throat—a laugh, sitting in Freddy's chair! What—what must Freddy's mother think of her!

"Oh, certainly!" Mrs Jones concurred. The large dark eyes, the only handsome feature she possessed, scanned with a fleeting gaze of inquiry the other woman's face. "I daresay, after your walk—"

"If you don't mind. Yes. Quite so. Tea is so very refreshing, don't you think?"

The temptation to say it was the cup which cheered but did not inebriate crossed her mind, but was combated.

The bread-and-butter handed to her with her tea was thick, the tea had not been creamed; but if food and drink had been fit for the entertainment of the gods, she did not think she could have swallowed. She lifted the bread-and-butter to her lips, then laid it, untasted, down again, she stirred her tea, and glanced at the clock upon the mantelpiece. For how long must she sit and talk inanities with this mother whose only child was lying fathoms deep beneath the sea? She had been there barely a quarter of an hour. For an hour and three-quarters, at least, she must sit there still, whatever the other woman thought of her, however she tried to rid herself of her company.

"You, too, have a son, I believe?" Mrs Jones was saying.

"Yes." She had an only son. His name was Connell. He was six years old.

"And very dear to you, I know!" The eyes of the woman whose only son was drowned shone with sympathy. They were speaking eyes, really beautiful with that light in them.

"Very dear to me," responded the woman in Freddy's chair. To her eyes came a sudden, unexpected rush of tears. Of her own child she felt she could not speak to this unconsciously bereaved mother.

"And six years old? Ah! Now I must show you what my dear boy was like at six."

She got up, and fetched from the mantelpiece a photograph of a tiny boy in a sailor's dress; a plain-featured, ordinary-looking little boy, with dark eyes too solemn for his age.

"Now, is your boy as big, do you think? We considered Freddy a fine boy. And whom do you think he takes after?"

"He is like you—about the eyes," Mrs Macmichel said. She gave the photograph hurriedly back. She could not endure to look upon the eyes closed now upon their "first dark day of nothingness."

Mrs Jones put the portrait tenderly in its place. "That big photograph standing above the clock was taken only the other day," she said. "When he was appointed to the Doughty, I wished so much to have him in his uniform. But the trouble I had to get him to have it taken! For no inducement in the world but to please me would he appear in uniform when not on duty, he said."

And now he lay, like Nicanor, "dead in his harness."

Mrs Macmichel was seated directly in front of the enlarged photograph. Its eyes looked straight into hers as she lifted them, with, it seemed to her, an infinite sadness.

"Is it not strange that we should both be mothers of only sons?"

It was not, in fact, a very remarkable coincidence, but the visitor conceded that it was strange.

"It ought to be a bond of sympathy between us."

"Yes."

Mrs Macmichel's eyes were turned uneasily upon the door at which the servant had suddenly appeared.

"Mrs Pyman is afraid she can't wait any longer now, ma'am. She wouldn't keep you more'n a minute, if you could speak to her, she says."

Mrs Macmichel put out a hand and gripped the arm of her hostess as she rose from her seat— "Don't—" she said imploringly, "don't go! We are so—so comfortable."

She could not but be flattered, although she could not help being surprised. "Tell Anne Pyman, I am sorry," Mrs Jones said to the maid, who, however, stood her ground.

"And cook say, the butcher have been, and can she speak to you for a minute, ma'am?" she asked.

The butcher! He who had brought the terrible news. In her eagerness Mrs Macmichel turned to the servant standing at the door.

"No," she said, "certainly not! Your mistress cannot come."

The miserable, not to be repressed chuckle of laughter took her again as the girl withdrew. "You must think me strange," she said to the lady, gazing at her with astonished eyes. "But I am strange. We are getting on so well. I don't like to be interrupted. Go on. You were saying—?"

"About the bond of sympathy: our only children. I'm afraid the bread-and-butter is too substantial; will you try a bun instead?"

"It is delicious!" Flora Macmichel said, and put the slice again to her lips, and again placed it unbitten in the saucer.

"There is," said the clergyman's wife in a lowered tone, "something awful—I mean in the sense of being full of awe—in being entrusted by God with only one child. Don't you think that much more will be required of us, and of them—our dear children?"

Mrs Macmichel had not thought of it in that light.

"You see, we have no others to share our devotion, to distract our attention. Our only one should be, as near as a mother can make him so, perfect."

"Wouldn't that make him a little—well—uninteresting?"

Mrs Jones's eyes blazed reproof as she answered: "Freddy is not uninteresting," she said.

Presently her voice dropped to a hushed whisper. "Then, there is the thought"—she said—"the haunting thought—should he die—should it please God to take him from us, we lose our all. All!" she repeated; and the word, spoken in that tone of heavy solemnity, dropped like lead upon Flora Macmichel's heart.

If she lost Connell there was still, in her case, her husband; but she thought of the husband of Mrs Jones, and was silent.

"I have a friend," she said, suddenly rousing herself to make one effort suitable to the occasion, "whose only little girl died last year. They thought her heart would break, but it did not. She—in a marvellous way she bore it. Never once did she seem to me to sorrow—painfully. The child, for long and long after she was dead, seemed with her, she told me." She leant forward in her chair; her voice, which was a rather harsh-speaking voice, grew low and earnest. Was it possible that she—she, Flora Macmichel—had joined the company of the preachers! "Don't you think that alleviations undreamed of are always sent?" she asked, smarting tears in her eyes, her voice breaking.

"Perhaps I ought not to say it," the other woman said, "it is my want of faith, of which I should be ashamed; but it seems to me that nothing—nothing—in this world, of course—could atone."

A bell clashed sharply.

By leaning back slightly in her chair, Mrs Jones could get, it seemed, a side view of the door.

"Dear me! It is the boy from the telegraph office," she said. "I never see him without the dreadful fear that something may be amiss. Isn't it old-fashioned of me?"

The flush which told of disease had deepened on her cheeks; she laid a hand upon her chest as she arose. "If you will excuse me for half a moment—?"

But Mrs Macmichel had sprung to her feet and was at the door before the other. "Let me!" she said hurriedly. "I—I have my hat on. You might take cold—"

"Excuse me!" Mrs Jones cried.

"You really must allow me!" said Mrs Macmichel.

There was quite a scuffle at the door as to which should go out first.

It was the younger and stronger woman who dashed across the hall and snatched the telegram from the boy upon the steps. She came back, crushing the orange envelope, unopened, in her hand. Full well she knew its contents. The authorities had not waited for the father's inquiry, but had wired the news.

"It was—was for me," she said, gasping out the intelligence.

The dark eyes of the elder woman questioned her sharply. "How strange—how very strange it should have been sent on here!"

"My husband knew I was coming to make—a long call. He sent it on."

Mrs Jones sat down again before her tea-tray, and in the speaking eyes was a dawning of suspicion—"I hope nothing is the matter?" she said. "You will read your telegram, Mrs Macmichel?"

Mrs Macmichel thrust the envelope into the pocket of her coat, and kept her hand upon it there. "It is from my dressmaker; she is always bothering," she said.

"But are you sure, as you have not read it?"

"Quite sure. I always know when they come from her."

The hand which seized upon her cup again was shaking. The slice of bread-and-butter was sodden with the tea which had been spilt on it as she had put it so hurriedly down. "What were we talking of?" she asked. "I—it was so interesting. Please go on."

"It was about our dear children," said Mrs Jones slowly. She looked with a gaze of awakening distrust at her visitor. Her thoughts evidently turned to her husband. "I will hear if Mr Jones has returned," she said. "He would be so sorry to miss you—"

She put out her hand to the bell. Mrs Macmichel stopped her hurriedly. "Don't ring!" she said, in the loud voice of alarm. "Please! I will stay till Mr Jones comes back, however long he is away. I promise."

Ah, if he would only come! Only half an hour lived through of the two hours yet! Yet, for worlds she would not be present at the meeting of the wife and husband, who then would—know!

"I will stay, if you will let me go the very instant he comes," she added. "If you tell me when you see him coming up the garden path, I will run."

"He is here!" Mrs Jones said, with an air of relief. "I heard the garden-gate; I know his step—"

Oh, not for ten worlds would Flora, who had ever shunned the sight of pain, see that meeting! She almost flung her teacup from her. She seized the other's hand.

"Good-bye! oh, good-bye!" she said; "I cannot possibly stay another minute. I am so sorry! Oh, Mrs Jones, will you please remember, I am nearly dead with sorrow—but I must go."

"She is certainly mad," said the other woman to herself. She was so astonished that she forgot to rise from her chair, but sat looking after her vanishing guest with eyes wide with dismay.

On the doorstep the clergyman and the lady encountered. He was panting as one, all unaccustomed to such exercise, who had run. There was a look of famished eagerness in his eyes, the unhealthy pallor of his face was beaded with drops of sweat.

"They told me—at the office—a telegram had been sent," he said.

She snatched it from her pocket and put it in his hand. "I kept it from her," she said. "Take it, and let me go."

And yet she could not go.

His shaking fingers had torn open the envelope, had clutched the enclosure. It wavered so, that, standing behind him, she put her arms round his arms—tall woman as she was—her hands over his, and helped him to steady it.

"Read it," he said to her; "I can't—I can't see."

So she read aloud to him, in a voice that rose on a note of triumph and finished in a sob, the single line of the message!

"Not on board the Doughty. Tell mother all right."

Mrs Jones, coming to the dining-room door, looked out for one instant on her husband, apparently clutched in Mrs Macmichel's embrace. In the next, the lady was speeding with her long stride down the path to the gate; the clergyman had staggered into a hall chair, a succession of sounds, something between sobs and hiccoughs, issuing from his throat.

"My dear, has she hurt you?" his wife cried excitedly. "She is mad—quite mad, I am sure!"

Her husband, catching sight of Mrs Macmichel's face as she entered, followed her upstairs to her room. She was lying, dressed as she was, on her bed, with her face hidden.

"My dear, what is the matter? What have you been doing with yourself?" he asked.

She had been to the Rectory, to call on the Joneses, she told him.

"Well?"

"The Doughty has gone down. All on board lost."

"So I hear. Well?"

"It was their son's ship."

"Well?"

"Freddy's." She sat up and laughed across the sob in her throat. "You stupid! I am crying because Freddy did not go down in the Doughty," she said.

A NERVE CURE

"Well, what a place!" Julia cried.

I had come to it because of an urgent need of change, because it was by the sea, because it was cheap, because the advertisement had caught my eye at a moment when I was weary of vainly protesting that I wished to go nowhere except to bed.

"To Let, during the months of November and December, a six-roomed cottage; desirable; furnished; free of charge, with exception of caretaker's wage."

A couple of letters from me, a couple in reply from the owner, who was going for the winter months abroad, and the affair was settled.

Then my people who—although for ten years I have earned my own living, and helped to keep some of them who have not earned theirs, although I am five-and-thirty years of age and an absolutely dependable person—have never let me have my own way in any single matter, insisted that Julia should come with me. She is my youngest sister. I have not a word to say against her, of course; only I know that the things I am content to put up with are never good enough for Julia.

"Well, what a place!" Julia repeated; the shifting of the accent did not denote, I was sure, a more favourable view.

It certainly was not a pretty cottage. It was also quite out of the town, in which we had believed it to be situated, standing at the extremity of an unfinished road which led halfway across the sandy waste lying between the town of Starbay and the village of Starcliff.

"A garden, back and front," Miss Ferriman had promised me in one of her letters. There were the gardens, sure enough, but almost as unfinished as the road. "An airy situation and uninterrupted view of the sea," the description had continued, and was faithful as far as it went. The wind, which happened to be blowing a gale, without obstruction of any kind to break its force, buffeted us remorselessly as, having descended from the car which had brought us from the station, we struggled up the path to the door. Half a mile of blowing sand, with sparse, wiry grass sticking through, was between us and the breakers; yet the ocean, cold and lead-coloured, was beyond, and not so much as a finger-breadth of impediment to check the prospect.

"Well, what a place!" said Julia again. "Let's go back, Isabella. Don't let us go in."

But, once inside, we found the sitting-room which was to be ours comfortable and prettily furnished; our two bedrooms—there were but three—were also all that was necessary. Mine faced the sea beyond the melancholy, level Denes, Julia, to my great content, choosing the one looking out upon the back. The little back garden with its stunted shrubs, the unmade road beyond, made a melancholy outlook, but one that suited Julia better than the sea-view.

"The sight of the sea at this time of year gives me the most awful feeling," she declared. She rounded her shoulders, and pressed her hands upon a chest made hollow for the occasion, and her knees gave way under her, to prove how strongly she was affected.

"Then, why did you come to the sea?" I asked, for I was a little tired of Julia's grumbling.

"I came to look after you and your nerves, Isabella," she reminded me; "and how could I possibly know I shouldn't like the sea in November till I had seen it?"

We had ordered tea to be ready for us, and after our long railway journey we were more than ready for the meal.

"The woman of the house is a most miserable, frightened-looking creature," Julia remarked. "It is to be hoped that, at any rate, she will provide us with decently cooked food."

On this score I had no misgivings. Miss Ferriman, in one of her letters, had laid special stress upon the fact that Mrs Ragg, the caretaker, was an excellent cook.

She offered us no solacing specimen of her culinary art, however. The round table in the bay-window of our sitting-room was spread simply with the materials for brewing tea and for cutting bread-and-butter.

Julia's eyes blazed with hunger and indignation. "This is your fault, Isabella!" she declared. "What did you order, pray?"

"Something substantial. It is very annoying," I could not help confessing.

Julia angrily jingled the little bell. "We want something to eat," she said, as the caretaker appeared. "Cook us two chops, please; as quickly as possible."

Mrs Ragg looked at us from the doorway with the same gaze of fascinated terror with which a half-starved crow might regard two wild cats taking possession of its cage. With her garments of shabby black, her black untidy hair, her long beak and startled eyes, she had something of the appearance of a bedraggled, ill-used bird of that species. Her trembling, clawlike fingers played with the buttons of her dress; her chin, a very long and pointed feature, seemed to elongate itself immensely as her mouth fell; she sucked in the sides of her thin cheeks, and looked with a helpless imploring gaze from Julia to me.

"You have no chops, I suppose?" I interpreted the beseeching gaze.

She had no chops, she confessed.

"What have you, then?" the unpitying Julia persisted. "What have you got for our breakfast tomorrow? for our dinner? You have provided something, no doubt?"

The hollows in each meagre cheek of the caretaker deepened, the effect of the still further elongating of her chin, the starting eyes turned from my sister to me.

"Julia," I said, with severity, "it will be better not to have two Richmonds in the field. I, myself, will, with your permission, give Mrs Ragg what orders are necessary."

Then, in a tone of severity which should have been at once an encouragement to Mrs Ragg and a reproach to my sister, I asked to have some eggs boiled for tea.

There were no eggs.

"Go and fetch some," the irrepressible Julia cried.

"I understood the two ladies were to do their shopping themselves," the caretaker tremblingly explained.

I said of course we would. "Press not a falling man (or woman) too far," I quoted to Julia, as, the unhappy Mrs Ragg having left us to ourselves, we sat down to our bread-and-butter.

Julia, although protesting in the finish that hunger still gnawed her vitals, ate half the loaf. I, who should have been content to put up with what remained of it for our morning meal, was unable to control my sister's raging determination to forage that night for food.

"I refuse to starve," she said.

There was, luckily for us, a full moon, or we might easily have lost the faintly indicated road, lightly strewn as it was with oyster-shells and broken bricks, and ploughed through the trackless waste of sandy desert all night. The outskirts of the town reached, there were several mean-looking streets to pass through, before we found a shop at which we thought it desirable to trade. As we walked, buffeted by the wind blowing in from the sea, Julia discoursed of the caretaker of Sea-Strand Cottage.

"That, mark my words, is a thoroughly bad woman," she declared. "She wouldn't be such a forbidding-looking creature unless she was wicked. It wouldn't be fair on the part of the Almighty to have made her so. I consider her aspect thoroughly sinister."

"Poor frightened, trembling old wretch!" I said.

"Exactly. Why does she tremble? What is she afraid of? In my opinion she is intending to murder us in our beds."

"You had better go home the first thing in the morning and leave me to my fate," I told her. To myself I said I did not believe the world contained another woman with the worrying capacity of Julia. It was because she was such a disturbing force in the family that they had been so eager for her to accompany me, I, not without bitterness, suspected.

At the shop where we bought our chops for breakfast and a chicken for dinner, I bethought me to enquire of the young woman at the entering desk if Mrs Ragg, the caretaker of Sea-Strand Cottage, was known to her. The reply was quite satisfactory. Their cart had always served the cottage; the woman in charge was a most respectable person; a couple of ladies who had taken the cottage in the summer had mentioned that she was also an excellent cook.

The chops were served to us the next morning charred black, uneatable. I pointed them out to Julia on her appearing, and, with a view to deprecating her inevitable wrath, frankly so described them. My sister regarded the lost hopes of our meal with a preoccupied stare; then turned upon me with the wide distending of her eyelids which I knew portended a new worry.

"What sort of a night had you?" she asked.

"Excellent. And you?"

"Frightful. My nerves are all on the stretch, in consequence. I give you warning, Isabella, if you drop your knife or chink your teacup and saucer I shall scream aloud."

"You didn't sleep?"

"Not a wink."

"Were there noises to disturb you?"

"Not a sound. That was it! Not a din, Isabella."

"That's all right, then."

"Is it? You know my room?—just a lath-and-plaster partition between it and hers—that woman's. I ought to have heard every movement, even if she turned in her bed."

"It was very thoughtful of Mrs Ragg to lie so still."

"She was not there, Isabella."

"Not there?"

"I'd stake my life on it. It worried me so at last—I had to listen, you know—that I got up and put my ear against the partition. The deadest stillness!"

"But even if she was not there, I don't see it is so very alarming."

"She says she was. I asked her just now if she was sleeping next to me, and she said yes."

"She was, then."

"She wasn't."

I poured out the tea with impatience. What a constant worry Julia was! Without appearing to cast a backward thought upon the chops, she buttered herself a piece of toast.

"Of course, at last, I did fall asleep," she admitted. "And that was the worst of all. Isabella, I dreamt of that horrible little room next to mine, and of the reason it was so still."

"Well?"

"I dreamt there was a dead woman in it."

I laughed at that, and Julia, pausing in the act of taking a bite from her toast, glared angrily at me.

"You are a nice, soothing sort of person to be sent away with one supposed to be in want of cheering influences!" I said. "You and your dream of a dead woman!"

"I dreamt one was there," Julia said, going on with her toast. "In my opinion one was there," she added, doggedly.

When she had finished her breakfast, and had withdrawn her thoughts from the engrossing subject of her dream sufficiently to grumble about the aching void where the chops should have been, she sprang up from the table and loudly tinkled the little bell.

"For Mrs Ragg to clear away," she explained to me. "While she is doing so, and you, Isabella, keep her attention engaged on things below, I am going upstairs to have a look at her bedroom."

"Absurd!" I ejaculated.

"Aren't you absurd?" Julia cried, and turned upon me with scorn. "To take up your abode in a little cut-throat hole like this and not to take the commonest precaution!"

She flew upstairs, then, and Mrs Ragg was in the room.

In order to obey my sister's injunction to keep the woman's attention I began to talk to her, asking her how long she had lived in Sea-Strand Cottage. I had just gathered from her grudging, mumbling speech that she had lived there since the cottage was built, when my sister was in the room again.

Julia watched the caretaker shovel the things on to the tray, and, sighing bitterly the while, drag wearily out of the room with them. She turned to me, then, with a nod eloquent.

"Locked," she enunciated. "The door was locked. Why—why should the woman want to lock her bedroom door when she is out of it?"

"She returns the compliment you have paid her, and thinks you not to be trusted," I suggested.

"If I have to climb on the roof and pull off the tiles, I'll see what is in that room before I go to bed tonight!" Julia declared.

Then Mrs Ragg came back for the tablecloth.

"I slept very badly last night, Mrs Ragg," said Julia.

Mrs Ragg sucked in her cheeks, sighed heavily, made no answer.

"And so did you, I'm afraid. You were very restless. You walked about half the night."

"Me, miss?" She had folded the cloth, but she dropped it from her shaking, awkward hands, stooped to recover it, dropped it again. "Begging your pardon, no, miss."

"Who, then?" Julia asked inflexibly.

The woman turned away with the cloth and shuffled hastily to the door.

"Wait," commanded Julia. "Who, then? There was no one else in your bedroom besides you, I suppose?"

Mrs Ragg hurriedly rejected the insinuation. She had had a pain in her chest, she remembered now, and had got up for remedies.

"Of course you heard me rapping on the wall and asking you to keep still? You heard that, at least, Mrs Ragg?"

"Yes," Mrs Ragg had heard that, certainly. She admitted the fact as if it had been a sin, with a look of actual horror upon her face.

"You heard?" asked Julia of me in a kind of triumph as we were alone. "There was not a sound through all the night. I never rapped upon the wall. Now, why is she lying? It may be nothing to you, but I mean to know."

Once more that morning, coming from our own rooms, dressed for walking, Julia tried the caretaker's door. Finding it fast, shook it, and turned from doing so to find Mrs Ragg, arrived on the scene in her felt shoes, standing behind her.

"Asking your pardon, miss, that is my room," the woman said; with a feeble kind of offence she went and put herself before the door.

"We have hired the cottage; I presume we have the right to look even into your room, if we deem it advisable," Julia said, with her haughtiest air. "So, you always keep your room locked, Mrs Ragg?"

"When strangers are about I do," Mrs Ragg replied; and although she was apparently afraid of us she gazed upon us with no goodwill.

As we left the house, Julia called my attention to the fact that the blind in the room next to her own was drawn. "All the same, I don't sleep again beneath your Mrs Ragg's roof till I've been into her bedroom," she declared.

I had come to Starbay for the benefit of the sea. Julia, however, would not allow me to make nearer acquaintance with it than that possible from my window, but dragged me into the town again. We put down our names at one of the circulating libraries, and, it coming on to rain, could think of no better than to go upstairs to the reading-room.

It happened to have only one other occupant. A man of early middle-age, who, with the marks of delicate health upon him, had a face which, like that of "my Uncle Toby's," invited confidence.

Julia, for a minute, as we settled to read, looked across the table at him with her direct, sea-green gaze; then turned to her paper and looked no more until she put the paper down and began to talk to him.

It was easy enough to begin with a question about a certain magazine. "Did they take it there?" and to follow on with half a dozen enquiries about the town, and the objects of interest in the neighbourhood. I listened for a minute or two, reflecting how to my young sister any human document, however casually picked up, exceeded in interest the finest book ever written, then went on with an article on Education in which I happened to be interested. I roused myself from my abstraction to hear Julia mentioning to the strange man the name of Sea-Strand Cottage as our abode, and describing in her exaggerated fashion its location and appearance.

"At the utmost end of Everywhere, and looking like secret assassination, nothing less, when you get there," my sister was saying.

The man, as it happened, knew the place well. "It was the advertisement of Sea-Strand Cottage which brought me to Starbay," he said. "But when I saw the place, I—"

"You didn't like it! No more did I!" Julia said.

"However, the caretaker seemed a comfortable sort of body, and I was assured an excellent cook," the man continued.

Julia, her hands in her coat-pockets, bent her supple body forward across the table, bringing her eager face nearer to the stranger's. "Did you see her?—Mrs Ragg?" she asked.

He had seen her.

"Well?"

"She seemed all right," he said; and Julia lay back, disappointed, in her chair again.

"To me she seems all wrong," she said.

When I thought the conversation had lasted long enough I took Julia away from the library. Mrs Ragg had declared herself unable to have our meal ready before three o'clock in the afternoon. We went into a pastry-cook's therefore, and Julia ate a fair supply of tarts and custards, and insisted on taking away with her a selection from the store. "You keep yourself in hand for the chicken cooked by Mrs Ragg; I intend to be independent of it," she said, and walked home with her indigestible provender.

As we neared Sea-Strand Cottage we saw, coming towards it from the opposite direction, our new acquaintance of the reading-room. We met by the gate.

"I have to do a constitutional of so many prescribed miles every morning," he said. "After our conversation just now, I naturally bent my steps in this direction."

"Do walk this way sometimes," Julia said, flashing her smile upon him. "If, after a few days, you should see nothing of us, you might bring a policeman with you and search for our remains."

He smiled too, and said he would certainly do so. "I saw two or three men here as I went by, just now," he said; "they might have been the assassins you are expecting, but they looked uncommonly like every-day carpenters and workmen."

"Coming out of the house, do you mean? Men?" Julia asked, instantly on the alert.

"Not from the house—from the outhouse," he corrected and nodded in its direction.

Julia and I had inspected this empty outhouse that morning, and had decided to have our travelling-cases moved there. As our eyes turned towards it now, Mrs Ragg came out from it and softly closed the door behind her.

"This is the Mrs Ragg about whose desirability we disagree," Julia told the stranger, who, with his hand to his hat, was bowing to us and moving on. He stopped for a moment, looked at the caretaker, looked back to us with a smile.

"The mystery is solved. Your Mrs Ragg and mine are not the same person," he said.

Julia, who had been round to the back of the house to make inspection, came running to me with the news that the blind was up in the caretaker's bedroom, and the window open.

"There is a ladder against the outhouse," she said. "You must come and help me to fix it, Isabella, and stand on the bottom rung while I climb to the window."

There was no need for such extreme measures, however. Going upstairs to escape from my sister's importunity, I found the door of the hitherto locked room invitingly open. This intelligence being communicated to Julia, she came rushing upstairs, and dragged me unwillingly into Mrs Ragg's bedroom with her.

A most commonplace, mean-looking room, the wind blowing through it from open window to open door. The bed still unmade, but the square box of a place otherwise clean and tidy.

"What a home of mystery!" I said, with fine sarcasm, to Julia. "Where's your corpse, my dear?"

Julia gazed with great eyes round the little depressing place. "It really is exactly like," she said slowly. "The bed stood just there. But on it, you know, Isabella—on it—"

She shuddered, and gripped my arm. "My teeth chatter. Come away," she said.

She was generous enough to share her confectionery with me, and her forethought in bringing it was amply justified. Mrs Ragg had been so much occupied all the morning that she had forgotten to put the chicken in the oven until she saw us at the gate, she told us.

"Of course we can't put up with this. We will leave to-morrow," Julia declared. But I, who had paid the caretaker a week's salary in advance, was of opinion we should have a little more for our money.

"Put the chicken back in the oven, and I will see to the cooking of it," Julia said, when we had sufficiently contemplated the more than half-raw carcase of the fowl. "My sister is an invalid," she continued; "I am anxious that she should not be quite starved. I will cook the chicken therefore, and you will be responsible, perhaps, for the bread-sauce, Mrs Ragg."

The woman, looking alarmedly at her, murmured the word "bread-sauce?" and sucked in her cheeks.

"You know how to make bread-sauce, Mrs Ragg?"

Mrs Ragg had to confess she did not.

"But how can you possibly have had a reputation as a cook!" my sister demanded. Her eyes continued to blaze forth the inquiry long after there was any hope of the woman making a reply.

"I'm afraid you are a helpless creature," Julia told her, with the stern pitilessness that belongs to youth. "I also do not know how to make bread-sauce, but I will make it. In the meantime, will you go up to our rooms, fetch down the empty packing-cases—you will find them extremely light—and place them in that shed across the yard we saw empty this morning."

Undoubtedly Mrs Ragg was a helpless creature. She stood uncertainly before us, her skinny hands playing tremblingly with the buttons of her dress, and did not attempt to move.

"Do you not hear me? Go at once," Julia commanded.

But I saw that the woman got no nearer to our rooms than the bottom of the staircase. She stood there, clinging to the rail, and looking aimlessly upward.

Running upstairs I brought the two light cases down myself.

"There is room for them in the kitchen," Mrs Ragg said. But, carrying one myself, I told her to bring the other across to the empty shed. Arrived there, however, we found the door of the shed locked.

"Fetch the key," I ordered.

She stood and looked at me, but did not move.

"Tell me where the key is, and let me fetch it."

The key was lost.

"Why have you taken the trouble to lock an absolutely empty shed?"

She had no reason to give. She had locked it, and the key was lost.

"She has some reason for not wishing us to go into that shed," Julia said, oracularly, when the circumstance was mentioned to her.

"Absurd!" I said, but I did begin to experience an uncomfortable suspicion of the woman.

"She has got those men locked up there," Julia continued, with her air of assurance.

"Nonsense! What for?"

"Murder," said Julia, laconically; and energetically crumbled bread for the sauce.

"What were two men doing here this morning?" I asked, with assumed carelessness, of Mrs Ragg when next we encountered.

She mumbled the words "two men?" and stared at me by way of answer.

"We were told two men were here this morning. This is a very lonely situation, Mrs Ragg. I suppose you would admit no one you don't know all about?"

She was, she said, always most particular.

"Then, who were these two men, and what were they doing here?"

She did not know.

"Two men here, Mrs Ragg, and you not know it?"

"They weren't here," she said; and I had to leave it so.

I offered to change beds with Julia that night, but she would not hear of it. "Your room is the more comfortable; keep it," she said. "While you insist on staying here at the peril of our lives, I will sleep as well as I can with a dead woman laid forth on the bed next mine, and two murderers shut up in the shed across the way."

Julia's talk is ever more extravagant even than her notions, but it was of a disquieting kind. Many of the absurd things she had said in the day recurred to me in the night, assuming a quite different value. So that, although I had longed for bed, I found myself, arrived there, quite disinclined for sleep.

Surreptitiously I watched the caretaker up to bed. She came upstairs, clinging to the balusters for support, a tired, worn-looking, elderly woman, with a lank, frail body, and a care-lined, miserable face. How ridiculous were Julia's suspicions! She not only did not lock her door to-night, but left it ajar. At intervals I peeped through mine to see if her light was extinguished; she had not—so poorly dressed she was—the appearance of one who would indulge in the extravagance of a candle burning all night. Yet, long after I knew by the creaking of the spring mattress Mrs Ragg had lain down, I saw the streak of light shining through the unclosed door.

Fears of fire were added to my other disquietudes. Standing on the landing, I was hesitating if to knock at her door, and remind her she had not put out her light, when I was conscious of a movement behind me. Starting round with a muffled cry, I encountered a tall white figure, which, with an answering cry, grabbed me by both shoulders.

"What are you doing here, Isabella?"

"How could you frighten me so, Julia!"

We clung together and scolded each other for a minute, then each returned to her own room. But I not to sleep. Listening acutely for every sound, yet shrinking from every sound as it came, I tossed and turned with wide-open, feverish eyes. Suspicious circumstances at which I had been disposed to laugh in the day, took on a sinister complexion in the watches of the night. The loneliness of the place, its distance from every habitation—details to which I held no special distaste before—got hideously upon my nerves at last. Supposing anything happened, in what a position did we three women stand! What chance was there of help?

In my mind I surveyed the prospect from my window. The trackless Denes, the wild, unfriendly sea. Shuddering, I turned mentally to the outlook from Julia's room. What of reassuring was there in the rudiments of an unlighted road across a desert of ugly waste lands?

I was thinking of the road, I suppose, when at last I fell on sleep; for my dream was a nightmare of toiling over it with Julia, in a frantic attempt to escape from some horror, none the less terrible for being undefined, ever close upon our heels.

It was some disturbing but uncertain sound that wakened me from this dreaming to an inner dream. Just a vision, seen in a flash and gone, of two men standing in a light thrown from an upper window, and looking up to it.

From this apparition so vividly presented to my brain, I was awakened by a repetition of the disturbing sound, soft but distinct now. I flew up in bed with a beating heart and the certainty that someone, somewhere, had thrown a clod of earth at a window—not mine; at the back of the house; Julia's, or Mrs Ragg's.

A minute, and I was out of my bed and into Julia's room. I laid a hand on my sister's shoulder. "Julia," I whispered, "wake up. I've had such horrible dreams."

The candle I held in a shaking hand showed the glinting green of Julia's eyes within their half-opened lids. "I'm so comfy," she muttered; "I'm having such a lovely sleep. Go back to bed, Isabella."

But I crept into Julia's bed, instead, and clasped her close for the comfort of her presence.

"I dreamt two men were looking up at a window," I said, "—do keep awake, Julia. I don't know why it seemed so horrid—nothing has ever seemed so horrid before. And—you're going off to sleep again, Julia!—you must listen!—someone flung something at a window. That was not a dream. I heard it quite distinctly."

"It wasn't at this window," Julia declared, in muffled tones. "What a nuisance you are, Isabella."

Then in an instant she flung off her sleep and was out of bed. "It must have been at Mrs Ragg's," she said. "I am going to see."

Shivering, I followed to the landing. The light no longer showed from Mrs Ragg's door, but the door itself was still ajar. Julia rapped sharply upon it and called the caretaker's name. When no one answered, she pushed the door wide, and we saw, by the light of the candle I carried, that the room was empty.

I scarcely knew why the fact that it was so filled us both with such dismay. Our faces were white in the candlelight as we looked blankly at each other; then, seizing hands, we scurried back to Julia's room. A rush of cold air met us on the landing and our light went out.

"An outer door is open," Julia said.

We shut and locked our own door and stood together in the darkness, gripping each other, intently listening.

Julia's senses are sharper than mine. "Someone is in the garden—at the back," she whispered. "I can hear footsteps—footsteps of more than one person. What shall we do, Isabella? I don't know yet what we ought to do."

Presently we were kneeling at the window. The moon had set, the night was quite dark. By degrees, straining our eyes in desperate anxiety, we made out the stunted form of a shrub or two planted opposite the house; we knew that the blackness of shadow at our left was the shed whose key had been lost.

As we looked, the shed door opened. We knew it by the light which suddenly streamed upon the night. It was the light from a lantern held high, a light flickering and uncertain. It blinked and trembled and swayed as if held in a shaking hand. We knew whose was the lean, lank figure, fitfully revealed, which held it.

"What can she be doing there?" we asked of each other, with chattering teeth, simultaneously.

Neither answered. There was no need. Too well we knew she was letting out the men whom, to have them handy for our murder at night, she had locked in, earlier in the day.

They came presently. The fluttering light gave us unsteady glimpses of them, and of some large and heavy burden they carried.

"What is it?" I demanded of Julia. My arm ached with her grip of it, but she did not answer. All her senses were merged in the sense of seeing. She could not hear, nor feel, nor speak.

Mrs Ragg, holding the lantern high, walked ahead of the obscure group, which slowly followed. The light illumined her stooping, meagre figure as she made her way down the path across the back garden to the gate. Only now and again, by the chance swaying of the lantern, a ray lit the heavy blackness of the mass moving in her wake.

She stopped with her lantern at the gate. For the minute it took for them to pass her we saw more plainly the figures of the men going heavily beneath their burden.

"What is it?" I found myself asking again, expecting no answer, needing none.

Very softly Julia pushed up the sash of the window, hung her head with its loose flowing hair into the night.

Presently, the form of Mrs Ragg came slowly back again, down the garden path. The lantern hung at her side now; its light streaming upward showed us her white and frightened face. Julia drew in her head, gently closed the window, turned to me.

"They have driven off—for the present," she said. "I heard the wheels. Before they return—perhaps—we shall have time to escape."

We had risen to our feet now, but we clung together still. "Julia, what was it?" I asked, for the third time, quite senselessly. For my eyes are as good as Julia's, and our opportunities of sight and judgment had been the same.

"It was a coffin," Julia said, and I knew that through the darkness her eyes glared with hardly maintained courage upon my face, and that she shut down her lips firmly over chattering teeth.

Space fails to tell of the remainder of that night: of how we dressed in feverish haste to escape, and then were afraid to go; of how, having assured ourselves—by the sense of hearing only, for we thought it best not to light a candle—of Mrs Ragg's return, and of her retirement for the second time to bed, and this time to slumber—we depended on our hearing also for the establishment of the latter fact—we sat and watched, shivering with cold and apprehension, through the endless hours for the reappearance of Mrs Ragg's accomplices, straining our eyes to stare in the direction of the garden path down which we believed they would come. Of how with the first faint light of dawn courage came to us to escape.

Julia remembered the name of the hotel at which our chance acquaintance of the reading-room had mentioned he was staying. As we did not know his name, it was by good luck that we encountered him on the steps of the Royal George setting forth on his before-breakfast constitutional. He showed himself politely sceptical of our story. How Julia's eyes blazed upon him in surprised and angry reproach for his want of faith, he has assured her many times since, he can never forget. We insisted that he should go at once to the police station and fetch constables to arrest Mrs Ragg on the charge of murder. The alternative course he proposed appeared to us weakly inadequate. However, he being a man and we being women, he had his way. We returned with him at once to Sea-Strand Cottage, the only concession he made to our fears being to take a policeman with him, to wait outside the house in case he should be wanted.

"The lonely situation has worked upon your nerves. You have dreamt a little and imagined the rest," he said, by way of overcoming our natural repugnance to return.

Julia gave him a scathing glance. "You will see," she said. She vouchsafed no further word to him, but with an indignant head held high, walked ahead of him and me as, side by side, we toiled over the uneven road, the policeman bringing up the rear.

The caretaker, characteristically oblivious of the fact that her lodgers, who, she had every reason to believe, were still in their bedrooms, would presently call for their breakfast, was leisurely eating her own over the newly-lit kitchen fire.

At sight of us, unexpectedly appearing before her, of our protector with his air of authority, of the policeman, who, contrary to instructions, introduced himself at the open door, Mrs Ragg rose with a wavering cry that was like a whine, from her seat. She sucked in her cheeks till they met, and with her claw-like hands grabbed her shabby frock where it loosely covered her bosom.

"You are not Mrs Ragg," our companion said.

She grabbed more convulsively at her dress, and made no reply.

"Where is Mrs Ragg?"

"She is dead, sir. Dead," the woman said, and sat down and began to cry. "She died the very afternoon the ladies came. I had the doctor to her. You can ask the doctor if you don't believe me. I'd have kept her alive if I could. She was my dear sister. I had only what she gave me—"

"And you undertook to impersonate her?"

The poor creature gazed at us with imploring eyes. "'Twas my sister that ordered it," she said, gasping with terror. "'Twas a pity the fifteen shillings a week the ladies were to pay should be lost to the family, my sister said. She put it in my head—she laid her orders on me before she died; she—"

"And she was laid forth in the bedroom next to mine?" Julia said; "and moved from there next morning to the shed in the garden."

"And from the shed taken at night to our brother's house, where she is waiting burial," the woman, now anxious to unburden herself, explained.

But what need is there to set forth any more of such talk? The rest of the story tells itself. And we have had perhaps more than enough of the pseudo Mrs Ragg.

Julia and I decided we had had enough also of Sea-Strand Cottage. We took up our abode temporarily at the Royal George. Our new-made friend—for after this adventure we could but look on him as a friend—had lived there for a month and could recommend it. It was in a busy thoroughfare of the town, houses on either side, at the back, over the way; men and women passing and repassing; plentiful gas-lamps, policemen within call. Ah, the blessed feeling of companionship and security! We had had enough of solitude, darkness, mystery, to last us for the rest of our lives.

However, the cost of living at the Royal George was greatly more than the cost of living at the Cottage.

"It is all very well for this man, who evidently has money to live in such a place," I said to Julia. "But we should quickly become bankrupt. At the end of a fortnight we will go."

"Make it three weeks," Julia said, "and I shall be engaged to the man with the money."

I scouted the idea, but stayed—perhaps to prove it impossible.

Or perhaps at my age I knew well that to the young and the confident nothing is impossible.

THE PRIVATE WARD

He had been seized with sudden illness in the suburban hotel in which he was staying, and being unknown there, had been removed to the Princess Mary Cottage Hospital. The dozen beds of the men's ward were full, and he had been placed in the private ward. He lay now on the narrow bed, sleeping heavily, the white, bright light of the spring morning showing mercilessly the havoc selfishness and reckless self-indulgence had wrought upon a once sufficiently handsome face. The emaciation of his long form was plainly seen through the single scarlet blanket which covered it.

The visiting doctor and the nurse stood, one on either side, looking down on him.

"What sort of night?" asked the doctor.

"Pretty bad," answered the nurse. The patient had been admitted the previous day, and she had watched by him through the night. "He was awake till three, and very restless."

"You repeated at three the dose I ordered?"

"Yes. He has lain like this since. When he wakes is he to have it again?"

"H'm!" said the doctor, deliberating, his eyes on the patient's face. "We will, I think, halve the dose. We mustn't overdo it; he seems susceptible to the drug."

He lifted his eyes from the unconscious face of the patient to the weary face of the nurse, and, as if struck by what he saw there, studied it with attention.

"You are more than usually tired this morning, sister," he said. "You must go at once to bed when I leave."

"It is always difficult for me to sleep in the daytime. I shall not sleep to-day," she said.

"But you are tired?"

"Dead tired."

The doctor observed her in a minute's silence. Her fine, almost regal form, at which few men looked and turned away, drooped a little this morning, seemed—but that was impossible—to have faded and shrunk since yesterday. There was, however, no sinking of the white eyelids over the pale blue eyes which, set in her darkly tinted face, were a surprise and a joy to the beholder. The eyelids were reddened now, and held wide apart, the eyes shining with a dry feverishness painful to see.

"If you go on night-duty and do not sleep in the day you will be ill," said the doctor, gently.

"Not I," said the nurse, roughly.

He was not, perhaps, sorry to miss in that handsome woman the show of extreme deference with which it was usual for the nurses to treat the doctors, but her brusqueness a little surprised him. Imagining that she resented the personal note, he turned, after a minute's quiet perusal of her face, to the patient.

Having given briefly his directions for his treatment and moved away, he stopped, looking at him for a minute still.

"His friends been communicated with?" he asked.

She shook her head. "By the look of him should you think he has got any friends who would care to hear?" she enquired.

Pityingly the doctor threw up his head. "Poor wretch!" he sighed. "What is his history, I wonder!"

To which Sister Marion made no reply. For she knew.

For the rest of the day she would be off duty. As a rule she took a brisk walk through the suburban town, passed the rows upon rows of neat little one-patterned houses, the fine, scattered villa-residences, with their spotless gardens, reached the common where the goats and the donkeys were tethered, the geese screamed with stretched necks, the children rolled and played. Plenty of good air there to fill lungs atrophied by long night hours in the sick atmosphere of the wards. Then, at a swinging pace home again to her welcome bed and a few hours' well-earned sleep.

To-day, beyond the white walls of the hospital, the sun danced invitingly, the spring breezes were astir. Sister Marion heeded them not at all. Having left the patient in the private ward to the nurse who succeeded her, she lingered listlessly in the wide, white corridor upon which all the wards opened, too preoccupied to remember that she was doing anything unusual.

There the doctor, having made the round of the wards, found her lingering still.

"Go to bed!" he said to her, authoritatively. "You will make yourself ill."

"Not I."

"Go to bed!" he said again, and, although his tone was not less authoritative, he smiled.

The feverish, pale blue eyes looked at him strangely with a regretful, wistful gaze, and he melted in a moment into unmixed gentleness. "Why are you being obstinate to-day? Go and lie down and get to sleep," he begged her.

"What does it matter if I do not?"

"It matters very much, to you, to your patients, to me. Will you go?"

She said yes, turned slowly away, and, passing down a passage leading from the central corridor, went to her tiny room. Arrived, she did not trouble to undress, but throwing off the cap which was tied beneath her chin, flung herself upon her bed.

"It is the last thing he will ask of me and I shall do it," she said.

She had known that she could not sleep. She put her hand above her burning eyes and forcibly closed the lids that remained so achingly open. In the darkness so achieved she must think out her plans; she must think how to get away from this place without attracting observation, leaving no trace of her removal, giving no clue to her destination. It was imperative that the step she decided on should be taken soon; she must form her project clearly, and there must be no blundering or mistake. But her overtired brain, refusing to work as she willed, presented only before her feverish eyes a picture of the young doctor coming in the spring sunshine down the hospital ward, a bunch of violets in his coat. How clean, and strong, and helpful he looked! And his voice—was it not indeed one to obey? It must be her fancy only that of late it had taken on a softer tone for her.

Her fancy! Her vain, mad fancy!

She flung over upon her bed and forced herself to contemplate what it was she had to do: To get away from the man who lay in the private ward; and from the place in which she had found a refuge till her evil angel had set him upon her track again.

Since the day, ten years ago, when she had married him, what a ruin her life had been! There had been, again and again, thank Heaven! periods of peace, periods of regained self-respect, of the enjoyment of the respect of others. These had been secured by flight only, by concealment of her whereabouts, and were of varying lengths of duration. Two years ago, with her hard-earned savings, she had paid his passage out to Africa. She had not believed him likely to earn the money to return, and had looked upon him as happily dead to her. Dead, indeed, perhaps. Until yesterday, when she had helped to lay him, unconscious, in the bed of the private ward. She guessed easily that he had learnt she was in the place, and had been about to seek her when he had been struck down.

If he should mercifully die!

Not he! she said, bitterly. Men sometimes died in delirium tremens. In every kind of illness, by every sort of accident, men died every day. Good and useful men, husbands of adoring wives, loving fathers of families, men needed by their country, by humanity, were swept mercilessly away. Only such carrion as this was left to fester upon the earth, to poison the lives of decent men and women. The doctor, standing above him, looking on the defaced image of what God, for some mysterious purpose, had made, had no thought but to restore to this foully-damaged frame the spirit and strength to do its evil work. Nurses, gentle and dutiful women, would give themselves to revive in all its corrupt activity the temporarily dormant mind and body.

Ought this to be? Where was the righteousness of it—the sense? Since that drug to which he was "so susceptible" was a deadly one, would it not be better to give him more of it? To rid society of a pest dangerous to its peace, to restore to one suffering, striving, blameless woman the happiness he had cost her?

"Would that be a crime?" she asked, and set her teeth and cried, "No, no," with hatred in her heart. Then, horrified at herself, flung herself over on her pillow, and, burying her face from the light of day, sobbed long with a tearless sobbing, bringing no relief; and so at last lay still.

She did not know if she had slept or only lain in the quiet and blank of mercifully deadened misery when, roused by the sound of her name, she lifted her head to find the matron of the little hospital standing beside her bed.

"We are having so much trouble with the D.T. patient, sister," she said. "He must not be left for a moment. I am sorry to wake you so soon, but will you go to him?"

She was so used to being alert and ready at the call of duty, that she forgot her plan had been to escape from the hospital at once, and in a minute was again in the private ward. The doctor was standing beside the bed, and Sister Marion saw he had been recalled because of the urgency of the case. For whatever reason, it was such a pleasure to see him again, to let her eyes rest upon the strong and kind and clever face—

And then, looking at him, she saw that down the broad brow and the clean-shaven cheek red blood was streaming.

He put up his hand to wipe the blood from his eyes, and the hand too, she saw, was gashed and bleeding.

He laughed at her look of surprise and horror. "This gentleman had a penknife under his pillow," he explained. "I have taken care that he does not do any more mischief."

He nodded in the direction of the patient, and Sister Marion, glancing that way, saw that the man lying on his back had his hands tied to the iron bed-rail above his head. In the reaction from the late attack he was lying absolutely still, and she saw, to her surprise, that in the eyes fixed on her face there was recognition.

"He is conscious," she whispered. "Come outside and let me attend to you."

He followed her to the ward kitchen, the room used by the nurses for the preparation of the patients' food, but empty now.

The doctor smiled and jested, but the blood flowed, the wound smarted, he was a little pale.

"He meant to hurt you?" she asked, through her set teeth.

"He meant to murder me, the brute!" the doctor said.

"Never mind," she soothed him; "I am accountable for him now. I will see to it he never hurts you again."

She felt herself to be a different woman; in some curious way emancipated. It had needed just the wounding of this man to change her. She was ashamed no longer to show him what she felt, nor had she any more a shrinking from doing what she now believed it right to do.

She stood above him as he sat in a new docility before her, and bathed the cut upon his temple, with lingering, tender touch, pushing back the hair to get at it. She knelt before him and dressed the cut upon his hand.

"I managed to do this myself in trying to get the knife away from him," the doctor explained.

With his unwounded hand he took an ivory-handled penknife, stained red with blood, from his pocket, and held it before her eyes. It had been a gift from her to the man who was now her husband in the early days of their acquaintance, before the thought of marriage had risen between them. With all the valuables he had pawned and lost and thrown away, strange that this worthless gift of the girl whose life he had ruined should have stuck to him; stranger still that after all those years she should be able to recognise it beyond possibility of doubt! He held it towards the basin of water as though to rinse it, but she took it from him and laid it aside.

"Let it be!" she said. "I shall know what to do with the knife."

The doctor's outside patients might be crying aloud for him; it was more than noontide, and he should long have been about his work; the patient in the private ward should have had Sister Marion at his side; but the pair lingered in the little red-and-white tiled ward kitchen, bathed in the warm rays of the golden afternoon sun. The dressing of the wounds was a long business, and to the ministering woman heavenly sweet.

Over the cut upon his forehead the short, dark hair had to be combed. By altering the place of parting this was easily done. And Sister Marion, looking down upon him to see the effect, thrilled to find eyes, usually cold and preoccupied, fixed in a rapture of adoration upon her face.

"No woman in the world has such a tender touch as you," he said. "My mother used to kiss my hurts to make them well. Will you do that too for me?"

Then the woman with murder in her heart stooped and kissed him tenderly as a mother upon his brow, knelt for an instant before him, and kissed his hand.

"Good-bye," she said, "Good-bye;" and without another word left him and went upon her business to the private ward.

The recognising eyes were upon her as she opened the door. "I did not have much trouble to find you, this time," the man said. "I didn't even come here of my own accord. I don't know anything about it, except that I feel infernally bad. Can't you give me something, Marion?"

"I will give you something presently," she said. "I wish to talk to you a little first."

"Not until you've untied my hands. What are they tied up for, pray?"

"To keep you from working mischief."

"Have I done anything to that long chap that went out with you? If so I'll make amends—I'll make any amends in my power."

"You shall make amends. Don't be afraid."

"You speak as if you had not a particle of pity in you; you are as hard and cold as a stone, as you always were—"

"Not always," she said, grimly—"unluckily for me."

"Any woman who had a grain of pity in her would pity me now. I feel so frightfully bad, Marion; I believe I am going to die."

"I believe you are."

He called on the name of God at that, and tried ineffectually to rise, and tugged frantically at the bandages which bound him. She watched him, standing at the foot of his bed, and could smile as she watched.

"You are afraid to die," she said; "I knew you would be. You were always a coward."

He cursed her then. His voice was feeble now; it had lost the strength of delirium. There was something awful in the sound of such words in such trembling, exhausted tones; yet Marion, listening, smiled on.

"I will not be nursed by you!" he cried. "I won't have you near me, glaring at me with your Gorgon stare. Send another nurse to me—send the doctor. Get out of my sight, Gorgon! Don't look at me. Go away!"

The door behind her had been standing a little ajar; she turned round and shut it. The window was open to the spring air; she closed and locked it. "Help yourself," she said.

"I'll rouse the place," he threatened, and tried to cry aloud, but his voice died weakly in his throat. He broke down at that, and began to whine a little.

"Have some pity," he wept. "I'm a suffering man, and you're a woman, and I'm in your hands. It's only decent, it's only human, to be sorry for me—to do something for me. My tongue's like leather; give me something to drink. A drop of water, even. Why should you begrudge me a drop of water?"

"There's none in the room," she said; "and I won't leave you to fetch it. There's only this." She held up to his eyes the quieting mixture the doctor had ordered. "There is only one dose, unfortunately. If the bottle had been full, I should have given you the lot, and there would have been no further trouble. As it is, you can drink what there is. The time has not come round for it; but time is not going to be of much matter to you, henceforth; we need not wait for it."

He cursed her in his fainting voice again, and again faintly struggled. But she held the bottle steadily to his lips, and he drained it to the last drop.

"That will quiet you," she said, and sat beside him on the bed. From the pocket of her apron she drew the penknife with which the doctor had been wounded. "Do you remember this?" she asked him. "There is blood upon it, but that is going to be wiped out."

He looked at her with eyes from which the consciousness was dying, and did not struggle any more.

"Do you remember it?" she asked again. "You had cut your name and mine on a tree in the garden of my home, and you asked for the penknife as a memento. Is it possible you can have forgotten?"

She spoke to him with great deliberation, holding the penknife before his eyes, and watching the drooping of the heavy lids.

"Strange, isn't it, that, so much having been flung away, you should have kept this miserable little keepsake with you till to-day? I suppose its small blade is its sharp blade still?"

Slowly she opened it, and stood up.

With an effort he opened his eyes upon her. "I am dead with sleep," he said, in a hollow, far-away voice; "but I can't sleep with my hands tied. Set me free, Marion! Set me free!"

"It is that I am going to do," she said.

She leant above him then, and, with fingers that never trembled, unbuttoned the wrists of his flannel shirt and rolled the sleeves back to his shoulders. How thin the arms were; how plainly the veins showed up in the white, moist skin. Across one that rose like a fine blue cord from the bend of the arm she drew the sharp blade of the knife. He gave but the slightest start, so heavy was he with sleep. She knelt upon his pillow, leant across him, and in the other arm severed the corresponding vein.

She had thought that the blood would flow quietly—how it spurted and spouted and ran! Before she could untie his hands and lay them beneath the blanket at his sides the white, lean arms were crimson with blood. At this rate, it would not take him long to die! She rinsed the blood from the little penknife in a basin of water, and turning down the blanket, laid it upon his breast.

"You have kept it a good many years," she said, mockingly. "Keep it still."

Some blood was on her own hands—how could she have been so clumsy! They were all smeared with blood; they—horrible!—smelt of blood.

She flew towards the basin to rinse them, but before she could reach it, without a warning sound the door opened, and the matron was in the room.

With the tell-tale hands behind her back, Sister Marion stood before her, intervening between her and the bed.

"Your patient is strangely quiet all at once," the matron said.

"He is sleeping," said the nurse.

In spite of herself she had to give way before the matron, who now stood by the bed.

"It does not seem a healthy sleep," she said. "He has a very exhausted look. And why is his blanket tucked so tightly round his arms?" She waited for no explanations, but smoothed the man's ruffled hair and looked down pityingly upon him. "Even now he has a handsome face," she said. "Ten years ago he must have been as handsome as a god."

Ten years ago! Who knew how handsome he had been then better than Sister Marion? In an instant how vivid was the picture of him that rose before her eyes! The picture of a young man's laughing face—gay, winning, debonair. A dancing shadow was on his face of the leaves of the tree by which he stood, and on which he had carved two names—

With an involuntary movement she was beside him, looking down upon the unconscious face; and wonderful it was to see that all its lines were smoothing out, and all the marks of years of debauchery. Even the sallow hue of them seemed to be changing in his cheeks. Extraordinary that the healthy colour of early manhood should reappear in the cheeks of a dying man!

In her surprise she called him by his name. Looking up, fearful that she had betrayed herself to the matron, she found that she was alone with him again, the door closed. There was absolute silence in the room, except a soft, drip-dripping from the bed to the floor. No need to look; she knew what it was. How short a time before the two streams from the veins, emptying themselves of the life-blood, met beneath the bed and trickled, trickled to the door! She flung a towel down to sop up the tiny flood, and saw it swiftly crimson before her eyes. She turned back to the bed, a great horror upon her now, and saw that the eyes of the dying man were open and upon her face.

"I loved you," he said. "Once I loved you, Marion!"

The words were like a knife in her heart. She groaned aloud, but could not speak.

"I have been bad—bad," he went on; "but I will atone. Give me time, Marion, and I will atone. Save me! Don't send me before my God like this, without a chance. You are my wife. You swore—swore to stick to me. Save me!"

In his extremity power had come back to his voice. He struggled desperately, half raised himself. "Save me!" he shrieked. "Don't send my soul to perdition!"

She flung the blanket off him, and tried with fingers, that only shook and helplessly fumbled now, to bind a ligature above the opened vein.

Misunderstanding, he tried to fling her off. "You are tying me again! Fiend! Fiend!" he cried. He dashed his arms about, fighting for life. Her enveloping white apron was splashed and soaked with blood. Even on her face it fell. As it rained, warm and crimson, upon her, she shrieked aloud.

In an instant the little room was full of surprised and frightened faces. "She has killed me!" the man screamed. "Killed me! She is tying me down to see me die!"

"I want to save him—now," Sister Marion strove to say above the clamour. No one heeded.

"She did this, and this," the man said, showing his wounded arms. "Ask her! Ask her!"

"It is true," Marion gasped. Oh, the difficulty of getting her tongue to form words! "But I want to save him—now."

"Too late," the matron said; and hers and all the faces—the room seemed full of them—looked at her with loathing, shrinking from her, as she stood before them, spattered with her husband's blood. "The man is dying fast."

At that instant one of the younger nurses who had been ministering to the figure upon the bed, lifted up a warning hand. "He is dead!" she said.

How the faces glared at her! Strange as well as familiar ones—crowds upon crowds of faces. Faces of the nurses who had been her friends, who had loved her; faces from out the past—how came they there with their heart-remembered names!—her mother's face—her mother who was with the angels of God! All the forces of Heaven and earth testifying against her who had done the unspeakable deed.

Was there no one on her side—no one who would shield her from the accusing eyes?

The cry with which she called upon the doctor's name in its frantic expression of utmost need must have had power to annihilate time and space, for while the sound of it still thrilled upon the ear the young doctor was in the room. She turned to him with the joy of one who finds his saviour.

Standing before her, his hands pressed firmly upon her shoulders, he bent his head till the strong, kind face almost touched her own.

"Murderer!" he whispered in her ear, and flung her from him.

She lay where he had thrown her; but someone's hands were still pressed upon her shoulders, a voice was still whispering "Murderer!" in her ear—or was it—was it "Marion" the voice whispered?

"Marion, how soundly you have slept—and not even undressed! It is eight o'clock, and time for you to go on night-duty. Doctor is going his evening rounds."

Only half-awakened, the horror of her dream still holding her, Sister Marion pushed the nurse away from her, threw herself from her bed, and flew along the corridor. From the door of the private ward the doctor was issuing; he stared at her wild, white look, her tumbled, uncovered hair. She seized him by the arm. "Doctor!" she sobbed. "The man in there has been cruel to me, but I want to nurse him—I want to save him! Never, never could I have done him any harm!"

"Why should you have done him any harm?" the doctor asked, soothingly. "Who would have harmed the poor fellow? Come and see."

He softly opened the door of the private ward, and with his hand upon her arm, led her in.

The matron and one of the nurses stood on either side of the bed, from which the scarlet blanket had been removed. The long white sheet which had replaced it was pulled up over the face of the recumbent form.

"He died an hour ago in his sleep," the matron said. "He did not regain consciousness after you left him. I have been with him all the time."

Sister Marion, with dazed eyes, looked down upon her hands—slowly, from one to the other. Clean, clean, thank Heaven! Looked at her spotless apron, at the sheet showing the sharp outline of the figure on the bed.

"Was there, upon his breast, a little ivory-handled penknife?" she asked.

But before they had told her, wonderingly, no, she had fallen on her knees beside the quiet figure and was sobbing to herself a prayer of thanksgiving.

"A sensitive, imaginative woman—she has been wakened too suddenly," the doctor said.

His gaze dwelt lingering upon her bent, dark head as slowly he turned away.

DORA OF THE RINGOLETS

"I wish I c'd du my ringolets same as yu kin, mother. When I carl 'em over my fingers they don't hang o' this here fashion down my back, but go all of a womble-like; not half s' pretty."

"Tha's 'cause ye twist 'em wrong way, back'ards round yer fingers," the faint voice from the bed made answer. "Yu ha' got to larn to du 'em, Dora, don't, yer'll miss me cruel when I'm gone."

The dying woman was propped on a couple of pillows of more or less soiled appearance; these were raised to the required height by means of a folded flannel petticoat and dingy woollen frock, worn through all the twelve years of her married life, but now to be worn no more. On the man's coat, spread for extra warmth over the thin counterpane, lay a broken comb and brush. Over her fingers, distorted by hard work, but pale from sickness and languid with coming death, the mother twisted the locks, vigorously waving, richly gilded, and dragged them in shining, curled lengths over the child's shoulders.

Because of the extreme weakness of the hands the process was a laborious one. A heavier pallor was upon the face, a cold moisture upon the sunken brow when it was accomplished.

"I'll kape on while I kin—I don' know as I shall ha' the strength much longer, Dora."

The child twitched her curls from the fingers that lay heavily upon them and turned on her mother fiercely. "Yu ha' got ter du 'em, then!" she cried. She glared upon the faint head slipped sideways on the pillow. "Yu ha'n't got ter put none o' them parts on, du I'll let ye ter know."

Her eyes were suddenly wide and brilliant with tears; the fading sight of the mother was dazzled by the yellow shine of them and of the richly-coloured hair. "My pretty gal!" she breathed; "my pretty Dora! I ha'n't got no strength, bor."

"I'll let yer ter know!" Dora cried with fury. "I'll hull yer pillars away, and let yer hid go flop, if ye say yer ha'an't got no strength. I'll let yer ter know!"

She stopped, because the sobs which had been stormily rising choked her. She seized in her red little hands the pillow beneath her mother's head. No word of remonstrance was spoken, the faded eyes gazing wearily upon the child held no reproof.

"What d'ye look at me, that mander, for? Why don't ye ketch me a lump o' the hid?" the child cried fiercely; then gave way to the suppressed sobbing. "Oh, mother, yu ain't a-dyin'? Yu ain't a-dyin' yit?"

She flung her own head on the soiled pillow; all the crisply waving, long ringlets flew over the mother's sunken chest; one fell across her parched lips. She moistened them with her tongue, and made a feeble motion of kissing. A tear slid slowly down her cheek.

"Not yit, my pretty gal," she whispered. "Mother ain't a-goin' ter lave yer yit."

"Promus! Yer ain't a-tellin' no lies? Yer'll stop along of me till I kin carl my ringolets myself. I ha' got ter have 'em carled, and there ain't no one else to du 'em for me."

The mother promised.

"There's Jim and Jack—they don't want ye, mother. Their hairs is short. They kin play hopstick i' th' midder, alonger th' other boys. Both on 'em kin put their own collars on. There's on'y me, what have carls, that'll want yer so. Mother! Mother!"

"Don' I kape on a-tellin' of yer I ain't a-goin'."

There was no time to sob for long on the mother's pillow. Dora was due at school. She wiped her crimsoned cheeks upon the corner of the sheet, stood up and put her sunburnt sailor-hat upon the carefully curled hair. She was neatly dressed in a brown woollen frock nearly covered by a white, lace-trimmed overall; she wore brown stockings and brown shoes. The mother watched her to the door with yearning eyes.

"My pretty gal!" she said.

The neighbour who waited on her in moments spared from her own household labours came in. She held a cup of paste made from cornflour in her hand, and stirred the mixture invitingly.

"It's time yu had suffin' inside of yer, Mis' Green," she said. "Yu ha'n't tasted wittels since that mossel o' bread-an'-butter yu fancied las' night."

She put a spoonful of the food, stirred over a smoky fire, to the parched lips.

"I'd suner, a sight, have a drink o' water," the sick woman said. "There ain't nothin' I fare ter crave 'cept water now."

"There ain't no nouragement in water, Mis' Green. Take this here, instids," the neighbour said firmly.

Two spoonfuls were swallowed with difficulty.

"Come! Tha's as ter should be! That comfort ye, Mis' Green, bor?"

The faint eyes looked solemnly in the healthy, stolid face above her. "There's nothin' don't comfort me, Mis' Barrett."

"An' why's the raisen?" the neighbour reprovingly demanded. "Because yu're a-dyin', Mis' Green, and yu don't give yer mind tu it. I ha' been by other deathbeds—the Lord reward me for it, as 'tis ter be expected He will—and I ha'n't never seed a Christian woman so sot agin goin' as yu are."

The reluctant one shut her eyes wearily; the dropped lids trembled for a minute, then were raised upon the same hard face.

"She don' look like a labourer's gal, Dora don't," she said faintly. "She ha'n't got th' mander o' them sort o' truck."

"What then, Mis' Green?" the neighbour inquired, stern with the consciousness of her own large family of "truck." The supposed superiority of Dora of the ringolets hurt her maternal pride and raised a storm of righteous anger in her breast.

Mrs Green did not explain; the discoloured lids fell again waveringly over the dim eyes, the upper lip was drawn back showing the gums above the teeth.

It was the mere skeleton of a woman who lay there. She had suffered long and intensely; no one could look upon her now and doubt that the hour of discharge was very near. The woman standing above her reasoned that if a word of reproof or advice was to be given there was not much time to lose. Often, from open door to open door (for the pair inhabited a double dwelling), often, across the garden fence, she had called aloud her opinion of her neighbour's goings on; she would seize the opportunity to give it once again.

"And why ain't yer Dora like a labourer's gal, then?" she demanded, shrilly accusing. "Oh, Mis' Green! Don't yu, a-layin' there o' your deathbed, know right well the why and the wherefore? Ha'n't yu borrered right and left, ha'n't you got inter debt high and low, to put a hape o' finery on yer mawther's back? Ha'n't yu moiled yerself, an' yu a dyin' woman, over her hid o' hair? Put her i' my Gladus's clo'es, an' see what yer Dora 'ud look like. Har, wi' her coloured shues, an' all!"

"They was giv' her," the dying woman faintly protested. "Her Uncle Willum sent them brown uns along of her brown hat wi' th' welwet bow."

"Now, ain't yu a-lyin', Mis' Green, as yu lay there o' yer deathbed? Them tales may ha' flung dust i' th' eyes o' yer old man, them i' my hid is too sharp for no sech a story. Di'n't I see th' name o' 'Bunn o' Wotton' on th' bag th' hat come out of? An' don't yer brother Willum live i' London, and ha'n't he got seven of's own to look arter? Ter think as I sh'd come ter pass ter say sich wards, an' yu a-layin' there a-dyin'! Ain't yer ashamed o' yerself, Mis' Green. I'm a-askin' of yer th' question; ain't yer ashamed o' yerself?"

"No, an' ain't," said Mrs Green, feebly whispering.

Beneath the flickering, bruised-looking lids, tears slowly oozed. The neighbour felt for a pocket-handkerchief under the pillow, and wiped them away.

"Fact o' th' matter, Mis' Green," she inflexibly pursued her subject, "yu ha' made a raglar idle o' that gal; yu ha' put a sight o' finery on 'er back, an' stuffed 'er hid wi' notions; an' wha's a-goin ter become on 'r when you're gone?"

"I was a-wonderin'," the dying woman said, "s'posin' as I was willin' to speer this here parple gownd o' mine, rolled onder my pillar—I was a-wonderin', Mis' Barrett, ef so bein' as yu'd ondertake ter carl my gal's ringolets, now an' agin, for 'er?"

"No," the other said, spiritedly, nobly proof against the magnitude of the bribe. "That'd go agin my conscience, Mis' Green. I'm sorrer ter be a denyin' of yer, but yer mawther's hid o' hair I ha'n't niver approved on; I can't ondertake it, an' so, I say, straight forrerd, at oncet."

The face so "accustomed to refusings" did not change, no flush of resentment relieved its waxen pallor or lightened its fading eyes. "'Tis th' last thing I'm a-askin' of yer," the poor woman said, weakly. "Try as I kin, I can't live much longer. 'Tis on'y nat'ral I should think o' Dora an' th' child'en."

"Yu think a sight too much on 'em, bor! 'Tis time yu give 'em up. Yu lay o' yer deathbed, Mis' Green, an' yu a mis'rable sinner; can't you put up a prayer to ask th' Lord ter have marcy on yer?"

"No," said Mrs Green.

"'No'—an' why not?"

"Cos I don' keer."

"Don' keer, Mis' Green?"

"No, Mis' Barrett, so's He look arter Dora an' th' child'en, I don't keer what He du ter me."

"Mother!"

No answer, but a quiver of drooping lids.

"Mother!"

At the sharp terror of the voice the lids lifted themselves and fell again.

"Yu ain't a-dyin', mother?"

"'Course I ain't."

"Yer promussed! Yer said yer warn't a-dyin'!"

"An' I ain't."

"Then don't kape a-lookin' o' that mander. Lay hold o' th' comb an' du my ringolets."

The comb was thrust within cold fingers which did not close upon it.

"If so bein' yer don't set ter wark and comb 'em out I'll shake ye. I'll shake ye, mother, du yer hare? Du yer hare, mother? Th' bell's gone, an' how'm I ter go ter school an' my ringolets not carled?"

They were not curled that morning, however, for at the sound of the child's angry, frightened voice Mrs Barrett came running upstairs and seized her and dragged her from the room.

"Yer baggige, yu! Ter spake i' that mander to a dyin' woman!"

"She ain't a-dyin', then," the child screamed as she was thrust from the house. "She ain't a-dyin', an' I want my ringolets carled."

Once, when Dora had announced in the hearing of a pupil-teacher that she was the prettiest girl in the school: "You ain't, then," the older girl had told her. "You are not pretty at all, Dora, but exactly like your brother Jim."

"Jim's ugly! You're a-tazin' of me!" Dora had fiercely cried.

"If you hadn't your curls you'd be Jim over again," the teacher had persisted.

She was a tempestuous little animal. She had flown to her mother with the horrid insinuation, had sobbed and screamed, and kicked the innocent, ugly Jim. If she had not her curls!

But she had them. Even this morning, when for the first time she must appear in school without having them freshly curled, the consciousness of their weight upon her shoulders was a comfort to the child. As well as she could without disarranging the set of it, she smoothed each long curl into order as she walked along. The sun of autumn shone, lying like a benediction upon the land whose fruits were gathered; among the hips and haws in the hedges the birds, their family cares all over, sang lightsomely, with vacant hearts. Happiness was in the air. Perhaps someone would say how pretty the curls were, to-day. Perhaps, as once, blessedly, before had happened, a lady riding slowly along the green wayside might pull up her horse to inquire whose little girl she was, to give her sixpence, to ask how much she would take for her beautiful curls.

Ah, with what joy on that happy morning Dora had galloped home to give the account to her mother! The sixpence had gone to buy the blue ribbon Dora wore among her locks on Sundays; but how the mother had cheered up! She had seemed almost well for half an hour that evening, and Dora had told the tale again and again.

"I was a-walkin' along, like this here, not a thinkin' a mite o' my ringolets, an' I see th' woman on th' horse keep a-smilin'. So I made my manners, an' she pulled up 'r horse. 'Whu's little gal be yu?' she say; 'an' where did yu git yer lovely hair?'"

Her mother had eaten two bits of bread-and-butter, that evening, and had drunk the tea Dora all alone had made her. How happy it had been! Perhaps it would all happen again.

Morning school over, she was putting on her hat among a struggling mass of children anxious to get into the open, where there was a great blue vault to shout under, and stones to shy, when the schoolmistress from the empty class-room called her back. The woman stood by her silently for a minute, one hand on the child's shoulder, the other moving thoughtfully over the shining fell of hair.

"Don't shout and play with the others to-day, Dora," she said at length. "Wait till they clear off, and then go right home."

"Yes, tacher."

The schoolmistress waited for another minute, smoothing the curls.

"You're only right a little girl, Dora, but you're the only one. You must try to be good, and look after poor little Jack and Jim, and your father—and be a comfort."

"Yes, tacher." Dora took courage beneath the caressing hand: "I like to be a comfit to mother best," she vouchsafed, brightly daring.

"But your mother—" the governess said, then stopped and turned away her head; she could not bring herself to tell the child the news of the mother she had heard that morning, since school began.

So Dora went, sedately for the first few steps, afterwards with a happy rush, the curls dancing on her shoulders.

"Yer mother is a-dyin', she 'ont be here long; you must try to be a better gal"; how often of late had that phrase offended her ears! She had met such announcements with a fury of denial, with storms of tears. She had rushed to her mother with wild reproach and complaint. "Why don't ye tell 'm yu ain't a-dyin', stids o' layin' there, that mander. They're allust a-tazin' of me?"

To-day no one had said the hated words; and mother would like to hear how teacher had "kep'" her at her side, and coaxed her hair. "I ha'n't niver seed her du that to Gladus, nor none on 'em," she would say, and would remind her mother how these less fortunate girls had not her "hid o' hair."

So, her steps quickened with joyful anticipation, she came running across the meadow in which was her home.

"Here come Dora," Mrs Barrett, who had been busy in Mrs Green's room, said to the neighbour who had helped her. Both women peeped through the lowered blind. "She'll come poundin' upstairs to her mother. There ain't no kapin' of 'r away; and a nice how-d'ye-do there'll be!"

The elder boy, Jim, whose ugly little face Dora's was said to resemble, was standing against the gate of the neglected garden. He did not shout at her, nor throw a stone at her, in the fashion of his usual greeting, but pulled open the rickety gate as she came up.

"Mother's dead," he whispered, and looked at her with curiosity.

"She ain't, then," Dora said. He drew his head back to avoid the blow she aimed at it, and shut the gate after her.

Jack, an ugly urchin of five, the youngest of the family, was sitting on the doorstep, hammering with the iron-shod heel of his heavy boot a hazel nut he had found on his way home. The nut, instead of cracking, was being driven deep into the moist earth. He did not desist from his employment, or lift his head.

"Father's gone for mother's corffin," he said.

The howl he gave when Dora knocked him off the step brought Mrs Barrett upon the scene. She pulled the girl off the fallen Jack with a gentler touch than usual.

"You come along upstairs, along o' me," she said.

There was not only the coffin to be ordered in Wotton, but suits of black for himself and children, besides the joint of meat to be cooked for the meal after the funeral. Mr Green did not hurry over his purchases, but went about them with the leisurely attentiveness of one anxious to do the right thing, but unaccustomed to the business of making bargains.

His wages had been "made a hand on," lately; there had been brandy and "sech-like" to buy for the missus; the neighbour to pay, leaving little more than enough for bread for the rest of them. But now, with this burying money—! The new-made widower enjoyed the hitherto undreamed-of experience of knowing that he might put in for a glass at every public-house he passed, and not exhaust it.

He treated himself to a tin of salmon to have with his supper, when he got back to Dulditch. While his wife had been well and about, she had been wont at rare intervals to supply such a "ralish" to the evening meal. Having the means to indulge himself, his thoughts had at once travelled to the luxury.

Yet, arrived at home, he had had too much beer to be very hungry, and the thought of the dead wife, up there, just beyond the ceiling, destroyed what little pleasure the feast might have held.

"Happen she'd been alive, she'd maybe ha' picked a mossel," he said to himself.

That she could be totally indifferent to the delicacy, even although dead and fairly started on her heavenward journeying, was a bewildering fact his dull brain could scarcely grasp. He got up from the table, and taking the unshaded lamp, walked heavily upstairs to look upon this marvel—his wife who was no more.

He was a stolid creature, but was shaken enough to give a sharp growl of fear when, from the other side of the rigid form upon the bed, a head was lifted.

"Hello!" he called. "Hello! What yu a-doin' here? Now then! Come out o' that, yu young warmint; don't, I'll hide ye."

The figure lying by the dead woman slipped to the ground. It wore a brown frock and a crumpled white overall trimmed with lace.

"Hello!" the man said again. He looked stupidly at his little daughter, then pulled aside the sheet which covered his wife.

In the waxen face, with lids still half-open above the dull eyes, with lips drawn back to show the gums, was little change. Beneath the chin a large white bow of coarse muslin had been tied. It was designed to hide the thinness of the throat, but gave, besides, a dreadful air of smartness to the poor corpse. Above the sunken chest the arms were crossed, but, over them, and over the thin hands, in a burning, shining mass of resplendent colour lay—

The husband held the lamp nearer, and bent his dull, red face to peer closer at the scattered heap— the miracle of bronze and red, red living gold. "Hello!" he said again, then moved the lamp to let its light shine on his daughter's face, and stared at her.

"Hello!"

"I ha'n't got no one now to carl my ringolets," the child sobbed, her voice rising high in the scale of rebellious misery; "my ringolets ain't no good to me no more. I ha' cut 'em off; mother, she kin have 'em. They ain't no good ter me."

The glare of the lamp held awry was upon the broad red face of the girl with the streaming, yellow eyes, with the unevenly cropped head.

"I thought yu was the boy Jim," her father said.

PINK CARNATIONS

"You see, they are my lucky flowers," she said. "I can't very well wear them on my wedding-dress, but I'm to have some to go away with. Jack's going to bring them down from town with him to-night."

I asked of Daphne, who had been the favourite of fortune from her birth, in whose cup of sweet no bitter had ever mingled, who had walked for all her happy days along a flowery path, what she meant by such nonsense.

She was ready enough to give me her absurd girlish reasons.

What she told me was the feeblest folly, of course; but even silly superstition must be pardoned to such a pretty person; and the words of a young woman who is going to be married on the morrow must be treated by a hopeless spinster, I suppose, with, at least, a semblance of respect. There had been an occasion, it seemed, long ago in her childhood, when she, having lost from her neck a locket which held her dead father's portrait, had found it, all search for it having ceased, on the carnation-bed where she had stooped to pick a flower. On the day that the news reached them that Hugh, her brother, had won the hurdle race at Cambridge (one of the chief triumphs, it appeared, of her eventless life) she had just finished arranging a vase of pink carnations for her dressing-table. Once, when her mother had been seriously ill and there had been a fear the disease from which she suffered was going to take a dangerous turn, she, Daphne, had been frightened and very unhappy. Longing for, yet dreading the doctor's arrival, she had watched him descend from his carriage, wearing a pink carnation in his coat. She had known at once that his verdict on her mother's state would be favourable; and it was. A burglar had tried to get in at Daphne's sitting-room window—at least Daphne, on what appeared to me insufficient evidence, declared that he had done so. The window-box had fallen to the ground, and had put the burglar to flight—that is, if there had been one. At any rate it was clearly proved that the window-box had fallen. It contained, of course, pink carnations.

And so on to many other instances, chief among which was the fact that the first time she had beheld the handsome face of the Jack she was to marry to-morrow she had worn a bunch of her favourite flowers in the bodice of her white silk dress. Afterwards, on the day of the County Ball, at which function he had proposed, he had sent her a bouquet composed entirely of pink carnations, and had chosen one of those blooms for his own buttonhole.

"Without knowing—without my having even mentioned to him that they brought me luck!" Daphne assured me, the dark, poetic eyes in her small face large with the mystery of it. "Do you wonder Jack agrees with me I must not be without them on my wedding-day?"

By her mother's command, and in order that she might not look, as I am assured many brides do look, a "perfect rag" on her wedding-day, Daphne was to rest for a certain number of hours, that afternoon. She was forbidden, even, to write one of the seventy still remaining out of the three hundred letters of thanks to the donors of wedding-presents.

She should have to work them off—so many a day—on her honeymoon, Daphne ruefully supposed. Jack would help. She would make him direct the envelopes. She bore a grudge apparently against the givers of the treasures under which the tables in the morning-room were groaning.

"If you could only know what it has been!" she sighed. "However hard I wrote I couldn't keep pace. No sooner had I wiped one name off the list than three more presents had come!"

From this onerous duty, however, she was now to desist, and from all fatigue of receiving the guests who were arriving by different trains throughout the day. She was to lie at her ease on silken cushions in that pretty room of her own, upon whose window-box the supposititious burglar had set his too heavy boot. I was amused to see that the white chintzes of the chairs and hangings were flowered with pink carnations, and that garlands of the flower, tied with pink ribbons, formed the frieze of the white wallpaper.

"Well, you were always a petted and spoilt child," I said to her; "and I suppose you are going to be so to the end of the chapter."

"Only more so," she said, with her youthful arrogance. "You can't think what a splendid hand at spoiling Jack is."

I laughed, told her to let me know how much he spoilt her in five years' time, and left her. For a servant had interrupted our conversation with the announcement that Mr Mavor, who had returned from town, would be glad to speak to me.

"Hughie? how absurd!" Daphne said, who wanted to go on talking to me about her lover. "As if Hughie could possibly have a thing to say to you which would not keep, Hannah!"

"It is to make me an offer of marriage I have not the slightest doubt," I told her, being of an age when a woman can make jokes of that kind about herself and pretend not to feel the heartprick.

I found the head of the house in the room which had been turned into a museum of objects of art— precious and not precious—for exhibition on the morrow. I had known the young man from boyhood, and I saw at once that something was amiss. He had left for town before my arrival that morning, and this was our first meeting, but he forgot to come forward and put out his hand. He stalked past me, instead, and banged the door by which I had entered; then he seized me by the arm.

"Hannah," he said, "I want to talk to you. I want your advice. We're in a devil of a mess."

"It's the wedding-dress, or the wedding-cake!" I said, staring at him. "One of them hasn't come!"

"It's about Marston. Something I only heard to-day. He must not be allowed to marry my sister."

"Hughie!"

He took his hand from my arm, laid it on one of the tables spread with the presents. There was a faint ringing of silver and china to show the hand was not steady. He is a self-contained, sturdily-built, matter-of-fact young man in the early twenties; quite unlike his sister, whose appearance is elegantly fragile, who is filled with nerves, and sensitive to the fingertips.

"I got a letter this morning," he went on, and for a moment fumbled in his coat-pocket as if with the intention, quickly relinquished, of showing it. "It was from a woman; telling me of certain incidents in Marston's career."

"Probably all made up. Lies."

"It isn't. Once for all, don't waste time in saying that. I went up this morning to the address she gave me. I saw her. She told me worse than she wrote—poor wretch! I didn't take it for gospel. I got confirmation, all round. There isn't room for the shadow of a doubt. She left her husband a year ago for Marston—"

"A year ago? Only a year?"

"A year. The husband got a divorce; this brute refused to marry her."

"Oh, Hugh!"

"It's worse. I can't tell you all. Sufficient that he played the traitor, the coward, the beast. Left her to face shame, and poverty, and—everything, alone."

"Can it be so bad! You are certain?"

He lifted the unsteady hand and laid it open, heavily again upon the table where the Crown Derby coffee services, the silver inkstands, muffineers and bridge boxes, whose donors had not even been thanked, jingled with a tiny music once more.

"Certain. Now, don't keep repeating that word, Hannah. I don't want to waste time producing proofs, but I've got them. It's as certain as death. And it's not the only thing. Once I was on his track—late in the day as it was—I learnt more. We live so in a hole, down here, and nothing like this has ever come near us. We've taken people for what they seemed to be—as I, ass that I was, took Marston—and never poked into their histories. The man's got a bad record, all along. Decent people have closed their doors in his face."

"What will you do, Hugh? What can you do now?"

"Do? Stop the marriage," he said. He glared for a minute upon the costly display on the table, then turned his back on it all, and carried his white face to the window. "My sister shall never marry that scoundrel," he said.

"Daphne's heart will break."

"I know." He looked out on the wintry landscape with gloomy eyes, and a resolutely held underlip. "That is what my mother says. I do not believe it; but if it is so, it does not alter what is the right and only course to take."

"What else does your mother say?"

He moved his shoulders impatiently. "That the wedding must go on; that it is too late to draw back." He turned swiftly upon me. "Could you have believed that my mother, of all people, could take such a view as that?"

"I can see how she feels about it. To break it off now is too hideously painful—"

"And what will it be for Daphne if it goes on? Don't you suppose her life with a brute like that would be hideously painful?" He held the back of his hand to his forehead for a moment and shut his eyes tightly as if in painful thought. "My poor little sister!" he said. "Poor Dapple!"

I sat down and stared stupidly before me, too overcome by the situation to be able even to think.

"Your mother says the wedding is to go on; you say it is to be stopped—"

He pounced upon me. "I am master here," he said.

He had always seemed a boy to me, and I had never known him to exert his authority before. His mother and young sister had taken their own way in affairs, and had never been hampered by the consideration that "Hughie" was a person of importance. Yet, there was no doubt about his position. Looking at, and listening to him now, I saw that he meant to have his way; and my conscience told me that his way was the right one.

A word or two more he said to me of incidents in Jack Marston's history; showed me how it had happened that these were only recently revealed to him; how, to the Mavors' circle he had been entirely a stranger; how the few friends of Hugh's who had had any acquaintance with the man had wondered at the sister's engagement, but thought it no business of their own.

"Have you made your mother understand you are determined in the matter?"

"I have told her I will shoot the man before he shall marry my sister."

"And what is she doing? Your mother?"

"She is raving like a madwoman in her bedroom."

The stupendousness of the situation, to which at moments I felt insensible, kept coming over me in waves of comprehension.

"Well, I don't wonder!" I said.

Long pauses fell between our fragments of speech. He stood before the square centre table, black-browed, staring at its glittering burden.

The footman appeared at the door. "If you please, sir, Hamley wishes to know if the dog-cart as well as the brougham and omnibus is to meet the 5.15 this evening?"

His master looked at the man with knit brows, as if making a painful effort to understand what was said. He pulled out his watch, and for a minute studied it.

"Tell Hamley," then he said, "not to meet the 5.15 at all. No one will come by that train. In ten minutes I shall want to send some telegrams."

The man, staring at the strange order, withdrew.

"You are going to stop the rest of the guests?" I asked.

"Of course. They were coming to the wedding. There will be no wedding."

"And Jack Marston? You can't telegraph this horrible thing to him!"

"Can't I? I shall."

"And Daphne? She is sitting in her room counting the minutes till he comes to her."

"Hannah, I want you to go and tell her."

"I, Hugh! Why should I be picked out to do such a horrible thing?"

"My mother will not. Daphne has always known you. You have sense—"

"I will not. So that is the finish, Hugh. I haven't got a stone for a heart. I would cut out my tongue rather than do it."

"Then, I must," he said, turned on his heels and made for the door.

Having reached it and flung it open, he looked back at me with his distressed, scowling face. "This is how one's friends fail one in an emergency!" he said.

His scorn, at the moment, was nothing to me, but I was beside myself with sorrow and dismay. Daphne, with her sweet, small face lying among her cushions, her dark eyes filled with visions of the lover who was speeding to her, of the joyful life just opening before her—and Tragedy, pitiless, relentless, awaiting her! Her messenger, oh so much more cruel than the messenger of Death, crossing corridors, mounting stairs, hurrying with the inevitableness of Fate upon her! Was there nothing to be done? Was there no hand to save?

Hugh was right. Boy as he was, he was acting as a man should act. His mother, who, to save her ears from the despairing cries of her child, to avoid the painful explanation to invited guests, the perplexity of interrupted plans, was willing that the marriage should continue, was weak, wicked even, perhaps. But I found it in my heart to wish that she might have her way, that the suffering, since there must be suffering, should be, at any rate, postponed.

The engagement had been a short one, and circumstances had of late limited my intercourse with the family; the bridegroom and I had met but once. Yet now his handsome face rose before me—a face whose only fault was that it was, perhaps, too handsome. I thought of the tales Daphne's mother had told me of his extraordinary passion for the girl with whom he had fallen in love at first sight. Women love love. No woman is too old to thrill at the story of a lover's ardour. The man was a sinner, no doubt; to Hugh he seemed a scoundrel; but—

I caught up with Hugh as he was going—very slowly going, poor boy—round the last turning to his sister's room.

"Hughie," I gasped, breathless with my haste. "You are right—but don't be brutal. Don't kill the child. Listen. Instead of writing to Jack Marston, let him come. Let him tell her himself. Give her a chance. Give him one, even. It is a cruel business, anyhow. Don't let's blunder into making it worse than it is."

I suppose as he had gone to the accomplishment of his heavy task he had become more appreciative of its difficulty. He was very fond of his sister, and must have shrunk with dread from the contemplation of her pain. Anyhow, his purpose had weakened. With a few words more I got him to acquiesce in the amended plan.

"How can we be certain he tells her? He will lie to her," he objected.

"We will take measures to be sure he does not."

"He is a specious beggar; she will marry him all the same."

"Then, if he has such an ascendency over her, would she not in any case? She is of age; her own mistress."

"But not from my house," the boy said.

However, in what I proposed there was respite; and, for better or worse, I had my way.

I could not return to witness the innocent happiness of Daphne, and I spent the rest of the afternoon in trying to soothe the agitation of Daphne's mother; listening to her tirades against her suddenly masterful son, hearing her protestations of faith in the rectitude of Jack Marston, alternating with her outbursts of anger and grief at his hitherto unsuspected villainy.

"Hugh will see him when he arrives, will confront him with the story," I told her. "I don't suppose he can utterly deny, but he can palliate. There will be nothing told to Daphne which she can't forgive. The wedding will go on."

Calm came to her presently, even cheerfulness—so mercifully is the mature heart case-hardened to bear its burdens. It is, I am sure of it, the heart of the young only which can break. Terrible things were hanging over the house. Sin and shame in the person of Jack Marston were approaching it by the 5.15 train. Its most idolised inmate was to be killed with disappointment, or to bind herself on the morrow to a life of misery, perhaps disgrace; but in the drawing-room was already a sprinkling of guests, many more were on their way. The wolf may gnaw at the vitals, but a hostess must wear a smiling face.

The omnibus and the brougham returned duly from the station with the last expected guests, vehicles containing their luggage and their servants followed; but the dog-cart, sent specially to meet Jack Marston, came back empty.

The master of the house heard the intelligence without comment. Presently he came across to me with an ugly look on his set face.

"The beggar has got wind of it, you see, and has made a bolt," he said.

I hardly know if it was a relief or not to find that this was not the case. One of the Mayors' newly-arrived cousins, who had seen the bridegroom at Liverpool Street, had been entrusted with a note to the bride which satisfactorily explained his absence.

I carried this note in to Daphne as she dressed for dinner. It was only a hurried scrawl on a leaf torn from a memorandum book, and, having read it, she passed it on to me.

"Four whole hours before he gets here!" she lamented. "Oh, Hannah! could anything have been more truly unlucky?"

"Darling," the pencilled lines ran, "I find those beggars in Covent Garden have not sent the carnations. I shall wait till the last minute, and if not here must go after them. I dare not come to you without the carnations! Have me met by the 9.30. Yours for ever, and ever, and ever—Jack."

"My dear, four hours isn't much," I reminded her.

"Four hours is a lifetime," she said.

She stared, positively with tears in her eyes, at her pretty reflection in the glass. "I don't know how I shall get through this evening," she said.

I don't know how we all did; but it passed somehow, although it did not pass gaily. Hugh was too young and honest to hide with any success the care that harassed him; his glum face at the head of the dinner-table was discouraging to the most persistent cheerfulness. Mrs Mavor did her best, but she was ill at ease, and, as must have been patent to all, strongly disinclined to talk of to-morrow's event. To Daphne, disappointed of her lover's presence and support, the gathering of the clans was an ordeal and an embarrassment.

Standing beside her when coffee was brought to her, I heard her ask of the servant if the dog-cart was yet gone to meet Mr Marston. He believed it was just upon the start, the man said.

"Let me know as soon as it goes, please," Daphne said, and presently the footman came in again with the desired intelligence.

I suppose the poor child wanted to follow in fancy the dog-cart along the silent roads and the dark lanes, beneath the starlit sky; to see it arrive at the little wayside station in time for the rush and roar of the train, dashing like a jewelled monster out of the desert of night; dashing off again, its great ruby eyes shining in its tail, into the blackness of space, having deposited the one precious item of its freight on the platform.

A half-hour before Marston could arrive Daphne slipped away. "I shall wait up for Jack," she said to her mother. "Send him, the instant he comes, to me in my sitting-room."

One by one the ladies of the party followed Daphne's example. The men went off into the smoking-room. Mrs Mavor and I were left alone. Her nervousness and excitement, suppressed hitherto, were now at fever heat. She moved about the room, pushing chairs into fresh positions, shaking their cushions, taking up and setting down, now this now that ornament, with trembling fingers pulling out and pushing in flowers in the vases, not improving their arrangement by any means.

"The question is what Hughie will do," she said for the twentieth time. "If only he would leave it alone! If he would not interfere! It has gone so far, only Heaven should intervene. You know,

Hannah, we all marry men with our eyes blinded. Daphne must take her chance like the rest. Supposing it was you, Hannah; if the man was a—murderer—and you loved him, and knew that he madly loved you, would you thank anyone for coming between? You'd marry him, wouldn't you?"

I declined to say how I should proceed with my murderer. If I had it in me to love a man against my reason and my conscience I could not tell.

"It's eleven o'clock," I said. "I thought you told me he would be here by half-past ten."

She ceased to fidget with the furniture, and came to the mantelpiece by which I was standing.

"The clock's wrong," she said. "Fast, a good half-hour." She seized the little gold carriage clock and shook it in her nervous fingers as if that would put the matter right. The door opened.

"Here he is!" she said, and started violently, almost dropping the clock.

It was Hugh who came in, his face pale, a fire of excitement gleaming in his eyes, his watch in his hand. "He should have been here half an hour ago. It is as I told you: he has made a bolt," he said.

"The dog-cart is not back?"

"No; but you'll see!"

"Are the men gone to bed, Hugh?"

"No, they're in there"; he gave a backward toss of his head in the direction of the smoking-room. "It all makes me sick," he said. "I can't sit there and hee-haw with them."

He took up his position between his mother and me, his hands on the mantelpiece, his foot on the fender, and gloomed down upon the hearth.

When the hands of the little clock showed that another half-hour had flown, the door was flung open and Daphne came in.

"Hasn't he come?" she asked. "I thought you were keeping him away from me, downstairs. Hasn't he even come?"

"The train is late," the mother said.

But Daphne was overwrought. She flung herself upon a chair, and twisting herself so that her arms embraced its back and her face was hidden, began to cry hysterically.

"There has been an accident," she sobbed, presently, lifting her head. "Hamley has overturned the dog-cart in the dark; Jack has been pitched out; there is no one to help,—and you all stand here! You all stand here!"

She insisted that her brother should go at once on his bicycle to see what was amiss. Her distress unnerved the boy, and softened him. He lifted her from the chair, and put his arm round her and led her to the door.

"You go to bed, Dapple-ducky," he said, calling her by the name he had given her in childhood. "It's all right, dear. Don't you be a silly. I'll go along at once and fetch him."

His stern resolve was shaken. If Jack Marston had come then he would have relented; I think the marriage would have taken place.

But he did not come. He never came.

Halfway to the station Hugh Mavor met the dog-cart returning, the groom alone seated in it. There had been an accident, he said; a couple of carriages had run off the line and overturned. He had waited for the surviving passengers to be brought in. The train bringing them had at length arrived; Mr Marston was not among them.

The accident had happened ten miles down the line. Hugh got into the dog-cart and drove to the scene of the disaster.

Mrs Mavor spent the night in Daphne's room. I awaited Hugh, sitting alone by the drawing-room fire, when he returned at four o'clock in the morning of what was to have been his sister's wedding-day. He came in, carrying a florist's tin box in his hand, and I read the news in his face before he spoke.

"Only three killed. He was one. I saw him. I thought I had to. It was awful."

He sank into the chair where Daphne had sat, hid his face on its back as she had done, while his shoulders heaved with painful sobbing. After a few minutes he turned to me.

"We shall have to tell her," he said. "That is the next thing to do."

He got up, and with shaking fingers, not knowing, I think, that he did so, pulled the string from the tin box, which lay on the table beneath the lamp, pulled it open.

"Everything else in the carriage seemed to be in shivers—but this," he said.

Inside, beneath the snowy wrappings of cotton wool, great perfect blooms of pink carnations lay. The spicy fragrance rose in our faces; in the light of the lamp the glowing flowers smiled in their faultless beauty.

"Poor Dapple's lucky flowers!" the boy said.

Those among us who know more of her dead lover than was ever told to Daphne are disposed to call them her lucky flowers still.

A LITTLE WHITE DOG

"There!" Elinor cried. "Now, how could you be so careless, Ted?"

"The blessed thing must have jumped of its own accord off the chimney-piece," Ted said. He looked down at his wife on her knees beside him, ruefully collecting the fragments of the broken vase. "I wasn't so much as looking at it, Nell."

"No! If you'd only had the sense to look at it!" Nell sighed. "But you will stand with your heels on the fender, and you push those great shoulders of yours against the chimney-board, and smash go all my ornaments—and a lot you care! However, something had to break to-day, and it might have been worse."

"How do you mean 'had to'?"

"That great awkward Emily threw down a soup-plate last night; and I—"

"No, not you, surely, Nell?"

"It wasn't my fault, of course. I was lifting the hand-glass from my dressing-table as carefully as carefully, and it just dropped out of my hands! 'That is the second,' I said to myself; 'now I wonder what the third will be.'"

"And why did you say anything so silly?"

"Have you actually grown to your enormous age, and not known that when one thing is broken in a house three are broken? Well, you have had an ineffectual sort of education!"

"You don't believe such rotten rubbish?"

"Don't you? When I tell you of the soup-plate, the hand-mirror, and now this vase? You can't call it nonsense, because there it is. A proof before your very eyes. You might as well say it isn't unlucky to see a single crow—"

"I'd sooner see one of the mischievous brutes any day than fifty."

"—That you may expect things to go pleasantly on the day you put on your petticoat the wrong side out—"

"I should expect them to take a comic turn on the day I did that, certainly!"

"What a ribald boy! Now, listen, Ted; be very attentive, and I will tell you a true, true story. You mustn't laugh the tiniest titter—ah, now, Ted! you won't laugh, will you?"

They were very young married people, and were not yet disposed to sit quietly apart and talk to each other. She seized him by the lapels of his coat now, and shook him to attention, while he, looking down upon her with the hardly yet familiar pride of possession in his boyish eyes, swayed his big frame in her grasp, flatteringly yielding to her small efforts.

"Are you going to attend, sir? Well, then—There was once a young man—"

"Who met a small vixen called Nell, and she fell in love with him and made him marry her."

"Ah, now, Ted, do listen!—A young man, and his mother told him never to walk under a ladder."

"And he did, naughty youth, and a bricklayer fell on him, and he died?"

She pleaded with him. "Seriously, Ted; no nonsense!" So he grasped her by the elbows and looked gravely in her face.

"It was mother's cousin Harold—really and truly—not a make-up."

"Hurry up, darling. I'm swallowing every word, and it's most awfully interesting."

"And he didn't believe that kind of thing—just like you, you know—ladders, and crows, and petticoats, and things. And he was going out to the West Indies to an awfully good appointment—hundreds a year! And his mother went for a walk with him on the last day. And they were building a row of houses—"

"Cousin Harold and his mother?"

"No. You know. And his mother said, 'Don't go under the ladder, dear'—and he did."

"Naughty boy! Naughty Cousin Harold!"

"You're laughing! Very well, just wait. To tease her, he would. 'Now, look here,' he said, 'every ladder I come to I mean to go under twice.' And he did. And his mother couldn't stop him, and she cried. And—that's all—"

"All? But where's the point?"

"I didn't say there was a point. You know about mother's Cousin Harold."

"I'm hanged if I do."

"He never, never came back."

"Goodness!"

"He never even got there."

"Break it gently, Nell."

"The ship he went in sank, and no one escaped to tell the dreadful tale."

"And supposing he hadn't walked under ladders, but was alive in the West Indies, what relation would he be to you and to me?"

She was proceeding to tell him in all good faith, but he stopped her. "And now," he said, "I will tell you a tale. But first, as my feelings have been considerably harassed, I will solace myself with a pipe."

She was being taught to fill his pipe, and to light it, and on this occasion was made to take a couple of draws to prove to herself that she had not properly cleaned it with the hairpin, according to instructions given last night. So that the story was long delayed, and when at length it came it did not amount to much.

"There was once an old man who gave a dinner-party."

"That was daddy," Elinor said, from the arm of the chair where she was now sitting with her shoulder against his.

"It was on the occasion of the marriage of his only daughter to a handsome and agreeable young man, the most eligible parti of the neighbourhood."

"That was you and me," Nell explained, contentedly. "Well, you are a vain old boy!"

"No interruptions, please," Ted went on, pulling at his pipe. "Although the occasion was one of rejoicing, there was a melancholy circumstance connected with it which cast a shadow over the otherwise sunshiny—'m—sunshine of the scene."

"You're as bad as a newspaper. Go on softly, or you'll never keep it up. I can't think what's coming."

"The guests sat down thirteen to table—"

"Well, so they did!" Nell recalled. "Now, that is really very clever of you, Ted. I'd quite forgotten. I was horribly frightened then—but I'd as clean as clean forgotten!"

"Well, there you are!" Ted said. "There's your moral."

"Where? Where?"

"Why, here we are, all alive and well and kicking; you and me, your daddy and mummy, your uncles and your cousins and your aunts."

"But supposing one of us wasn't!" Nell remarked sagely. "When you ask your thirteen to dinner and one dies it must be horrid; and I should think your guests might—might bring an action against you."

She was holding the hand he had just put up to meet hers, which was round his neck now, and a thought suddenly struck her. "But the year isn't up yet, Ted," she said.

The dinner had been an epoch in their young lives; they both remembered the date was the eighteenth of October. He pointed to the silver calendar on the chimney-piece, to which the parlour-maid attended. "This is the eighteenth again," Ted said. "There aren't two eighteenths of October in one year."

Elinor was back in memories of the event. "Do you remember Aunt Carrie, and how ill she was? At the very verge of the grave. And how afraid mummy was she should notice there were thirteen? Now, here she is as well as any of us, and going to get married again. Ah! What are you doing, Ted?

"No, Ted! Oh, no, please! My hair will come down!"

"I'm getting another hairpin."

It was such pretty hair, he was always pleased to see it hanging about her ears, as had been its fashion when he had first met her—not so long ago. So he fought her for the hairpin while she ducked her head and threw it backwards, and laughed, and struggled in his grasp; to submit, of course, at last, to yield up the hairpin, to roast it, red hot in the fire, to watch it burn its malodorous passage through his pipe.

That ceremony over, she got him his boots, and would have laced them for him, and kissed them too, if he would have let her, and did grovel at his feet to arrange the roll of his stockings for him.

"You have got nice calves, Ted!" she told him. "I don't think I could love even you if you had sticks of things like Robert Anstey's."

"Oh, Bob's legs'll do all right," Ted said, loyally. He stamped a foot into the second boot, and in doing so ground some of the broken vase beneath his heel. He filliped her cheek, then, smiling into her eyes—

"You and your old woman's superstitions!" he said. "Perhaps you don't know I've a—what d'ye call it?—a portent in my own family—or had when I had a family," he told her, bending again over his boot. "Well, I have, then!"

"And what's a portent, silly? I daresay it's nothing to boast of."

"It's a little—white—DOG!"

He barked the last word at her, loud and sharp, his face suddenly projected into hers. She fell backward and sat on her heels.

"Ted! How horrid of you! What does it do?"

"I haven't the faintest notion."

"Are you making it up?"

"Not I. They all made it up. My father, and my grandfather, and the whole tribe. They stuck it into each other, and tried to stick it into me, that whenever one of us is going to die he sees this beastly little hound."

"Ted!" she was clinging to the calf she admired now, in an agreeable ecstasy of shuddering. "I wish I had a ghost, too."

"You shall have mine, with pleasure."

"But why didn't you tell me before?"

"I clean forgot it till this minute. My father told me about it when I was quite a little chap."

"But is it true, Ted?"

"Of course it isn't."

"And did they really see it?"

"They said they did. You may bet your life they didn't."

When he was ready to walk round the little domain he had inherited from his father, Elinor accompanied him to the gate. "I wouldn't have a little white dog for a ghost!" she said to him, slightingly, as they parted. "Anyone could have as good a ghost as that if they tried!"

"Everyone couldn't have an ancestor who had tortured one to death to spite his wife!" he said.

"You can see a dozen little white dogs any day," she taunted him.

"I saw one more than I wanted yesterday when I was out with my gun," he admitted. "That new little beast of Anstey's ran in front of me into every field and frightened the birds. I hardly had a shot."

"Tell Bob to keep it at home," advised Nell.

"I must," Ted acquiesced, and went.

In the course of the morning Bob Anstey, who always appeared some time during each day, came in. Elinor found him standing up by the chimney-piece, manipulating the silver calendar.

"You're a day too previous in your calculation," he said. "This isn't the eighteenth, but the seventeenth, madame."

"Well, how funny!" Elinor cried. "Now I wonder how Aunt Carrie is! I shall have to tell Ted the year isn't up, after all."

To Anstey that was rather a cryptic utterance, but he asked for no explanation. These two were full of little jokes, of allusions, of reminiscences, interesting to them, in which he had no part, close friends as they were.

"Can you spare Ted to me for an hour or two this afternoon?" he asked.

"She could not," she said, smiling; "she could never spare Ted."

"Then come along with us yourself, madame. I want Ted's opinion of that mare I've got my eye on at Wenderling. Your ladyship's opinion would be of value, too."

"Ted has nothing to ride. Did you hear that his horse had wrenched its shoulder yesterday? A wretch of a little dog ran out of a cottage and got mixed up with Starlight's feet. Ted jerked the horse round to spare the dog—and Starlight is as lame as a tree."

They would bicycle then, he decided. The roads were good. They would get into Wenderling in time for tea, and take it easy, coming home in the dusk. They must remember to take lamps. They would start at three.

She agreed to all arrangements, swaying herself idly in the rocking-chair Ted had bought for her; a pretty slip of a girl with a happy, almost childish face. Anstey little thought as he looked at her how often and often through all his life he would with his mind's eye see her so again!

As he was going through the door she called a laughing reproach to him. "Your abominable dog spoilt my husband's sport yesterday, Mr Anstey. Why do you keep such a wretch?"

"Which dog?" he asked, pulling up, smiling at her.

"Your horrid little white dog."

"I haven't got a little white dog," he said, and laughed, and went away.

After all, Elinor did not share the expedition to Wenderling; for at lunch-time it came on to rain, and Ted would not let her get wet. He was proud of seeing her rough it sometimes; he delighted to take her hunting on days when no other lady was in the field, to see her face, rosy and eager, her bright hair darkened with the wet, the raindrops hanging on her hat. He kept her beside him, standing silent and patient in a certain soppy, sodden spot by the river, waiting for the chance of a wild duck flying homeward above the low-lying mists of the fens. What did not hurt him could not harm her, in her youth and strength and spirit, he thought.

"She has the pluck and the staying power of a man," he was proud to tell Anstey; but was proud, too, now and again, to exercise his new prerogative of taking care of the wife who was such a recent, dear possession. Quite unexpectedly, he would veto some proceeding she proposed.

"I won't have you doing it," he would say with dignity. And she was equally proud to obey.

"Ted says I mustn't," or "Ted says I may." What, in those golden hours, did it matter which?

She walked with him, bareheaded, through the drizzling rain to the house where the bicycles were kept, and felt the tyres with him, and rubbed a spot of rust off the handle bar, and walked beside him again, he pushing the machine, down the drive to the road.

"It's a beastly day," Ted said, with an eye cocked at the low-hanging, steel-coloured clouds. "If Bob wasn't so keen on my seeing this horse, I'd chuck it and stay with you."

"Come home soon," she begged him; and, "You may be sure I shall come as soon as I possibly can," he promised her.

"It wasn't Bob's dog that bothered you the other day," she told him as he stood ready to mount, his foot on the pedal; "Bob hasn't got a little white dog."

"It must have been that brute that ran out from Barker's under Starlight's feet the other day, then," he called, and was off.

Nell stood by the gate and watched him till he joined his friend, and, in spite of the faster falling rain, she watched him still. Before they reached the bend of the road Ted turned his head; she waved a gay hand to him, and he, hesitating for a moment, wheeled round and bicycled back.

"Did you call me, Nell?" he said.

Of course she had not called.

"Bob knew you hadn't, but I thought I heard you call; and then you held up your hand and beckoned me."

"Nonsense! Nothing of the sort!" she laughed. "Be off, Ted. I shall never get you home again if you don't start."

"You'll have me home in a twinkling," he promised. And in a flash was gone.

She turned and ran back, with head bent beneath the downpouring rain, light-hearted, to her home, not knowing, never guessing that on that handsome, smiling, healthy face of her young husband she had looked her last.

For when, a couple of hours later, borne on men's shoulders, he was carried to his home, he was so crushed and mangled out of his likeness as his wife had known him that, even by force, they prevented her from looking upon him.

When time had elapsed—Elinor, for some part of it mercifully numbed or unconscious, could not have told if hours, days or weeks—Bob Anstey, at her request, was brought to her. He had been in waiting, knowing that, sooner or later, that meeting, if they did not die with the pain of it, must be lived through.

He had expected to see her lying helpless and strengthless with hidden face. She was standing up against the darkened windows at the end of the long room furthest from the door. He started, walking slowly, almost as if he was groping his way, among the familiar chairs and tables, in her direction. But when half the space was traversed, and she still stood there, uttering no word, dully watching him, his courage failed, and he stopped short. It was the sight of Ted's chair, his pipes on the bracket beside it, the picture of him, smiling, in the silver frame on the mantelpiece, which unmanned him. He had prayed that he might have strength to support the girl-widow in this interview; and he found himself suddenly giving way before her, sobbing like a child; while Elinor looked on tearlessly from afar, dangling the tassel of the window-blind in her hand.

When at length he somewhat mastered his grief and looked up, she had come quite close to him, but she did not speak.

"I thought you might like to hear," Anstey said, in sorrow-muffled voice; and she nodded her head for him to go on.

"He—talked of you nearly all the way," he began. "He said how—"

She stopped him. "Not that," she said, "not yet. The other—the other!"

By some instinct he knew what she meant. "It was going down the Wenderling Hill," he said, "just as we got into the town. You know that steepish hill? Halfway down was a brewer's waggon. We were going at a good stroke, not saying anything, for the moment. We got up to the waggon. 'There's that infernal white dog again,' he said. And I heard him call loudly, 'Get out of the way, you brute!' He swerved violently on one side, as if the dog were in his path—I don't know how it happened; God knows why it happened!—he was flung right under the wheels. He—thank God, he did not suffer, Nell, or know a moment's terror or regret. He died instantly."

Elinor was silent for long. She sat, with brow clasped tightly in both hands, looking intently upon the carpet at his feet, trying, he thought, to understand, to get into a mind too confused to work receptively what he was saying to her. Presently, still tightly holding her head, but with more of comprehension in her face, she looked up.

"And the dog?" she asked him. "The little white dog?"

"It's a strange thing about the dog," he told her slowly. "There wasn't one!"

"And besides all that, the poor little woman is ill," he said. "She didn't complain much, but she looked like a ghost to-day."

"What is the matter with her now?" his wife asked.

She was lying back in her chair as if she, herself, were a little tired, and her long white hands busied themselves with four knitting-needles from which depended the leg of a knickerbocker-stocking intended for the shapely limb of Everard Barett.

He looked quickly at her with an air of suspicion and offence. "Now?" he repeated. "What does 'now' mean, spoken in that tone? I don't want to talk about Vera if you don't want to hear. You call the little woman your friend, and ask in that tone, 'What's the matter with her now?'"

Mrs Barett knitted on in silence during the agitated minute in which her husband kicked away the chair on whose seat his feet had been stretched, sat up, punched the cushion behind him three times with a vicious fist, and, finding it even then fail intelligently to support his head, flung it across the room.

"'Matter with her now!'" he snorted to himself, in a tone as unlike that mimicked as possible.

"Vera seems to be generally full of complaints, that's all," the wife said.

He gave her a furious glance, and stretched a hand backwards for the newspaper that lay on the table behind him. "We will change the subject," he said, loftily.

"She has her husband, who is devoted to her," Mrs Barett reminded him, disregarding the remark.

For answer the man moved impatiently, and angrily slapped one of his slippered feet over the other.

She smiled upon her knitting. "I daresay her husband isn't the style of man you admire, but he is devoted to her all the same," she said.

"Pappy idiot!" Mr Barett ejaculated. He worked himself deeper into his chair, and held his newspaper before his face.

His wife knitted on, and presently said, as if of the outcome of her thought, "I will go in and see Vera to-morrow, of course."

The newspaper rustled defiantly as it was turned over.

"You know very well, Everard, if Vera is really ill there is no one more sorry than I. Of course, I shall not neglect her."

He was mollified by that, and lowered the paper sufficiently to gaze over the top of it into the fire. "It would be rather unfair if you did; and, considering all the little woman did for you when baby was born, a little like ingratitude into the bargain," he said. "You can't have forgotten all she did?"

No. She had not forgotten, Mrs Barett admitted.

"Here every day of her life, and sometimes all day long—neglecting her own home, and—"

"I remember perfectly, dear," said Lucilla. "What of it?"

Her husband repeated the question in a tone of exasperation, got up, threw away his newspaper, fidgeted about the room, moving the chairs out of his way, staring at the ornaments. "What of it?" he asked. "I suppose, knowing she was there, and seeing after things—saving me bother in giving orders, coming between me and that infernal nurse, and so on—was a comfort to you, wasn't it?"

Mrs Barett, intent on her knitting, made no reply.

His position was strong; he repeated his question: "Wasn't it, I say?"

"It was a comfort to you, I suppose," Lucilla said, then. "We will leave it there."

He gave her a quick glance, angrily questioning. He had temporarily anchored against the fender now, and stood with his heels on it, his hands in his pockets.

"I suppose that it was a comfort to me was something, at any rate?" he asked. He shrugged an angry shoulder. "I was the one that had to go through the misery of it, I know that. I shan't easily forget the time before, when Billy was born, and I was shut up for a solid three weeks with your mother! Heavens! going about with a face like a funeral! Looking at me as if I was a monster every time I took up my hat to go out! I should think Vera Butt was a comfort to me! It wasn't as if you had been really ill. You know you were always saying you wanted to get up and come downstairs to be with us, weren't you?"

"I certainly should have liked better to be with you," Lucilla admitted.

"Well, and Vera said, 'Here's Luce lying tucked up as jolly as a sandboy, why shouldn't we be jolly too?'"

"Exactly; and she wasn't fretful, or complaining, or hysterical once, all the time, was she?"

His thoughts travelled back over the memories of the weeks of which they spoke; the weeks in which he had first begun to find Vera attractive. He saw the face which in that time he had, not without surprise, discovered to be pretty; he thought of the fun they had made between them, and heard her chattering, gay voice, and listened to their mingled laughter. A smile moved his lips for an instant; he looked up, caught his wife's eye, and had a sudden feeling of looking foolish in her sight.

"She was a good little woman, when we wanted her, and I'm sorry if she's ill. That's all," he said. "The Butts aren't very well off, and she doesn't get the comforts a woman wants in illness."

"I'll go and see after her to-morrow," Lucilla said.

It had become the custom of Everard Barett to go for a stroll the last thing at night, to get a "mouthful of air before turning in," as he said. When, later on this evening, he looked in upon his wife before starting for his walk, he found her standing by the hearth, gazing thoughtfully down into the fire.

"If you're thinking of dropping in at the Butts," she said, "you might take a few grapes to Vera. There are just a couple of bunches left. Shall I get them?"

He was putting himself into his topcoat, and he reddened a little with the exertion. "Oh, grapes?" he said; "I took them this afternoon. I saw them standing about, and—"

"Oh, that's all right," Lucilla said. "So long as she had them! And is that where the violets went? I wanted some in, to-day, and gardener said they had all been gathered out of the frame. Did you take the violets, too, to Vera?"

"I daresay I did," said Everard, turning his back.

"You daresay?"

"Well, I did, then. How should I know you wanted them, or that there was going to be a piece of work about a handful of violets?"

With that he went, and pulled the door to with a slightly unnecessary emphasis.

Everard Barett was the sleeping partner in a large manufacturing firm in that provincial town. He drew his comfortable income from this source, but had very little else to do with the business; and so it was that time hung heavily on his hands. Yet, every now and then, a business zeal would seize him, or a weariness of doing nothing, and he would have himself driven down to the great malodorous factory by the river, to put away a few hours. From thence he would return in a far more cheerful spirit than was his on his unoccupied days.

On the morrow of the above conversation he came back from such a dutiful visit, and going into the drawing-room in search of his wife, he found, lying on the sofa drawn up to the fire, not Lucilla, but the lady who of late had dwelt so dangerously in his thoughts—Vera Butt.

She had assumed a charming attitude, which she only changed to throw out a welcoming hand as he came forward. "Here I am," she said. "It's really me. Isn't Luce an angel?" She smiled at him, showing all her teeth, stretching back her head on the pillow to bring her full, round throat into prominence, shutting her eyes. "Oh, it is good to be here!" she said.

It was good to see her there, he murmured, but not without a little embarrassment. For, it is one thing for a man to make love to another man's wife during a half-hour's call at her house, and another to do the same when she has taken up a permanent position in his own wife's drawing-room.

"I'm to stay here till Fred comes back," Vera told him, opening her eyes upon him. (Fred was the husband.) "He won't be home for another fortnight, at least. Are you prepared to tolerate me for a fortnight?"

He thought he was, he smiled; he sat down on the divan not far from her sofa and gazed at her in a rather shamefaced way.

"In a company of three, one must be de trop. I only hope it won't be me," she said.

She was such a nice little woman! With anyone else he might have thought it "good cheek" to imagine it possible his wife or he could be de trop in their own house.

"What talks we'll have!" she went on. "Do you remember when Luce was ill we laughed so loud at some ridiculous thing you said when we were going up to her room that the horrid nurse came out and was rude, and asked us to be quiet?"

Everard remembered the occasion with resentment. It was he who had made the witty remark, certainly, but it had been Vera who had boisterously laughed.

"I never laugh, at home," she told him. "And if Fred does, I am ready to fly. I can't bear any sudden noise. Luce is going to have nurse take the babies always down the back stairs, for fear I should hear them as they come out and in. She has given orders they're not to come into this part of the house at all while I'm here."

"Of course not," Everard said. But he thought of his little Billy, who was two years old, and who was allowed to spend half an hour with his father twice each day. His son was very near to his heart. He wondered how he should make up to Billy for those lost half-hours.

"It is delightful!" Vera said. "I think I should like to lie here for ever, only the firelight to see by, and you sitting just there to talk to me."

"We mustn't talk if it hurts your head," Everard said, with tender caution.

"Well, you to sit there and keep silence, then," she amended.

The divan was not very comfortable. He could not echo her wish that he should sit so, for ever, silent.

"How is the poor head to-day?" he asked.

"It is like fire," she told him. "Feel."

She hitched herself upward, leant on her elbow, and stretched her neck forward, bringing her face within easy distance of his own. What could he do but kiss her forehead?

He had a very gay look when he burst in upon his wife, who was dressing for dinner.

"So you got her here?" he said. "Isn't that giving you a lot of trouble, Luce?"

"We mustn't think of the trouble," Lucilla told him. "I shall not be able to be with her always, but fortunately you and she get on so well—"

"Oh, I daresay I can find time to sit with her, now and then, if that's all you want me to do," he acquiesced, looking down his nose.

"She seems really sadly," Lucilla told him. "Her head is bad, and her nerves—she's all nerves! Then, she has a sort of seizure, now and then—"

"Heavens!"

"Yes. She suddenly becomes, she says, rigid. Can't move hand or foot."

"I say, that must be bad. And what do we do then, Luce?"

"Well," said Lucilla, calmly surveying herself in the glass, and turning her long neck to get a view of her elegant back, "in that case you will have to carry her up to bed, and I shall have to undress her and send for the doctor."

"I carry her!" he said to himself, doubtfully, again and again as he dressed. "She's something of a lump for any man to carry."

He was considered a handsome man by himself and his friends; by no one could he be considered a fine one. Lucilla—he admired her long, graceful figure still—was as tall as he, and he knew himself lacking in muscular strength. "I hope she won't become rigid here," he said.

She had all her meals served in the drawing-room, and she partook of every course, and had a really fine appetite. Plates with biscuits, with grapes, basins with beef-tea, glasses of milk, champagne bottles, were always standing around her sofa.

"It is making rather a piggery of the place," Everard said more than once to his wife.

It was a matter of importance to him, because he found he was expected, both by his wife and Mrs Butt, to spend all his time there. Lucilla, with her nursery, her conservatories, her interest in parochial matters, had never been exacting; he had come and gone without explanation, as it pleased him. But a half-hour unaccounted for came, with Vera, to mean a sulk, to mean tears, to mean, eventually, a nagging such as in all his life Lucilla had never given him. Certainly, if he had prized Vera Butt's society in the days when he could get very little of it, he had his fill now.

A meal being over, Lucilla would say—"I have such and such a thing to do; you go in, dear, and keep Vera amused for an hour." And the hour would stretch to two hours—till the next meal, even. And during that time Vera gave him no rest. She would call upon him incessantly to tell her things, to amuse her.

"Surely something interesting must have happened! Does nothing ever happen in this house?" she would pout. "You used to say funny things—do you remember how we laughed when Luce was ill? Say something funny now, to keep me going?"

He, with inward resentment, would decline to be funny at command, and she would pass on to the reproachful stage, and so, by easy passage, to the stages of tears and sulks and semi-insensibility; when he would have to dab her forehead with eau-de-Cologne, and rub her hands, or to lift her head higher with his arm beneath the pillow.

"I'm a married man, but I never was called on to do this kind of thing before," he would say to himself.

And at last—"I'm hanged if I'm not getting fairly sick of it," he said.

Then came a day when, before going to his place by the invalid's sofa, he ran up to the nursery and fetched Billy down.

"All nonsense," he said to himself as he carried the child, perched on his shoulder and delightedly holding on by his hair, downstairs. "She screams and cries enough herself; suppose Billy takes his turn!"

"Look here!" he said as the pair entered, "here's Boy Billy come to see you."

Boy Billy struggled down from the paternal shoulder, ran across the room as fast as his fat legs would take him, and with a delighted cry of "mummy! mummy!" hurled himself upon the lady on the sofa. To fly back to his father, with outflung arms and a scream of terror, when, instead of the fair, blooming face of his mother with the auburn waves of hair, the sallow cheeks, the tossed black hair, the great dark eyes of Mrs Butt met his infantile gaze.

The howl that Billy gave in the first pang of that disappointment was certainly out of place in a sick-room. Everard, with one glance at the figure on the sofa, flinging itself into a sitting posture, and gazing at him in an outraged frenzy, caught his boy in his arms and fled with him upstairs.

"My's mummy! My's mummy! Billy wants my's mummy!" the child screamed.

His mummy was sitting over the fire in her own room, and her husband, bursting in, deposited Billy on her lap. The sobs died away against her breast, but Everard went down on his knees and smoothed and patted the beloved little head, and talked the foolish language of consolation his fatherhood had taught him.

"Ugly lady!" the child cried, in his broken voice. "Not Billy's mummy—ugly lady!"

"Billy's is a pretty mummy, isn't she, darling?" the man tenderly said.

"Billy's mummy loves her precious boy," Lucilla murmured.

"'Oves daddy, too," the child sobbed, feeling the father's touch.

She smiled upon the kneeling young man. "Loves dear daddy, too," she said.

It had been only a foolish flirtation—just the snatching at something to fill his empty days. Everard Barett's heart had been his wife's all along. He knew it for a certainty, looking at the woman and her child together, kneeling before them, with a sudden conviction of his own unworthiness, and folly, and absurdity.

"We all love each other, little man," he said. "If we three stick together, we're all right, Boy Billy—we're all right, Luce."

He got upon his feet presently. "I'm going to the Works this afternoon, dear," he said. "And after dinner I thought I'd go in and take a hand at bridge with the Worleys. I'm afraid you'll have rather a time of it, poor old girl."

"I'm afraid you will, when you come home again," Lucilla said.

He dropped his voice to a whisper. "I say, haven't we had almost enough?" he asked. "A fortnight's a deuce of a time! She's all very well, but it's jollier when we're alone, Luce. I want us to be alone again."

When he came home to dinner, his wife met him in the hall. "Everard," she said, "it's come."

"In the name of heaven, what?"

"The Rigor. You know. She can't move. Can't stir hand nor foot. All the afternoon she was in a terrible way, crying, and—well, actually fighting me. Then the Rigor came on."

"I'll run for the doctor," he said. He had an aghast face.

"All done. He's here. He's waiting for you to carry Vera to bed."

"Let him carry her himself!" Everard said, fiercely. "Look here, I'm best out of this. I'll go and dine somewhere."

"My dear, you can't run away like that," she said, and, of course, prevailed.

It was as Lucilla had said. Vera was rigid. She looked up at Everard with a smile of satisfaction at that fact. "What do you think of me now?" it seemed to ask. "Am I the sort of woman to turn your back on, and neglect?—a woman who at once becomes as stiff as a broomstick?"

"She must be got upstairs and undressed," the doctor said to Barett.

"Lean on me and try to walk," Barett implored the patient.

She gave a defiant smile. "If my life depended on it I could not move a toe," she said.

"If I took her head, and you her feet?" Everard suggested to the doctor—a plan at once negatived by Vera.

"I won't be carried in that fashion," she said. "I am not a long woman, like Luce," she added. "Fred carries me with perfect ease."

"I think you can manage it, Mr Barett," the doctor said.

There was no help for it. Everard stooped to the task. He ought to have been a happy man, perhaps, with that burden in his arms. It was not as such he described himself to his wife afterwards.

Halfway up the stairs he tripped, and she screamed.

"Grip me! Grip me! Don't let me drop over the balusters!" she called.

He laboured on, the cords bursting in his forehead, his legs bending, his throat swelling, his arms two seats of agony. Lucilla, who had gone before, cleared the mats out of his way. "It isn't much farther," she whispered.

"He is not grasping me right," Mrs Butt cried in a terrified voice. "It's not how Fred grasps me. I am as easy as a child when he carries me. Oh! I shall drop—he is going to let me drop!"

He thought he was, but made a superhuman effort, and tottered on. Having reached level ground he stopped, then started on again with a staggering run. In piloting her through the bedroom door he banged her head against the frame, and Vera gave a howl of rage and pain.

The next minute she found herself hurled upon the bed.

She remained as she fell, upon her face, uttering suffocating moans of angry shame and misery.

Everard waited not a second to watch her there. He reeled from the room, and reaching the landing again, sank down there, ignominiously, sitting on the carpet, his back to the wall, a wreck of his spruce, dapper self, having bodily and spiritually reached the bounds of endurance.

They telegraphed for her husband. "Let him come and take her home, and carry her himself!" Everard said, savagely. "It's his place to carry her, not mine. We've done our part—let her go."

He came as soon as the train could bring him. Lucilla was able to tell him truthfully that his wife had lain and called upon his name all night.

"He is kneeling by her bedside and kissing her, and crying over her," Lucilla told her husband, running down to him, her own eyes wet with tears. "Isn't it a mercy he loves her so?"

"There's nothing whatever the matter with her, you know," Everard said. "The doctor's just been telling me. Nothing whatever."

"I knew that all along," Lucilla told him.

He took her hand and looked in her face, and his own grew red. "Confession is good for the soul, and you and I should have no secrets, Luce," he said. "That little woman upstairs—you'll think me an awful ass. She and I—she—"

Lucilla nodded, without looking at him. "I knew that all along, too," she said.

"You knew? Yet you asked her here?"

He held her before him, and looked in her face, and kissed her.

"I don't believe any other woman would have done that. That was a risky thing to do, Luce," he said.

"But it answered," Lucilla said to herself as she turned away.

TO BERTHA IN BOMBAY

He is a big, heavily-made, healthy-looking man of young middle-age. He came into the coffee-room as I was sitting at breakfast, and having looked slowly round the room, he placed himself with much deliberation opposite me, at the little table which I had secured to myself. The act did not prejudice me in his favour. There was room and to spare at a large centre table where a dozen men were sitting; two of the smaller tables were empty. There was something about him I need not bore you by describing which stamps the colonial man. From such, one knows what to expect. He called for a carte and ordered porridge and a sole, and they were some time in bringing his breakfast.

However, as you know, I have not arrived at thirty years without having learnt to endure a prolonged gaze with perfect appearance of indifference.

"I hope you have no objection to my sharing your table?" he said; and I replied, as I went on with my meal, that I had none.

"You have an open window, and a view of the sea," he remarked, and I assented, and added that on such a morning these things were desirable.

Then his porridge came, and I proceeded with my toast and marmalade, and the letter I had from you in Bombay, which lay beside my plate. Your writing is never too legible, Berthalina, and my head and eyes were aching, that morning, and I felt less rested than when I had gone to bed. My limbs ached too, and while I looked at those crossed lines of yours, without gathering the sense of what I read, I was wondering if, in the broiling heat of this sultry weather, I had taken cold, and was going to be laid up in this strange place, alone in a hotel. Have I told you that, since the cramming for this last horrid exam. has sent me, to an extent, off my mental equilibrium, I have a constant terror of falling ill? It was that which had given me such a fit of horrors when I saw my bedroom, the night before. Here, by the orders of a peremptory doctor, for change of air and the sea-breeze, I find myself, after vainly tramping the town for lodging, in a tiny back room of a huge hotel, with a window which will only open two inches at the top, and a ceiling and four walls crushing in on me like the lid and sides of a coffin! For prospect, I have a window like my own, at about five yards' distance, a few feet of red brick, and a leaden water-pipe!

If I were to be ill in this hole! The fear of it kept me awake and feverish for hours; but falling asleep at last, I had the most vivid and delicious dream. I felt myself irresistibly called by something—I don't know what, the murmur of the sea, perhaps; and I thought I escaped from that entombment, and walked in my night-gown down a long corridor, to a door at the other side of the house. The door yielded, in that ridiculous way in which all obstacles yield in dreams, and I went through a room which I should know again among ten thousand rooms, to the window—a big window thrown wide open; and through it the sea—the sea—the sea! Such a sea! As effulgent, moon-silvered, glorious, as we may look on in Paradise, Berthalina, if God hears the "silly sailor-folk," as Kipling has undertaken that He will.

Ah! The sea, as revealed by the coffee-room window, sparkling in sunshine, dotted with fishing-boats, the white bathing-machines defining its margin, is but a vulgar thing, compared with the sea of my dream.

"Do you believe in ghosts?" The man opposite put the question quite unconcernedly, but I was back in the description of your triumphant dinner-party, and was unpleasantly startled. I answered with a little temper, therefore, that of course I believed in them; and I did not encourage him to further conversation by a glance in his direction.

Had I seen any? he inquired; and I answered "Hundreds." After a minute, repenting of my incivility, I put your letter down, and told him that that was why he saw me getting my breakfast before him. And I even explained—for why need a self-respecting woman be disagreeable even to an unknown colonial in an ill-made flannel suit, and with rough hair?—that I had been working too hard lately, and that the shades of people, dead or in distant lands, well-known and half-forgotten, had taken to appearing before me, when I lifted my eyes from my book.

"In fact, I have come here to get rid of ghosts," I told him; and he said he hoped I had not come to the wrong place. "Why, you surely don't think 'The Continental' haunted?" I inquired.

Then he told me, with an appearance of perfect gravity, that a ghost had visited him last night.

"It is just possible that my ghosts have lost their way in this bewildering place and have strolled in to you, by mistake," I suggested.

"You don't happen to have seen any since you came here?"

"I only came last night."

"And you didn't see one?"

"No! Do I look as if I had?"

"Not the ghost of a terrified man, for instance, flying up in bed?"

"Good gracious, no! Why?"

"I thought you might have done," he said, and went on with his breakfast.

You'll say he talked such nonsense to get me to look at him, Berthalina; and of course I did. He has not the appearance of a seer of ghosts: a huge, heavy man, with a hump on a big, characterful nose; a powerful jaw, and very quick, blue eyes beneath shaggy eyebrows. The talk of ghosts seemed out of place on such firm lips.

"Was your ghost that of a terrified man, etc.?" I asked him, in spite of myself.

He gave a vigorous shake of his head. "Thank heavens, no!" he said. "In that case I shouldn't have given it two thoughts."

"Of what then?"

"Of a beautiful woman."

He spoke with much deliberation, and his eyes upon my face were serious.

"What was she like? Describe her."

He turned away to reach a bit of bread from a neighbouring table. "She was very much like you," he said.

You may be sure I let him see then that he had gone too far.

I was standing by the door of my disgraceful little bedroom, dressed for walking, when I saw him again. He was mounting the broad stairs with his head bent, and not wishing to pass the man on my way down, I waited till he had disappeared within the door of his room. That door, with the width of the house between, was directly opposite mine. As it opened, there came to me the first glimmer of the light which was to burst on me in all its terrible force a minute later.

When he had reappeared, in his great loose grey flannels, his straw hat on his head, a book in his hand, and had gone downstairs, I flew along the corridor and pushed open the door of the room he had left. Berthalina, it was the room of my dream! Those details which had impressed themselves so clearly on my sleeping vision last night were here in the flesh—well not exactly in the flesh, but—. I stood at the window, wide open from the bottom; the sea lay sparkling in the sunlight—

Of course, you remember the time when I stayed with you, my dear friend, after that crisis in my stupid life of which you and only one other knew? You haven't forgotten how I terrified you nearly to death by walking in my sleep to your room? and how, afterwards, you insisted on keeping the key of my bedroom door under your own pillow? To the best of my belief I have never sleep-walked either before or since that time. The certainty came to me now, as I stood at the man's window, that I had done it again last night!

"And what have you been doing with yourself, all day?"

I had turned my back on the pier bands, on the crowds of the esplanade, and had wandered as far as my legs would carry me along the beach—a hard, smooth beach of yellow sand—and was sitting there, with only the waves for company, when the voice of the man I had successfully dodged all day spoke at my back.

"You were not at lunch, nor at the table d'hôte, to-night," he added; and I did not consider that the statement demanded comment.

He came and sat beside me, and gathered up his knees into his arms and looked out to sea. "I suppose the beach is free to all?" he remarked; and my silence did not gainsay him.

"I am like you," he went on: "I care nothing for all that," he jerked his head in the direction of the town and the populace. "I'm never afraid of my own company. And you?"

"I prefer it to all other company," I assured him, and told the lie with the acrimony of truth.

"And you have been by the sea all day?"

"I have been tramping the town looking for rooms."

"You are not comfortable at the hotel?"

"I prefer apartments."

"Perhaps for a young woman, alone, it is better."

Now for my opportunity.

"I have not been alone until this morning," I told him steadily. "My sister left me by the early train; before breakfast."

"You probably miss her very much?"

"I do. She scarcely ever leaves me. We have everything in common. She is my twin-sister. You could scarcely tell the one from the other, apart."

The information did not flow from me as I desired, but was, rather, gasped out—or so it seems to me on looking back.

I felt him turn his eyes on me—they look absurdly blue and youthful in his sun-reddened, middle-aged face—but I think I mentioned this before. You know how I love a man's hair clipped to the bone, Berthalina? My dear, this one wears his in a mop! I must admit, however, it is a soft kind of hair, and does not arrange itself badly.

"We even share the same bed," I went on. I had to twist my fingers together painfully to maintain the necessary levelness of the indifferent voice. "But that is a matter of precaution."

"Of precaution?"

"My sister is—a sleep-walker," I said, and waited, with the sound of the sea and the band and the multitude in the near distance booming in my head. "Even last night—I awoke to find our door open," I added. "She had wandered in her sleep."

I had said it; but I declare to you, Berthalina, the effort left me weak as a baby. Before you make up your mind to a career of perfidy, dear, go through a course of physical training. You want the strength of a Sandow, I assure you.

I waited with inward trembling for his comment. He made none, but pointed out to me instead the colour of the brown sail of a little fishing-boat almost stationary on the placid sea, the light of the sinking sun upon it. A big steamer came into sight upon the horizon-line. A bare-legged man, pushing a shrimping-net before him, waded through the shallow waters, close inshore.

"This is very pleasant," he said. "You did not mention if you were successful in obtaining rooms?"

I shook my head. "But I leave here in four days."

"And until then?"

"I must remain at the hotel—where I think it is about time I returned."

He rose, as I did. "Have you any objection to my walking at your side?" he asked, and walked there without waiting for permission. "I am a lonely man, and a stranger here," he volunteered. "And you?"

I told him that I was used to being alone; that there was no one now belonging to me—

"With the exception of your twin sister who never leaves you," he reminded me, and went on at once to tell me of his life, which had been passed for many years in Australia. His sister who lived with him died there eight years ago, he is forty years old, he has made money, and has come home for a holiday.

All this, and much more I learnt. He seems quite eager to impart personal information—or perhaps I did not learn it all then, but afterwards. For there has been no getting away from the man, Berthalina; you may believe that my will was good.

At night, I got the chambermaid to lock me in that atrocious little cabin of mine. (Oh, I know you are laughing, Berthalina; good gracious! what a fool I feel about it all.) I knew that he was an early riser, and I did not go down the next morning till I felt sure that he would be enjoying the sea-breezes, and that the coffee-room would be nearly empty. There he was, patiently keeping guard over the table in the window! He strode across to me (he is so huge and self-assured and important-looking, that everyone turns to watch him, and the waiters fly at a glance). "I have kept our table," he said, "and I have taken the liberty to order for you the same breakfast you had yesterday."

After that, I gave up trying to avoid him. I had put everything right in his mind, and it was only for four days! Then I must be getting back, and looking out for ways and means to earn the money I have borrowed to pay my fees and keep me at the hospital. Oh dear! How it all weighs on my mind!

"And so you are going to be a doctor?" he said once, I don't know at which meeting. How can I tell—there were so many!

"I am a doctor," I corrected him.

"Well, I am a doctor too," he said. "And perhaps that is the reason I loathe the thought of any woman meddling in that profession."

"I don't particularly like it myself," I told him. "It was necessary for me to be something, and I had enthusiasm enough to begin with; but—"

"What is your sister?" he asked me suddenly; it took me by surprise, but I told him, with blushes, that she was a doctor too.

"I wonder what my brother will say to that?" he pondered. "You look surprised. Is there any reason I should not have a brother? He is a doctor like myself, and shares my prejudices."

"Those prejudices don't affect my sister," I took courage to remark.

"They should. No decent woman can afford to despise the prejudices of a decent man. The place of a young and beautiful woman is not—"

"I did not tell you she was young or beautiful. I—she—we are thirty years old; and 'pretty,' 'interesting,' 'fine-looking,' are the most complimentary epithets which have ever been applied to us."

"We don't all see with the same eyes," the man said.

It was on our last evening that I sate on a chair in the hotel gardens; he came and smoked his cigar beside me.

"You go to-morrow?" he said.

I nodded.

"And you don't purpose to tell me where you go?"

I shook my head. How can I have him coming to my place with that story of my sister—?

"So here, for ever, we say good-bye. I go back to my practice in Sydney; and you—?"

I said nothing to fill up the pause.

"Four days!" he mused, and was silent.

The band was playing on the pier; the strains of that pretty thing Hayden Coffin sings in The Greek Slave came sorrowfully to us across the sea and the sand. The people in their smart seaside costumes went trooping past.

"Not a face I know in all these thousands," he said, and waved the hand which held the cigar to include pier, parade, beach. "Not a face known to you. Under such circumstances two people get to know each other in four days as well as in years of ordinary intercourse. When I say good-bye to you, I shall feel that I am parting with a very dear friend. A friend I shall hardly know how to replace, or even to live without. After four days! Absurd, is it not?"

"May I tell you about my brother?" This was after a long pause, during which I had been inwardly shrinking from the dreary struggle before me, and wishing—wishing—wishing that life was all holiday. "He is my twin brother. Curious, isn't it? You don't think so? Oh, of course we know there are twin brothers as well as twin sisters; but—. Still, let me tell you a rather curious fact with regard to him.

"The night before that morning when I had the happiness to meet you, he was staying in this hotel— he left by that convenient train before breakfast, you know, the early one—and he had a strange experience. He was lying awake in bed—the moon was very bright, it was that which kept him awake—when the door of his room opened, and a woman, young and beautiful, in her night-gear, with her dark hair, 'straight as rain,' hanging down her back and over her shoulders, and with eyes full of all my brother loves to see in a woman's eyes, came into his room. He is not a nervous man, and he saw at once the woman, who in the moonlight was lovely as a vision, walked in her sleep. He held his breath, fearing to disturb her. She went to the window, stretched out her arms to the sea, bathed her hands and her adorable face in the moonlight, drank in, in grateful breaths, the cool sea air, and passing silently through his room, left him as she came.

"You think that an interesting experience for my brother, do you not? But I have not quite finished.

"My brother is a man not without sentiment, although he has attained to middle life without marrying. He has more sentiment, in fact, than in his young days, when he decided it was best for man to live alone. He has seen cause to doubt the wisdom of that creed. He is not without regrets and longings, thoughts of what might have been, and what might yet be. Fairly successful and happy in his career, he has yet come to think that a woman's love and companionship are perhaps just those things he has missed which might have crowned his life.

"Having arrived at such a pass, he was moved by that vision of the night—mightily moved. And he swore to himself that the woman who had come to him like that—a living, breathing, beautiful woman, and yet almost in an angel's guise—was the woman he would seek out and marry, if he could prevail on her to have him.

"Tell me what you think of that resolve of my brother's," he asked me presently. He turned from watching the passing crowd and looked for the first time in my face; and then he got upon his feet. "You will perhaps give me your opinion later?" he said. "You will think about it, and let me hear when I come back?"

I did not wait for his coming back. I went to my room and stayed there. I don't know if he looked for me at our table in the window next morning, for I did not go to the coffee-room for breakfast. And by eleven o'clock I was sitting in the ladies' drawing-room—empty as Sahara at that hour—with my hotel bill in my hand, wondering how it was possible that such a little, little holiday should have cost so very much.

Then he came into the room. He sat down opposite to me at the round table, and I saw that he had a telegram in his hand.

"I have bad news for you," he said. "Your twin sister is dead."

"Oh!" I breathed. What could I do but sit there turning red and white, and looking like a fool before him?

"It is a sad and curious coincidence that my twin brother expired at the same instant. What is there for us to do but to console each other?"

He reached out a hand, palm upwards, to me across the table. "You will find life pleasanter as a doctor's wife than as a doctor," he said. "And—"

But I have told you enough till next mail, Berthalina. By that time, perhaps, you will have prepared yourself for the rest of what he said to me, and what I answered.

I wonder if you will think I have been a sensible and self-restrained woman all my life to act like a rash, precipitate fool in the finish?

I wonder!

AUNTIE

"And now, pray, what are you gnashing your teeth about? You never rested until I'd made Auntie promise to stay with us. I didn't wish for her; she didn't wish to come; but, as she's here, the least we can do is to behave decently to her."

"Who said we shouldn't behave decently to her?"

"Well, to see you standing there cursing and gnashing your teeth while you brush your hair!"

"I don't curse, or gnash my teeth, or even brush my hair in public, do I?"

"Oh, of course, it's the wife who has the monopoly of all such pleasing demonstrations!" the wife said. Then she pushed her arms through the short sleeves of the blouse she was going to wear, in honour of Auntie, at dinner that night, and presented her back to Augustus Mellish in order that he might perform a husband's part and fasten the garment.

"You, who have never been in her delightful home at Surbiton, don't know the luxurious sort of life Auntie leads," Mrs Mellish went on. "Travels with her maid, generally; but I told her we could not put her up. Keeps four servants; never does a thing for herself, but is pampered and made much of in every way. Money, of course. There isn't anything in Auntie to call forth all that devotion."

"Money is a useful thing," the husband said. "I wish your infernal dressmaker wouldn't make your things so tight. That's the second nail I've broken, confound it!"

"Gnashing again! If I were to swear and go on in that ridiculous way over every little thing I do for you, I wonder what you'd think of it! Brushing your hats, ironing your ties, putting your trousers into stretchers—and if I ask you to fasten a few buttons, you blaspheme. If you had the worries on your shoulders I have on mine! Cook's in one of her tempers to-day, just because I was anxious for things to go without a hitch, for Auntie. There's a piece of salmon, at half-a-crown a pound, bought because Auntie would think just nothing of the price, and is all the year round accustomed to salmon; cook is certain to send it in bleeding or to boil it to a rag. You, at your office all day long, with nothing to think about, and when you come home everything running on oiled wheels—"

"Oh, I've heard all that before. My life is all perfect joy, according to you," Augustus said. And in such inspiring intercourse the Mellishes passed the few minutes of their tête-à-tête.

In the drawing-room, Auntie awaited them: a large, matronly-looking spinster, with a heavy face and frame, a non-intelligential gaze from dull brown eyes. Not a promising visitor, from a social point of view. She was expensively attired, her garments rustling richly when she moved. Her dark hair was fashionably piled on the top of her head.

She sat in a chair farthest from the window which she regarded distrustfully, it being slightly open. In the railway carriage coming down she had felt sure there was a draught, and now her neck was a little stiff.

She thought slightingly of Grace's drawing-room; indeed, the whole establishment wore a paltry air, to her thinking, who had a predilection for the ornately massive in style. But if Grace had been foolish enough to marry a lawyer, in a town already too full of lawyers, and he young, and with his way to make, what could she expect? Alfred's daughter should surely have done better than that, Auntie said to herself.

Still, later on, she was bound to admit that the lawyer and his wife did their best to make her comfortable, and showed her every attention. Augustus, or Gussie, as Grace instructed her to call him, seemed an agreeable person, although no one could consider him a good-looking one—not half good-looking enough for Grace, who had been considered a beauty. So black he was about the shaven portion of his face, his close-cropped hair, and great eyes, so white everywhere else. Auntie, who associated health with a brick-red complexion like her own, decided that he could not be a strong man. She spoke to her niece about him after dinner.

"He's chalk-white," she said.

Grace was not at all alarmed for her husband's health. "He's always like that," she said. "He's never had a day's illness. I do hope you and Gussie will like each other, Auntie. I can tell you, he's bent on pleasing you."

"He seemed agreeable," Auntie said. "Has he got nerves?" she asked.

"Nerves!" repeated Grace, opening her eyes. "Dear, no! Only like other people's. Why?"

"I only asked the question," Auntie said. "When he isn't talking or eating, his mouth still works; and when he smiles he shows his gums. I thought it was nerves."

"Oh, that's just a habit he's got. He only does it when strangers are present."

"I hope Henry won't catch it," Auntie said. "Children are imitative."

"No fear about Henry. Henry takes after me—colour and all," Mrs Mellish said. She was a brown-haired woman, with cheeks like a damask rose, and Henry was the only child of the house, and was away at a boarding-school.

During the evening a neighbour and his wife came in. He and she and the two ladies played bridge, while Gussie looked on or fidgeted aimlessly about the room, taking up and putting down again books and papers, looking into empty ornamental jars, continually comparing his own watch with the drawing-room clock.

"To tell you the truth, he always goes out in the evening," Grace informed Auntie, while seeing her to her bedroom. "He has his club, you know. They play rather high. I don't think he cares for our careful little game. If you don't mind, I think I shall tell him to go there to-morrow night. He does worry me so when he prowls about the drawing-room."

"Let him go, by all means. I don't mind at all," Auntie acquiesced.

"I knew she'd win. They always do, when they've money, and don't want to," Mellish said to his wife, talking over the evening's game. "Played threepence a hundred, didn't she?"

"Isn't it mean of her!" Grace said. "With a purse full of sovereigns—for I saw them when she gave it to me to pay the cab—and thirty more, she told me, in her jewel-case. By the way, the servants asked for their wages again to-day, Gussie."

"Oh, I daresay! Ask your aunt to pay them."

"I should like to see myself stooping to ask such a thing of Auntie!"

"You don't mind stooping to ask money of me every time you open your mouth."

"I wonder you can dare to say it! I haven't had a penny from you, for a week. I hadn't even the half-crown to buy the child the new paint-box he wrote for."

"Henry? Does he want a paint-box? He shall have it, poor little chap. I will see about it tomorrow."

"Once he's gone to the office, don't you see him any more, all day?" Auntie asked, as the front door closed on the master of the house, next morning.

"Not till dinner. He has a biscuit for his lunch, or goes without it. He isn't a man to care for food at any time."

"No. He isn't what I call a restful man," Auntie said, and spread herself more at her ease in her chair. "He isn't one, I should say, to enjoy the comforts of home."

"Oh, as for that, I don't care for a man always in your way among the chairs and tables," Mrs Mellish said. "Gussie isn't a woman's man, you see, Auntie. He's about as clever as they're made, Gussie is; and when they're like that they're men's men; and I like them better so."

Grace's red cheeks were redder. She was a quick-tempered, high-spirited young woman. "Hands off! he's mine," her manner, more than her words, said to Auntie, who would have liked to listen to a few wifely confidences as she and her niece sat tête-à-tête through the long morning.

They lived in a provincial town, and on the second night of Auntie's stay they went to the theatre, at which a London company happened to be performing.

Grace loved the play, and was in high spirits, making an extra toilette for the occasion. She was not half through it when her husband, who had hurried over his dressing, left her and went downstairs. He had heard Auntie, who was always too early for everything, and made a merit of it, leave her room. He found her in the drawing-room, pulling a pair of long white gloves over her large hands and arms.

"I have been stupid enough to leave myself short of cash," Mellish said, beginning lightly at once, almost before he had closed the door behind him. "I wonder if you could oblige me, Auntie, with a few pounds for a couple of days? Say ten or fifteen? Just to carry me on till my money-ship comes in."

Auntie, working on her tight gloves, looked at him; his tone was carefully careless, but his face, which she had called chalk-white, was surely whiter yet. His question being asked, his lips still moved.

"How Grace can bear to sit opposite to him at meals every day, I don't know!" Auntie said to herself. "He gives me the creeps."

She drew in her lower lip loosely beneath her teeth, her gaze grew blanker; never a clever-looking woman, now she looked a fool. Slowly she shook her head.

"No. I am afraid I can't," she said. "I'm afraid I can't spare it. I only brought as much as I should want to get me back home again."

There was a minute's unbroken silence. Gussie's smile, always so pronounced, spread across his gums till his face looked as if it were cut in two.

"I can let you have half a sovereign," Aunty suggested.

"Oh, thank you; it's of no consequence," Gussie said, making a gesture of refusal. He walked about the room as if hurriedly seeking for something he never found.

Auntie, with her unintelligent gaze divided between his movements and the glove which so reluctantly covered her arm, offered a tardy explanation.

"I never lend money," she said. "It was my father's dying request that I never should. I owe it to him to regard it."

"Quite so; of course," Gussie said. "The matter just came into my head. I merely mentioned it. Pray don't give it a thought."

As they drove to the theatre, Auntie remarked that she should insist on paying for her ticket and her share of the cab, a suggestion at which Gussie and Grace were hospitably offended. She asked, then, if the house was safe, left with only the maid-servants to protect it. In order to reassure her, Augustus informed her that he was intending to go home once in the course of the evening to make sure that things were all right.

"Not that it matters to me," Auntie told him; "for I have brought my valuables with me—jewellery and money, too. I always take them with me, in strange places. I could never enjoy the play if my mind were not at rest. I wear a bag concealed in the skirt of my dress on purpose."

"Ah! I wish I could make Grace as thoughtful!" Gussie said.

"Give me Auntie's money and jewels, then see!" Grace cried.

"And I suppose you go to bed with them, too?" Gussie admiringly inquired. "Grace has never so much as carried up the plate-basket."

He was quite right. Auntie did go to bed with them, always putting the bag containing them under her pillow.

"A wise precaution!" said Gussie.

"I'm a heavy sleeper," Auntie explained. "A robber might break in and take my property, and I never hear him; but let him touch the pillow beneath my head, and I'm wide awake on the moment."

"Yes, but—" said Augustus Mellish, and smiled, "a few drops of chloroform on a handkerchief held over your face, Auntie, and where would you and your jewellery be then?"

They were at the theatre, by that time, and Auntie did not answer. But when she went to bed that night she thought of what Grace's husband had said. She had a little difficulty with breathing, being a stout woman, and a horror of suffocation. The idea of that handkerchief held over her face was terrible. She loved her money and her jewels, but loved more her comfort and her life.

"Once they stopped my breath, I should never wake up again!" she said to herself; and, deciding to alter her usual procedure, she returned her treasure from the bag hidden in her skirts to her jewel-case.

The play had been a moving one. Grace, very susceptible to emotion, had laughed and cried beside her; but Auntie was a phlegmatic person. The comedy was just make-believe. She thought more, as she undressed, of Augustus's request for a loan than of the heart-stirring episodes of the drama. She had been wise not to begin lending him money, but to say at once, straight out, "No." He had asked for only a few pounds; if she had given them, he would have gone on to ask for more, in all probability. Auntie liked Grace well enough, rather better than most people, perhaps; but Grace had pleased herself in getting married; the man she had taken must keep her. He had no claim on Grace's Auntie.

With such thoughts in her mind, as soon as her head touched the pillow, she slept.

She awoke with a sickly, suffocating smell in her nostrils; and her eyes opened wide upon a face bent above her own. She had slept with a small lamp burning beside her, and by its dim light it seemed to her that the face was black.

As she gazed, the face receded. Its owner drew backwards, pulling one empty hand from beneath her pillow. The other hand held the handkerchief whose odour she had felt upon mouth and nostrils.

Auntie flew up in bed. "Burglar!" she cried.

It was the only word spoken between them. The whole incident was over in a half-minute. By the time that epithet had burst without volition from her lips the robber, with his black-veiled face, had slunk to the door and was gone.

With an agility she had not displayed since girlhood, Auntie sprang from the bed, and, clutching the bag containing her money and jewels, furiously rang the bell.

Mrs Mellish, in her nightgown, came running into the room.

"Oh, Auntie! Are you ill? Are you on fire?" she cried.

The stout lady, strengthless and breathless, was lying in a chair, the jewel-case clasped laxly with one arm.

"A robber has been here," she gasped. "A robber, with black on his face, and a chloroformed handkerchief."

"Oh, Auntie! Auntie! Never!"

"Where is your husband? Is he in your room?"

No. For Augustus, ever a restless sleeper, had thought he heard something stirring in the room beneath, and, later, a footstep on the stair. He had risen, therefore, had taken the pistol, which always lay loaded by his side, and gone down to investigate.

Auntie opened her mouth to speak, but closed it without a sound; her eyes, with their most vacant stare, were turned upon her niece; she gathered her underlip loosely beneath her teeth.

It was not until the servants, also aroused by the bell, but having waited to dress, came to Auntie's room, that Mrs Mellish was at liberty to run down to seek her husband.

There was no doubt about the house having been entered, she said, on her return; Auntie had by no means dreamt the burglar.

("No!" interpolated Auntie, with a solemnly emphatic shake of the head.)

A window broken in the kitchen, and a wide-open sash had showed the exploring Gussie the means of ingress. In the dining-room it was evident that a couple of glasses of brandy had been drunk, but none of the silver on the sideboard had been touched. Too clearly, Auntie and her possessions had been the objects of the attempt.

Auntie nodded gloomy affirmation, trembling and gasping in her chair. Where was Gussie, she asked; and showed relief and satisfaction when told he had gone to give notice of the affair to the police. But not even the promise that the servants and Grace would sit beside her and watch her while she slept would induce the poor lady to go to bed again.

"Not in this house. Never again in this house," she protested.

And even when morning brought a cessation of panic and a certain sense of security to all, she could not be persuaded to change her mind.

"I should die if I ever trusted myself to fall asleep under this roof again," she said. "Let me get away from it as soon as possible. I am fifty years of age, but I've never had a bad shock before in my life. I won't risk a second."

The swarthy, fat, foolish face was pale and flabby and aged from the night's adventure and the sleepless hours following.

"Auntie, I am sure you are not well enough to travel," Grace said. But, with a grim determination, Auntie persisted.

"The first train. I should like to get away by the very first."

"It isn't our fault, remember," Grace said, firing up. "It isn't as if we arranged a burglary for you, Auntie."

There was a train at 10.15 a.m., and of this Auntie would avail herself.

No policeman came to the house. Augustus did not return.

"He and the detectives have got on a track, and are following it up," his wife said. "Trust Gussie!"

When the ladies were about to sit down to breakfast, and still the master of the house had not returned, Grace was a little surprised. The neighbour who had played bridge with them came in. He had heard of the burglary, and was come to offer assistance, he said. He picked up a couple of newspapers lying by Mr Mellish's empty plate.

"You let those alone! Gussie hasn't seen them yet," Gussie's wife said. The Mellishes were on terms of great intimacy with the neighbour.

"I'll take them, all the same," he laughed. "Send Gus to me for them if he wants them."

"I tell you what! I think I'll just 'phone up to the office to see if Gussie's there," Grace said. "I don't see the fun of being kept in the dark like this. I should like to know what's going on, and if they've caught anyone."

The face of the friendly neighbour changed as she disappeared to carry out this intention. He walked close to Auntie and whispered in her ear:

"Don't let her get hold of a newspaper," he said. "There's disagreeable news. I heard it last night. Mellish has got into a scrape—forgery, they say. I hope to heaven he's got away—H-s-s-sh!"

There was no need of the caution. Auntie, with the grand talent for silence which distinguished her, sat with a sucked-in lip looking heavily after the retreating neighbour, when Grace returned. Grace, bright and pretty in her neat morning blouse, made a laughing dash at the papers in the neighbour's hand. He flourished them a moment above her head and retired.

"Gussie's not at the office," Mrs Mellish said. "He's on the track of your burglar, Auntie, you bet. He'll catch him, too! You'll be wanted to identify him; could you swear to him, do you think?"

Auntie very hurriedly declared her inability to do this. "All the upper part of his face was covered," she said.

But she thought of a black-shaved chin below the mask, and a jaw that had worked silently, in a way of late familiar to her; and she found herself quite unable to do justice to her niece's eggs and bacon.

At the door of the first-class railway compartment by which Auntie was to travel Grace stood.

"Gussie will be furious when he comes back and finds you gone," she said. "He'll catch the man, to the deadest certainty. He's got the brains of the whole police force in his own head. You should have stayed to enjoy the excitement."

Auntie, whitened and flabby-looking under her smart violet toque, reiterated the statement that she could not have stayed another night.

"It's been a great shock. I feel as if I might never recover from it; and I wish with all my heart I had never come," she said.

"Well, since you wish it, I wish it, too," Grace retorted, kindling. "We must console ourselves that it has not been for long, and try to forget all about it."

"I shall be glad to be back in my own home," Auntie said.

She looked so changed from the well-satisfied, prosperous Auntie whom Grace had welcomed to her home two days before, that Mrs Mellish's resentment faded as she regarded her.

"You are sure you like best to travel alone?" she asked her, with anxious kindness.

Yes. Auntie preferred her own company. If a man got in at any of the stations, she said, so upset were her nerves, she would certainly be ill with the fright.

So Mrs Mellish found the guard and intimated to him that the lady wished to be undisturbed. Auntie stopped him when, in his officious zeal, he was about to lock the carriage door.

"I can't bear the feeling of being locked in," she said. "It makes me lose my breath."

She leaned out of the window, and kissed her niece with more demonstrativeness than was her custom. "You know my address if you—want anything. Good-bye," she said.

"Good-bye," Grace said, and shook a hand at the window. "Don't forget to eat your sandwiches— you had no breakfast, you know. You've got some brandy-and-water in your flask, remember. Take care of yourself. Good-bye."

"Silly old goose! Making such a fuss, at her age!" she said to herself as she walked away. "Well, after all, it's a relief she's gone. I'm sure I never wanted her. It was Gussie's idea, not mine."

Evidently the story of the burglary had got about. Mrs Mellish noticed several people turning to look at her with unwonted interest as she walked along.

On inquiring of the servants, she found the master had not returned.

On his dressing-table, as she took off her hat, she noticed a neat little oblong parcel lying. It was addressed in Augustus's writing, "To my darling Henry, with all his father's love."

Grace smiled to herself. "Gussie remembered the paint-box," she said. "He never forgets the boy."

She took the little parcel, and posted it to her son.

As the train sped on, Auntie, expanding herself in her corner, felt a revival of health and spirits.

She had escaped, thanks be to God. But for her mercifully awakening before the chloroform had taken effect, she would at the present moment be lying a corpse on the visitors' bed of her niece's house, done to death by her niece's husband. Once under the chloroform—she was certain of it— she could not have revived.

She could not endure to think of the house in which she had been attacked, and on which she had now mercifully been permitted to turn her back. The sun had shone brightly within its spotless windows this morning; fresh flowers had decked the breakfast-table; a neat servant had brought in the coffee. Grace, at her end of the table, pretty and rosy and young, had talked away, only pleasantly excited by the night's adventure, in her quick, alert manner. And over it all was hanging this cloud of ruin, horror, disgrace! Let Auntie banish the ever-recurring picture, if possible, from her mind. Surely she had done well to get away!

But as the train sped on, Grace's image, pretty, brisk, capable, floated persistently before her eyes. She heard her quick speech, her laugh. She was Auntie's own flesh and blood—Alfred's daughter. Some people, who did not appreciate how keenly she felt discomfort, and how dreadfully anything at all unpleasant upset her, might say she should have stayed at Grace's side, and not left her alone to face what was coming: they might say it to each other, that is. No one had the right to censure Auntie.

"What good could I do? I should only have been in the way," she said; "best to keep out of it all."

The train sped on. At every station the attentive guard walked by, turned an observant eye, touched his cap. The old girl was good for two-and-six at the journey's end, perhaps; also, perhaps, she would thank him and give him nothing. A guard can never be sure. Still—!

How could Grace, who had been such a nice bright little girl, and who used to go to Auntie for her holidays, years ago, and give very little trouble, considering, have tied herself to that mouthing black and white man, with his restless little shaking hands, endlessly fidgeting? When she partook of a late supper Auntie sometimes had bad dreams, and awoke with her heart beating into her mouth. She knew what her nightmare would be for the future!

There were Grace's sandwiches. To divert her thoughts she took the little packet from the bag which held her money and jewels, and drew out also her silver flask. Years ago her doctor had told her never to travel without a little brandy. She looked at the sandwiches, unscrewed the flask, but found sight and scent to be enough that morning, and put both aside.

It had seemed a long journey, but now London was near. They stopped at Broxbourne. Auntie was not quite sure if this station they flew by was Ponder's End or Angel Road; she put her head out of the window to try to catch the name on the lamps and benches, failed to do so, and lay back again in her corner.

What was that? A stirring, a bulging outward of the valances of the opposite seat. Something was emerging. A man. Dragging himself forth on his stomach, gathering himself up to his hands and knees, rising to his full height, collapsing, a dusty, degraded bundle of clothes, in the further corner of the carriage.

"Guard!" shrieked Auntie. "Gua—!"

The word died on her stiff blue lips. She, too, collapsed in her corner, and lay stonily staring at the face staring back at her: a face with desperation in its hunted eyes, with black chin, and chalk-white cheek and brow, and a mouth restlessly mumbling with no sound.

Beside the man, on the flat-topped division of the seat, a pistol lay; but the fingers of the small white hand which held it were nerveless. In his bearing was no menace—only the unstrung droop of despair.

So they faced each other without a word—the man and woman who for the last two days had played the rôles of attentive host and gratified guest.

And the train sped on. Away from the sunny little house, the dainty, capable housewife, the security, the shelter, the heaven of home; away from peace and guiltlessness; away from a life in which the "gnat-like buzzings of little cares" had once been its heaviest burden, to a life in death of danger, of degradation, of bottomless despair.

As the train slackened speed for the next station, the man arose, dropped the pistol in his pocket; his hand stole out to the handle of the door. Cautiously he looked forth over flat landscape of building site, of brickfield, of the huge tanks and lush vegetation of sewage farms. Gently he pushed the door a little open, and, holding it, paused, as more slowly, slower still the train sped on.

There was a shrinking touch upon his arm, and Auntie, livid, heavily breathing, pointed to the silver flask filled with brandy, to the parcel of sandwiches Grace had cut for her, chatting happily the while, that morning. The man took them without a word, and pushed them in the pocket of his coat.

The train was slackening still. Auntie grasped her bag, with weak, half-paralysed fingers drew out the bag of money and jewels for which the man had groped last night beneath her pillow, put it in his hand. There came a sound in Augustus Mellish's throat that might have been a sob or a strangled word; then the door opened wider; a moment, and he had slipped from sight.

The station was passed, and the train sped on, bearing Auntie, sole occupant of the carriage, her journey nearly done.

At St Pancras the guard, the chances of half-crown or no half-crown still agitating his mind, came to the door of the first-class carriage he had taken under his special supervision. He touched his cap with a smile expressive of felicitation that, thanks to his unremitting care, the lady had reached the end of her travels undisturbed and in peace from intrusion.

But Auntie was lying back in her corner, dead.

WILLY AND I

When we were little—Willy and I—oh, such a weary long year ago!—we lived in a big house, in a wide, quiet street in the old town of Norwich. Now, although the house was so big, there was allotted to it only a small square of garden; a garden exquisitely kept and fostered; a garden to smell the roses in, blushing on their neat rows of standards; to walk in, holding father's or mother's hand; even, wondrous treat! to take our tea in, sometimes, sitting demurely, we two, with a couple of dolls and a few lead soldiers from Willy's last new box for company, at the little round table whose root was buried deep in the ground beneath the red may-tree. A garden for such mild pleasures, but not for play. A garden that was the delight of our city-bred father, who protected the sprouting mignonette seeds from depredations of snail and slug, who trained with tenderest care the slenderest shoots of sweet-pea and canariense, who tied and pruned and watered with his own hands when office hours were over. A broken toy would have been as great an offence in that treasured spot as a stray cat; a little footmark on the verbena bed, a kicked-up stone on the gravel walk, were punishable offences. No room for us two children there.

And so, besides the nursery where our toys and books were kept and where our soberer hours were passed, there was given up to our use at the top of the house a large attic, which was called our play-room.

It is quite desirable for children to run wild at times, it is good for them to shout, to scream, to jump, to ramp—good for girls as well as boys. And if you girls who read this have not a big garden where you may do these things unmolested, I counsel you to demand respectfully of your parents a play-room such as was this of ours. I don't for a minute advise you to copy Willy and me in aught—for we were often and often a naughty pair—I only suggest that your parents should copy ours in making over to you an empty room.

We had not many toys there. On looking back I think we spent our time mostly in struggles on the floor, rolling over and over each other with screams and shouts; with roarings as of wild animals emphasising the fact that we were not Willy and his little sister Polly, but a great large lion and a huge black bear in mortal combat. We played at French and English too. It takes a lot of yelling from lusty lungs, a lot of stamping and jumping on hollow boards, for one little girl to represent at all adequately a mighty and victorious army. Of Willy, as not only his countless followers but as Napoleon at their head, a good deal was also required. With all our vigour, we were only ordinary flesh and blood and we always grew tired at last, and then we sat down quietly upon the floor and looked through our closed window at the window opposite.

There was only a narrow passage between our house and the next; walking through it with outstretched arms you could touch the house walls on either side. Unless you leaned quite out of the window, so high up were we, you could not see the little dark-paved court beneath; and a close wire screen covering the window was believed to prevent the possibility of our looking out at all. But Willy, to whose bold, adventurous spirit I felt my own but a feeble companion, had contrived with his pocket-knife to undo the four screws which attached the wooden framework of the screen to the window-frame. So that the obstacle being at will removed, and I holding desperately to his knickerbockered legs, the boy could look out upon the black pavement beneath, or drop a marble from his pocket upon the head of a passer-by.

It was not the dark passage, however, which as a rule claimed our attention, but the window exactly opposite our own. We could see quite plainly into the room, and its occupant could see into ours.

This was a small young man with a pale face. So much I remember of him; and the fact that the sight of prominent dark eyes and a runaway chin always recalls to me this episode in my childhood's career, inclines me to believe that that conformation of features was his.

The room had been empty like our own till one day a bed had been set up in it, and a chair and a washstand; and after that the young man had appeared.

"It isn't his play-room, it's his bedroom; he's another lodger at Miller's," Willy informed me.

When we were not at play we used to sit at the window and watch him. He did not go to an office, like our father. He seemed to have nothing to do. Sometimes he stood before the window and looked across at us, but oftenest he lay on his back on his bed and stared at the ceiling.

"I should jolly well like to have my bedroom up here, and never take off my clothes when I go to bed," Willy said, enviously.

It is curious to remember what a new interest that silent watcher of us gave to our gambols. It was with one eye on the pale young man at the window that I marched to the tune of Old Bob Ridley on the field of Waterloo; and Willy became so painfully realistic in giving me my quietus, when I lay dying and at his mercy after the battle, that I had to turn on my face and cry secretly, he hurt me so.

One day—a very sunshiny day, I remember, the sky above our neighbour's roof was a bright blue— we were holding a lively representation of a circus we had visited the day before. Willy, with the carriage whip brought up from the hall, took the place of the gentleman in the ring, while I as the piebald palfrey galloped on all fours spiritedly round the place, or pranced proudly on my hind legs, to command. We were spurred on to more vivacious action by the knowledge that our neighbour had opened his window wide, and was standing before it. When we tired of our equestrian performances, and took up our position opposite him, he, for the first time, nodded and smiled at us, and presently motioned to us to throw up our window likewise.

Proud and pleased at this mark of attention, we speedily tore down the screen, and, both of us going to work together in our eagerness, flung the window wide.

"Nothing like being friendly with your neighbours," the young man said. "You seem pretty lively across there—how do you do?"

We said, both at once, that we were quite well, thank you; that this was our play-room; and we asked him how he liked being a lodger. We asked him many things, besides. Was he ill, or only very tired, that he lay on his bed so much? Did he have his dinner up there, or did he go down to get it as we did? Did he eat what he liked, or what Miss Miller liked to give him? Was he fond of Miss Miller? We hated her because once she had seen Willy leaning out of the window and had told father, who had had the horrid screen put up.

I don't remember what answers he made to all these questions, piped forth in eager little voices, whose words tripped each other up in their hurry, but I know he said he thought the screen a babyish contrivance and advised us, now we had taken it down, not to put it back again. I reminded Willy that father would be very cross if we did not, and Willy reminded me that father being out for two nights, that didn't matter. We cautioned our neighbour not to let Miss Miller know the window was open or she would be at her tale-telling again, and he, on his part, advised our keeping the fact of his being now such friends with us secret from the servants. He hated servants, he told us, as much as Miss Miller; and Willy admitted that ours were certainly sneaks and not to be trusted. I told him that Willy and I often had secrets, and volunteered the information that I had once kept one from mother for two whole nights!

He should think we were very lonely with father and mother away, and only cats of servants left to us, he said; and asked what we should like best in the world to play with.

We both with one breath cried "a kitten;" because that was the one coveted treasure which had been persistently denied us hitherto.

Then he said that he most fortunately happened to possess the sweetest kitten in all the world, of which he would be happy to make us a present; and Willy said, in deep-toned satisfaction, "would he really, though?" and I got on my feet to jump for joy.

It was just then that nurse's voice came calling us to say good-bye to our father and mother. So we slammed down the window in our new friend's face, and pushed the screen back into position, and, bursting with our secret, Willy and I went galloping down the stairs.

Oh, those uncarpeted, twisting stairs! Now that Willy and I have "grown up and gone away," do they creak gaily beneath the happy feet of children still, I wonder, or only groan with the heavy tread of sober grown-ups? Often and often now, while

"In the elders' seat

Resting with quiet feet,"

I fall asleep and dream I come to the foot of those enchanted stairs, where for my little companion and me stupid law and irksome restraint ceased, and the liberty we craved began. Then, once more, Willy and I, whose hands will never meet again on earth, mount hand in hand to the region we loved.

We drove with our father and mother to the station, and, coming back, found we had the tiresome formality of our nursery tea to get through before we were free to make tracks for our happy hunting-ground above.

The young man was waiting there, before his open window, his hands in his trousers-pockets. We tore down the screen, flung up our own window. "Have you got it?" we called to him, breathlessly. "Is it there? The kitten?"

It was in his coat-pocket; a little sandy kitten which trembled exceedingly through all its fluffy fur, and piteously mewed. He held it forth to us, finger and thumb about its tiny neck, across the narrow way; but stretch as far as we could we could not reach it. Willy undertook to catch it if it were thrown, but the young man said that for worlds he would not endanger the life of the kitten, and I implored him to run no risks.

"What is that standing up by the side of your bed?" Willy asked him, pointing. "It was not there before—that long board?"

It was a plank, the young man informed us. He was going to make it into a box. He was a carpenter by trade. Didn't we know it?

We told him no, and artlessly informed him we had thought he was a gentleman, assuring him politely at the same time we were glad he was not.

Then Willy suggested that the plank should bridge the space from his room to ours, and that the kitten should be induced to walk on it.

The young man welcomed the idea as an excellent one, but feared when Kitty saw the great depth below she might turn giddy and fall. Done in the dark, now, she would not see, nor have any fear.

But nurse made us go to bed before dark we told him, and we so longed for the precious kitten.

We should know it would be there, he said. Leave the screen down, and the window open all night, and we should know it would be there, and could bring it its breakfast, the first thing in the morning.

With this prospect we were obliged to be content; but although at present, separated from our new treasure, we stayed in its neighbourhood as long as we could, learning from the obliging young man many wrinkles for the education and upbringing of the kitten, which would have to live in the play-room, its bread and milk obtained by cunning and subterfuge from under nurse's nose.

Inexpressibly I longed to have the little thing in my possession; for with its present owner, despite his love for it, it seemed less happy than I could wish—stowed away, heedless of its feelings, in his coat-pocket, or exposed on the narrow window-ledge, where it shivered, and mewed, and squeezed up to shelter, in an agony of terror lest it might fall.

We stayed with it until we were called to bed, but it was not of the kitten alone we talked. It gave us much pleasure to find what interest our new friend took in us. He even troubled to inquire where, exactly, in our house, which was built like Miss Miller's, did we sleep—how near to mother's room, how far from the servants? As you went up from the back passage to the great square front landing, our mother's door was the one that faced you—he knew that—

We laughed, and told him no, and cried out in our new delightful friendliness how stupid he was! That was our nursery door, and then came our night nursery, and then mother's, and—so on.

It was with much reluctance we tore ourselves away when nurse called; the wind from the open window blew chill upon us as we nodded good-bye to our friend. He waved the mewing kitten to us in farewell. It protested loudly, its little fluffy hind legs clawing despairingly at the empty air.

In the afternoon of the next day our parents were home again, brought back by a telegram which told them that their house had been robbed, the strong box in our mother's room broken open, and all the easily portable articles of plate taken from the housemaid's pantry.

We had policemen in the house, all the morning, policemen were closeted with our father when he came home. Willy, in a suddenly disorganised household, free from nursery rule, trotted about, proud of his courage in thus daring, at a policeman's heels. Now and again, I would hear him coming at a rush upstairs to report progress to me, who would not leave the play-room.

All the bars of the doors and shutters were untouched. The thief must have been let into the house, the policeman said; and our father, who trusted all his servants, was furious with the policeman.

A policeman wasn't a man to be afraid of when you knew him; why wouldn't I come and see this one? He—Willy, quite a hero that morning—would take care of me.

Then away, with excited face and flying feet, downstairs again. And presently, a quieter step upon the stairs—a step I knew well then, hear often in the lonely silence now, shall surely know amid the sound of all the myriad feet that tread the golden floor when I hear it again—and my mother was in the room.

"Where is my little girl, and what is she hiding away for? And what have you got in your lap, and why are you crying, Polly?" she asked.

Then she turned back my little skirt which hid it, and there was the kitten; sobbing wildly, I flew up and pushed it into her arms.

"The man—the man at the window—promised it," I cried, incoherently. "And I wanted it because it was so unhappy—and we left the window open—and I loved it so. And it had to walk the plank—and Willy and me thought it was asleep, and I picked it up—and it was dead."

Soon, lying with the dead kitten in her arms, I had sobbed out something of the story. "It is a secret—a secret," I told her, wildly; "don't let Willy and the man at the window know I told!"

She carried me away, before the policeman and my father had mounted to the attic. It was Willy, shaken and frightened now, who had to tell the story of the unscrewed screen, the open window, the plank laid across.

They said it was the young man at the window who came over on the plank, sitting on it and pulling himself along; they said he brought the kitten, as he had promised, having first choked the life out of it lest it should mew, and wake the house. They said that when they caught the robber, Willy and I would have to go and look at him and say, "That is the man." We used to lie shaking in our beds at night, dreading the hour when we should be called on to do this duty.

But they never got the jewellery back, they never caught the robber.

As time went on, Willy, who was always brave for his age, grew braver, and would often declare he, if policemen were present, and the robber in hand-cuffs, would not be afraid to look upon him; but be sure that I, who thought of the murdered kitten, had never a wish to see the young man with the prominent black eyes and the runaway chin again.

I made a pilgrimage to that wide street the other day, and stopped before that big old house where we two had lived as children, where I had played so contentedly second fiddle to Willy. Willy, who was so eager to act the leading part, so determined to enjoy, to do, to conquer; Willy

"Whose part in all the pomp that fills

The circuit of the summer hills

Is that his grave is green!"

I stepped into the narrow passage between the two houses, and looking up, saw that the present neighbours, friendlily inclined, had slung a rope across from window to window, upon which towels hung to dry. I could see only the projecting ledge of the window through which our little faces used to peep and the projecting ledge of that upon which the kitten had shivered and mewed. But I looked long at these, and at the tiny slip of blue sky above, and then came home and wrote this story.

A BROKEN BOOT

"Oh, the insufferable eyes of these poor might-have-beens."

Every morning of the spring and early summer he had walked down that sun-and-shadow-flecked suburban road, and rested on that particular iron chair. The butcher's and fishmonger's boys going their rounds, the policeman on his beat, the postman wearily footing it, the daily governess returning from her morning's occupation, had become used to his appearance there; and he watched each one going upon his or her business, wistful-eyed.

To-day, on one of the chairs planted by the thoughtfulness of the ever-solicitous Town Council at intervals along the road, a tramp had also placed himself. He was a tramp of a dirty and unprepossessing appearance, and having cast a sidelong glance at the well-dressed, handsome, and distinguished-looking young man beside him, he had begun in hoarse, faint tones to beg of him. The voice was evidently that of a hungry man; but to the appeal no response was made, unless there was reply of a sort in a painfully crimsoning cheek and an averted gaze. The tramp pointed to his feet, the ragged boots grey with dust of weary miles, the naked toe peeping through. The gentleman faintly shook the head that he continued to hold aside. With an effort the tramp got upon his feet.

"D—n you!" he said. "May your belly go as empty as mine. May hell-fire blister your feet as mine are blistered!"

The man left alone upon the iron bench looked after the tramp shuffling painfully away, with no anger or condemnation in his eyes, only a submissive sadness.

"Poor devil!" he said. "Poor devil! What a beast I must seem to him."

Once again his fingers, hopeless as his eyes, felt over the region of his coat and waistcoat-pockets, wandered nervelessly to his trousers-pockets—empty all! How many a time had they flown there in the last few weeks to make the same discovery—a discovery causing a shock at first, surprise, incredulity, anger; of late, mechanically only, quite hopelessly.

And only a short time ago his pockets had been so well lined! He had been in debt, it is true, but money had been forthcoming for who cared to take. No beggar, however "professional," however visibly lying, had ever asked of him in vain. He had squandered, in a society his father's son should never have known, the fortune his father had left him; his extravagance had been mad, his self-indulgence unlimited; but it must be told of him that the occasion on which he most bitterly felt his present poverty was such an one as this. He missed so much—all that made life worth living in that foolish whirl "from gilded bar to gilded bar" which was all his manhood's experience: his credit at his tailor's, the cigars he had smoked and given away, his daily games of billiards (the one thing at which he had excelled in all his wasted life was billiards, his fingers sometimes itched with the longing to feel the cue in his hand again), all the thousand extravagances of such a young man's day. But up to the present it was this alone which made poverty intolerable,—the having to refuse when Want asked of him.

He watched the tramp hobbling painfully into the distance, and in his pale blue eyes came that pricking which is of tears.

"His blistered feet!" he said. "His blistered feet!"

And then very slowly he lifted one of his own long legs and laid it at the ankle upon the other knee, and touching his slender, high-arched foot very gingerly, he bent his head and examined his own boot.

Yes; there, sure enough, was the crack in the leather he had first discovered yesterday, and which had caused him a sleepless night. The first crack in his last pair of boots!

The lower lip of that small mouth which had been used to laugh at such foolish nothings, and which now so easily drooped to grieving, fell open as he looked. The crack was quite close to the sole and was scarcely noticeable yet, but it would take—how few days! to widen to a considerable gap! Then the people of the town in which he had been born, through which he had ridden his father's horses, and driven his father's carriages, would notice that he walked about in broken boots! To-day he had been careful to come by back ways to that favourite road whose sunshine and shadow he had run over so often as a boy; to his seat on that chair which was placed beneath the hedge of the garden in whose house he had been born.

Three months ago, when to his overwhelming astonishment it was first made clear to him that he had no longer a penny under heaven, he had gone in his bewilderment to his brother, a man whose share of the patrimony had not been squandered—had been put out to usury rather, bringing in thirty, forty, a hundredfold—a man living in luxury and holding the respect of his fellow-townsmen.

"You can come to me," the brother had said. "Eat at my table, sleep beneath my roof. I shall not turn my back upon my brother. But I shall not pay any bills for you, nor shall I allow you a farthing of money—you have shown us the use you make of money. You will find it inconvenient to be without, and I advise you therefore to get work."

So, for three months he had availed himself of his brother's hospitality, and the brother had kept his word. For three months he had crossed in the muddiest part of the street because he had feared to look the crossing-sweeper in the face, he had avoided the placarded blind man, the paralytic woman who had known him well. He carefully made détours to escape these, and the shoeblack boys with whom he had been held in high favour. As for the people of his own class—the world is not all unkind, but it is very busy, very forgetful—none remembered to seek him. He had been surrounded by associates of a sort; and he found himself quite alone.

For the first week or so he had thought it would be an easy thing to find employment; a few rebuffs where he had looked for a helping hand, a curt refusal or two, seemed to show him it was an impossibility. He had no knowledge of book-keeping, he could not take a clerkship; business men, with a mere glance at his handsome, delicate features, at the shrinking, deprecating glance of his eyes, at his white, nervous fingers, his faultless dress, decided that he was no good.

"Work? Yes. But at what can I work?" he had asked his brother at length, flushing and hesitating; for since he had been a recipient of his bounty he had become afraid of his highly-respected relatives, and of the wife who looked at him with hard eyes as he took his place at the table.

To that question no answer but a sour smile of a dragged-down lip and a shrug of the shoulder had come, followed by the reminder that there was always a crossing to sweep.

"I would rather sweep a crossing than lead the life you are leading," the brother had said.

And the other had acquiesced. It would be better, certainly; but—

For a young man of aristocratic appearance and faultlessly cut clothes to take a place at a crossing in his native town, and beg of the passers-by, some of whom would be personal friends, for coppers, requires moral courage; he had been all his life, hence his misfortunes, a moral coward.

So, of late, only spasmodically, and with a hopelessness that prepared defeat, did he make efforts to find occupation. But he was not naturally an idle man nor in all directions incompetent, and he watched the people passing to office, shop, workroom, with a gaze which had grown unspeakably wistful.

When the hour for the midday meal arrived, he had been wont to return to his brother's house, but to-day he had something else to do.

The road being emptied of the stream of passers-by which flowed more fully at that time, he got up and walked to the gate of the house where he had been born, and looked long within, upon the garden. It had always been a beautiful garden, full of flowering shrubs, and wide lawns, and winding, box-edged paths. Very little had it altered since to him it had seemed all the world, and he had the fancy to follow now about its sunny, shadowy ways into all its pleasant haunts, the figure of a little boy who had played there long ago.

It had been a lonely child who had played there, his only brother being too old to play, and he had gone about the garden-ways, carrying his absurd jumble of childish fancies, incredible aspirations, baby ambitions, on untiring little feet. It pleased the young man at the gate to follow him in fancy, from spot to spot, always in the sunshine, always with flowers around him, and the whisper of trees about him, and the song of birds overhead.

Leaving behind him the gay flower-beds upon which the creeper-covered house looked forth, into many a leafy nook and shrub-bound fastness the phantom little form ran happily. Where the trees grew tall and close above an undergrowth of shepherd's-parsley and blue-bell had been a favourite resort of the child's. When the eyes of the young man followed him there, and saw him stop beside the smooth trunk of a silver birch, he knew that a new knife had been given him that day, and that he was going to carve his own name upon the bark. He knew that, the task being accomplished, the child would fetch his mother, and lead her to the tree to see how deep the knife cut, and how always—always the name would be there!

Once, being tired with overmuch play, the child had fallen asleep against that tree, and had wakened to hear his mother's voice calling,—

The young man came back to the iron bench, his figure drooping. The lower lip had fallen open, showing the small, regular teeth. Into the face, "accustomed to refusals," into the wistful gaze of the pale blue eyes, something of awe had crept. Presently he put up his boot upon his knee, and once more his eyes fell upon the crack in the side. He moved his foot within the boot—certainly a bulging showed; by to-morrow the stocking would be seen.

To-morrow! Yes. He nodded his handsome head with eyes upon the boot and breathed the word to himself.

How long ago it seemed since this tragedy of the broken boot had befallen! Could it have been but yesterday? Was that possible?

His great need had developed his strategical powers, and accident had seemed to further his design. Quick upon the discovery, he had encountered his brother's page on his way to his brother's shoemaker, bearing that relative's shoes to be repaired. Seizing the opportunity, he had hastily divested himself of his own boot and had added that to the page's burden.

His spirits so easily arose; such a load by that simple manoeuvre had been lifted from his heart! He pushed his feet into his slippers and came whistling downstairs to lunch. He had a perfect ear, and his whistle was most melodious and sweet; the canaries in the dining-room windows awoke and joined in shrilly. His brother, standing, with sour, sarcastic face, upon the hearth, held fastidiously between finger and thumb an article which apparently it was not agreeable to him to touch.

"I met Payne taking my boots," he said; "he had managed to get hold of one of yours by mistake. I rescued it. I think we don't employ the same bootmaker."

The young man's cheek did not burn any longer as he recalled that incident. He felt nothing now, no anger, no bitterness. To such as he it is so easy to forgive. Forgiveness had ever flowed from him in sheer weakness. It had been the habit of his life to love and admire his brother—he loved and admired him still. He did not think that he himself would have been quite so hard on a poor devil in his place; but his brother was a strong man and he a weak one—no doubt his brother was right.

It was certain he was not a cruel man—did he not owe him the bread he ate? Had he not shed tears over the death of a dog a day or two before? The dog had been in incurable pain, and a pill which had been procured from the chemist had caused that pain instantly to cease. The master had given the order of execution, and had turned away from the gaze of the suffering brute with the waters of sensibility in his eyes.

And how quietly the dog had died! One instant in convulsions of pain, and the next still—quite still! The young man who had carried with him from childhood a great dread of death had been much impressed. After all, could it be so terrible?

Only one little pill had sufficed to produce that great change—would suffice to kill two or three dogs, the chemist had said. But the young man had brought away with him a second dose for fear of accident. As he looked with unseeing eyes at the broken boot, his finger and thumb held the second little pill securely in the corner of his waistcoat pocket.

He was afraid of death; but, as a child believes, he believed in God. Through the recklessness, the wildness, the "joyous folastries" of youth there had clung to him still the feeling that God was above him; there beyond the stars; he had felt His smile sometimes, or grown cold beneath His frown. He had not read, nor thought; nor had he listened to clever talk on the absurdities of a worn-out faith, the uselessness of an obsolete creed. His business had been with enjoying himself simply—with none of those things. Of every other foolishness on earth his lips had babbled, but not blasphemies. He had not trodden the downward path with lingering steps, he had gone precipitately to his ruin; but at least his eyes had been on the stars.

It was for this reason, perhaps, that, although he sat there, a miserable failure, driven by the heartless might of the world to the last extremity, there was yet a light upon his brow, and about his weakly-parted lips a sweetness sometimes absent from brows and lips of more admirable men.

If he went, beneath scented lime-tree, past gay-flowered border, to peep through a certain wistaria-festooned window he should see his father with pipe and book in the accustomed chair, the mother would look up from her sewing. A recollection came to him of how once in those childish years which had been so much with him of late a sudden sense of overpowering loneliness had come upon him as he played. He had rushed to that window to comfort his little soul with the sight of the familiar faces, and had found the room empty. He recalled the terror that had fallen upon him, the horror of desolation. He would not risk the shock of disillusion. He saw them quite plainly, as his eyes seemed fixed on the broken boot, but he would not disturb them. No. When the time came and he entered the gate he would not go near the house, but would make his way through the shrubbery in which the lawn ended, and would seek that wilderness which had been his playground.

The wild hyacinths were blue about the roots of the tree on which his name was cut—how low down the sprawling letters were!—the pet name by which his mother had called him. If he fell asleep with his back against the trunk she might come and call him by it again.

It was because he had not slept all night that he was so tired. He had tossed and turned, tossed and turned upon his bed, seeking in his muddled, ineffectual brain for an escape from the disgrace of the broken boot. Quite suddenly there had presented itself to him the way of escape—the only way— the way he intended to take.

The feathery leaves of the shepherd's-parsley would wave above the broken boot. He would fall so blessedly asleep—so blessedly! The dog, he remembered, had not stirred.

The present master of the wistaria-covered house was driven past him, as he sat in the roadside chair, to turn in at the familiar gate; the afternoon sun, sinking towards evening, shone on the smart phaeton, the glossy-sided horse. Lesser men walked by him briskly to their humble dwellings, little children, belated from school or at play, rushed on. He grudged to no man his success, he looked on without bitterness at the joy of life—he blamed no one, envied no one. He had gone astray somehow, and was stranded and lost; but it was without rancour, or enmity, or spite that he, a lonely outsider, watched the "flowing, flowing, flowing, of the world."

So, at length, he rose from his place, pushed open the gate, laying a tender touch upon the latch that such dear hands had pressed in days gone by. So he made his way, going with unerring step, beneath the overbranching of copper-beech, lilac, and red may, to the flower-carpeted wilderness where, with bluebells about its roots and feathery foliage waving high around its trunk, stood that silver birch-tree upon whose smooth bark he had long ago carved his name.

WHEN DEEP SLEEP FALLETH

Ten days of honeymooning passed in a big hotel at Brighton. Ten days of feeling himself—he who, living, a man of wealth, in a small provincial town, was used to find himself talked about, looked up to, considered on every side—curiously unimportant and of no account. Then back with his bride to the imposing if somewhat gloomy-looking old house to which a dozen years ago he had brought home his first wife.

They had left Brighton early in the morning, and reached home as the winter's afternoon was closing in. In the drawing-room, where many a time she had seen his wife perform that office, the Bride poured out tea for him.

"At last," he said, and stood upon the rug before the fire, cup in hand, and smiled at her. "This is pleasant, isn't it?"

With a smile up at him, and a full glance of the dark melancholy eyes he so much admired, she let him know that indeed she thought it pleasant.

Her costly fur coat, one of his wedding-gifts to her, was tossed over the back of her chair; the firelight gleamed on heavy gold ornaments at wrists and throat. She had been a poor woman, clothing, not dressing, herself, till in her eight-and-thirtieth year all the fine things which money could buy were suddenly lavished upon her. So soon the feminine mind accustoms itself to that change! Every woman is born to fine raiment, meant to be softly swathed, richly decked, daintily tired. Cheated of her inheritance though she be, it is as natural to her as her own skin when at length she comes into it. The Bride felt a sense of well-being, but no strangeness.

The room in which she sat was perhaps a little overcrowded with beautiful things. In the days which were past, which she did not trouble too much to remember, she had sat here on Sunday afternoons—her one holiday, and always spent with the good-natured wife of the man she had married—and had told herself that the room bore too evident stamp of the wealth of the master of the house, and the too sumptuous tastes of the mistress. Yet, now that it was her own, so desirable in itself seemed each piece of furniture, so beautiful each ornament, it would be difficult, she felt, to decide what to banish.

The man's gaze followed hers, speculatively, roaming over the costly objects. He was by no means anxious to make a display of his wealth.

He dreaded above all things the charge of vulgarity, distrusting his first wife's taste, not being quite sure of his own. A compactly built, well-featured man of middle size and pale complexion; a man careful and correct in speech, manner and dress; in his gently reserved, modest bearing giving no sign that he had raised himself far above his origin, that his wealth was new.

"Do what you like here," he said to his wife, as if reading her thoughts. "Alter the disposition of the furniture—do away with it altogether. I am by no means wedded to things as they are."

He crossed as he spoke to a rosewood cabinet placed against the opposite wall. On its polished surface, above its innumerable little shelves and drawers, a Crown Derby tea and coffee service was set forth. Standing in the midst, propped between a basin and a cup, was the unframed photograph of a woman. This the man removed. Holding it loosely between his finger and thumb, still talking to his wife, he returned with it to his old position on the hearth.

"I have not set foot in this room since—for a year," he said. "I thought I would leave everything till you came. Do just as you like."

"You are so good to me—" she began, and then started forward in her chair. "Oh, don't, don't, love!" she cried. "Don't burn her picture!"

She was too late. For one instant the face of the first wife looked up at her, smiling, fat, fatuous, from the heart of the glowing coals, then, with a stab of the poker, wielded by a remorseless hand, vanished in the blaze.

"Oh, love!" she sighed, reproachfully, "Oh, love!"

"Why not?" he asked, with a smile which went no further than his close-set lips. He put down the poker on the hearth and rose up again. "She must have laid in a stock of hundreds of those photographs," he said. "The servants appear to have an inexhaustible supply. In spite of—discouragement—they kept my dressing-room and study-table garnished with them till I ordered them to desist."

The new wife looked away from him into the fire in a minute's silence. "It seems cruel," at last she said, with an obvious effort. "I wish you had not burnt it, love. At least, not to-night. In this big house there should be room for me and—her photographs."

When she found that their bedroom was to be the same which he and his former wife had occupied, she was uncomfortably surprised.

The servant who showed her to that apartment in time for her to change her dress for dinner was the middle-aged woman, calling herself parlour-maid, but who had acted as lady's-maid, factotum, confidante to the dead wife. She had made confidantes of all who would listen, poor woman, pouring out the secrets of her heart, and, as far as she knew them, of her husband's heart, into any stranger's ears.

"Can I be of any assistance to you, madam?" the maid had inquired; and madam, in order not to give offence, accepted for a time her services.

"I like to do my hair myself," she said, "but if you brush it for me I shall be glad."

She did not like this servant who had been on terms of close familiarity with the other woman; while, outwardly acquiescent, she allowed herself to be buttoned into a dressing-gown by the hard, bony fingers, in spirit she protested.

As the pins were taken out of the heavy dark hair, and the braids untwisted, the eyes of the new mistress and the eyes of the old servant met again and again in the glass. And the thought came to the bride: how often in that same glass those slanting eyes of the maid must have encountered other eyes! Eyes of shallow blue beneath a fringe of yellow-dyed, tousled locks.

The reflection was not a comforting one, and warm and cosy as was the brightly-lit room, she shivered. Hastily casting down her gaze it fell upon a photograph of her husband, taken ten years or so ago, shrined in its silver frame amid the silver accessories of the dressing-table. In order to break a silence which was getting on her nerves—

"Is that the picture which was always here?" she asked.

"Always," the servant replied. "It stood opposite one of my late mistress, taken at the same time, and framed in the same way. After my late mistress's death my master wished to have her photographs removed. He destroyed many of them. I think he destroyed the last to-day."

"Now, how in the world did she know that?" the Bride asked herself, guiltily conscious of the tell-tale face in the looking-glass, reddening before the servant's inquisitive eyes.

"After all, I will brush my hair myself," she said hastily. "I am used to doing it."

The servant, with no sign of either pleasure or displeasure on her shut-up, solemn face, withdrew.

"The silver-backed brushes on the table are those of my late mistress," she said from the door—"my master's last present to her. In the drawer beneath the looking-glass I think you will find your own brushes."

She found them there, and, lying beneath them, face upwards, a photograph of the dead wife.

The two women for years had called each other friend, but the Bride started back from the smiling presentment of the face now as if it had been some loathable thing. Started back, and shut the drawer.

Yet, in a minute had recovered herself, had taken out the picture, and laid it on the table before her, forcing herself to look long into the face that from among the medley of silver-topped bottles, pans and jars, smiled up at her.

As she looked, an inexplicable feeling of uneasiness and insecurity took possession of her. The fat, fatuous, and smiling face! It seemed to look with an air of contemptuous toleration upon her as an interloper; to say with its shallow gaze—"These are Mine. All this is Mine. It is I, you understand, who am mistress here."

Fascinated by this fancied new expression in the once expressionless eyes, the Bride looked and looked again—looked till the happy present slipped away from her and she was back in the unhappy past. The humble friend, her own poor toilette so soon made, sitting, by gracious permission, to watch the magnificent toilette of the other woman. In her bitter heart she felt again the scorn which her mind had always secretly held for this poor-witted, vulgar creature, who had not the brains to adapt herself to her husband's altered circumstances, who angered and shamed him beneath his still exterior, to his face, and gave him away to the first who would condescend to listen, behind his back. Who had sat before the dressing-table, watching in the glass the wide expanse of her bare bosom and white arms, and had boasted of her jewels and her dress. Babbled of things which should have been sacred between her husband and herself. How that woman sitting beside her, with the poor dress and the melancholy, dark eyes, hated her! With what an agony of pity she pitied the husband! Of what good were money, position, power to him with such a wife as this! She hated her. Hated her, as she sat before the glass, smiling at the reflection of her fair big arms and neck; hated her as, later at the dinner-table, she watched the husband's face, listening against his will to the woman gabbling forth some bit of information which the dullest-witted present knew she was expected to keep to herself.

Still lost to her surroundings in her reverie, the Bride heard again the outburst of foolish laughter with which the wife had once publicly declared her husband could keep nothing from her because of his habit of talking in his sleep. What she wished to know that in the daytime he would not tell her, she got from him at night by asking questions he never failed to answer while he slept.

She had hated her; and at last the poor creature, whose smiling face lay there beneath her fascinated gaze, had known it, and with the inferior force of her inferior nature had hated back. She had learnt—who knew how?—of the love between the woman who had been her friend and her own husband. The eyes had smiled no longer then.

The Bride lay back in her chair, motionless, while before her mind's eye rose the altered face of the woman who, deceived for long, was deceived no more—who knew! With her there had been no self-respecting reticence, no decency of secret tears. She had heaped insult upon the woman who had wronged her, she had led her husband a life of hell.

That time had been, mercifully, of short duration. A little illness of which no one took account, had ended all for the unhappy wife, had been the beginning of a joy beyond words for the other two. She had kept her bed for two days, suffering from a nervous attack, accompanied by excruciating neuralgia, and had died quite suddenly from the bursting of a vessel on the brain.

It had been, of course, in this room she had died. Upon the bed, there. And her husband, sleeping beside her, had not known that she was dead. Slowly the Bride, as if fearing what she might see, looked over her shoulder. The room, with a bright fire, and lit by electric light, was as cheerful as day. But as her eyes, slowly travelling back again, met their own reflection in the glass, she saw in them a haunted look which frightened her. She flew to her feet; snatching the portrait from the table, she hurriedly crossed the room and flung it to the flames.

"He is right. Why not?" she said. "To burn a picture is nothing—nothing! And it has given me horrible thoughts."

It was difficult to banish them.

When the newly-married pair were alone in the drawing-room after dinner, and she was seated at the piano, she asked him, through the chords she was softly touching, if there was not another room in the house they could take for their sleeping-chamber.

"Certainly," he said; "most certainly if she wished."

He, himself, had not slept there since the night of his first wife's death, he told her. Told her, too, that before leaving for their wedding-trip, he had given orders to have one of the other rooms prepared against their return. The reason this had not been done, the invaluable parlour-maid had informed him, was because the wardrobe he had particularly desired to be moved there had proved too big for the niche which was to have received it. Wardrobe or no wardrobe, however, since she wished it, they would migrate on the morrow.

"You do wish it?" he asked her.

She nodded, softly striking her chords.

"I wonder why? You are no more superstitious or fanciful than I."

She shook her head, bending forward to study the score of the music on the desk, one of Sullivan's operas they had heard together at Brighton. He, sitting close behind her, his chin touching her shoulder, had fixed his eyes on the music too, although he could not read a note of it. "Horrid thoughts came to me there," she said. "I don't think, love, I shall ever like to be alone in that room."

He named the invaluable maid. "Have her up to dress you," he advised.

The Bride shrugged her shoulders, and her fingers moved more quickly in a livelier movement. "We will change the room," she said.

Later, he had placed himself on the rug at her feet, and she, leaning forward in the armchair drawn over the fire, had her arm about his neck while he talked to her of himself, she questioning. Of his early life he talked, and what had been for and what against him; of his later success, and his old ambitions.

"All achieved now," he said, and turned to smile at her the curious, characteristic smile accomplished by a twist of a closed lip.

"I have not bored you?" he asked her with anxiety, when the evening was over. "Except to you, I have never in my life talked of myself. It is a luxury in which I must not too much indulge."

She reassured him with the zeal of the newly-wedded, much loved and loving wife. "Promise me that you will always tell me all, that you will never keep a secret from me," she said; and he promised, smiling upon her with his twisted lip.

"If you do," she cried, fondly threatening, "I shall know it, Sleep-talker! I shall ask you in your sleep and you will tell me all."

That, under those circumstances, he should probably tell her much that had no foundation in fact, and much that it would by no means please her to hear, he warned her.

She fancied by his tone that he was annoyed, and hastily asserted that she had been in fun, that not for a moment could she seriously entertain such an intention.

"What you do not wish to tell me, be sure I do not wish to hear," she told him.

He stood by the open drawing-room door and watched her as she ran lightly upstairs.

Conscious of his eyes following her, the knowledge of his love and admiration warm at her heart, she went into their brightly-lit bedroom. For years she had lived such an unloved life, watching her youth fade, fighting only for bread to keep herself alive in a world where none wanted her. Since, in this man's eyes she was still so young and fair, let her look at herself!

She crossed the room to the looking-glass with a quick, exultant step, but having reached the dressing-table, drew back with almost a cry. Standing on it in its old place, facing her husband in his silver frame, was the silver-framed portrait with the elaborately-dressed fair hair, the smiling, shallow eyes of the first wife.

The Bride stifled the little cry upon her lips, but with her heart beating thickly, fell back from the dressing-table, and leant against the foot of the bed.

A moment's thought reassured her. There was nothing, after all, disturbing in the reappearance of a photograph which had been displaced. The invaluable maid with her slanting eyes, with, perhaps, her stupid devotion to a memory, was responsible.

At the thought the Bride's nerves steadied themselves, but her anger arose. She moved to the bell— but stopped. Better not to create talk among the servants by the order she had meditated; rather let this portrait of the dead wife follow the rest.

But when she held it, frame and all, over the fire, she relented and drew it back. "It is not like me to be a superstitious fool. I will not," she said. "She is in her grave, and I am—here. In a way I did not wish, but could not help, I spoilt the last year of her life. She is dead, buried out of mind, shovelled away under the earth, that a joy undreamt of might come to me. This poor triumph at least she shall have, to keep her old place on the table. I will never dress in the morning without remembering I am in her place. When I prepare for my bed at night she shall not be forgotten."

"'Les morts que l'on fait saigner dans leur tombe se vengent toujours!'" she quoted to herself as she undressed; and while she prided herself upon being above superstition, decided upon the above method of propitiating the Shade.

In the night she had a dream which bathed her in the sweat of terror. Opening her dreaming eyes upon the dressing-table which faced the foot of the bed she saw the figure of the dead wife standing there. Its back, clothed in its long nightdress, was turned to her, but in the glass which had so often reflected it she saw the foolish, fat face, the over-curled, fair hair. She saw, too, that the figure held in one hand its own photograph, while, with a pencil held in the other it wrote, smiling the while its own fatuous smile, on the reverse of the picture.

In her dream the Bride knew this vision to be a dream, a knowledge which by no means lessened the horror of it. "I must awake or die!" she said, and in a minute seemed broad awake.

It was morning; the sunshine flooding the room shone, with a brilliance which hurt the eyes upon the silver frame of the picture on the dressing-table. Nothing else was there; all the silver-topped pans and jars and bottles had disappeared; even the companion photograph was no longer to be seen; only the face of her one-time friend smiled and smiled and seemed to beckon from the strangely brilliant, dazzling frame.

With the horror of the dream no whit abated, the Bride rose heavily from her bed, dragged mysteriously attracted feet, that yet seemed weighted with lead, across the floor to the dressing-table; picked up in a hand that fumblingly obeyed the motion of her will, the picture.

Upon the back, written in the dead woman's familiar scrawl were the date of her death, and the words, "Died by my own hand."

In the desperate effort to cast the picture from her paralysed grasp, the Bride awoke.

She was really awake at last, and lying, faint with the dews of remembered terror, upon her bed, her head upon her husband's shoulder.

Thank God, awake at last! How horrible that had been!

Clinging to him in terror at first, she presently extricated herself from the man's encircling arm, and switched on the light. She dared not lie in the darkness with the thoughts that assailed her. Never for one instant before had the possibility of the wife's self-destruction occurred to her. Yet, all at once, how probable, how almost certain it seemed.

Died by her own hand! How easy it would have been! An overdose of the opiate the doctor was giving her to ease her pain. And she, weary of life—life made suddenly hideous to her; all her foolish vanities killed, her delight in herself, her belief in her friend, her faith in her husband. The gilding all stripped from the bauble which till then had made her happy. How possible! Nay, was it possible longer to doubt it?

And who was responsible? The woman who lay in her place, staring out into the room which had witnessed that foolish, harmless life, which had witnessed that tragic death; and the man sleeping beside her. They two.

Slowly, lest she should disturb him, the Bride raised herself upon her elbow, looked upon the sleeping face.

It was a face still unfamiliar to her in sleep. The always close-shut mouth was open, the straight-cut upper lip was strained tightly over the gums with a look almost of suffering, the eyes and temples looked as if sunken in pain. Feeling her gaze upon him, the man's lids half lifted themselves, an incoherent word or two fell from the stretched lips, the head moved restlessly upon the pillow.

Did he too guess this thing? Did he know?

"If he does he will never tell it to me," the Bride said to herself, knowing well he would spare her that pain.

In the next moment she was leaning over him, calling him in soft, distinct tones by his name.

"Love," she said, "do you hear me?"

He moaned, turning upon his back. The heavy jaw came fully into view, and the too thick throat which in the daytime the tall, close collar hid. With a light touch she swept the hair which, clinging low over his brow, so disguised it, backward.

"I hear," he answered in the thick, difficult voice of the sleeper.

"Love, I love you," she said. "Tell me, do you love me?"

A pause; then, "With my soul," he answered heavily.

"And—that other wife? Tell me, love."

The answer had always to be waited for, and seemed to come in unwilling response to the command of an intelligence afar off.

"Hate—I hated her," the sleeper said.

"She knew it—at last. Did she—did she kill herself? Tell me the truth, love, as you love me."

No answer but a strangled muttering, a head that moved as if in pain. The eyes watching him saw that the sleeper was tortured.

"But this once," she said to herself, "I must ask—I will know."

She bent over, without touching him, and put her lips down close to his ear. "Swear to tell me the truth," she said in her distinct, arresting whisper.

Long she waited, watching lips that writhed before speaking, eyes that seemed to ache to open and were sealed by an invisible hand. At length in the low, stumbling, unwilling voice came the response—"I swear."

"Did—she—kill—herself?"

"No!"

"Oh, love! Are you certain? Will you swear it?"

"I swear it," said the muffled voice.

"Why are you so sure? Why? Oh, tell me! Listen: she said she died by her own hand."

"A lie. It is a lie. I killed her."

Hours later, the light of morning, outshining the electric light, found the woman, the heavily slumbering man beside her, gazing, with a stricken face and eyes which looked as if sleep had been banished from them for ever, upon the new, unwelcome day.

Brightly the rays of the ascending sun struck upon the silver-framed portrait on the dressing-table, upon the smiling presentment of the fatuous-faced, shallow-eyed, dead wife.

THE EXCELLENT JOYS OF YOUTH

"No head without its nimbus of gold-coloured light."

He had that delicately tinted infantine complexion which only accompanies red hair; his eyes were brightly blue; his features well chiselled, with the exception of the lips, which were clumsily cut and loosely held together. He came down to breakfast in a not very agreeable mood, for he had been drinking for the last week, and this was the first time he had been thoroughly sober for that period. His head ached, his tongue was hot and leathery; he kept his hands in his trousers-pockets because they shook heavily, and he did not want the lodging-house servant to see.

The pockets were quite empty. He could not tell where the last few pounds had gone—if he had lost them at that game of poker he remembered playing before he fell asleep, or if they had been stolen since. He did not remember, and it would be worse than useless to inquire. Not a penny was left to him, and he had not a notion where a penny was to come from—even to pay for the breakfast which he had no appetite to eat.

With a heavy gloom upon his face, he stood and looked at the meal spread for him for several minutes before he sat down to table. There was smoked haddock, and he shook his head at it; scrambled eggs, and having looked at the dish he hastily covered it from sight. Beneath the sideboard a few bottles of soda-water were lying. He opened one, and, there being no glass at hand, poured the contents into his breakfast-cup, then drank with a thirst which threatened the cup as well as what it held.

Then he sat down to the table and stared at his reflection in the teapot.

"God! What a fool I've been," he said. "And what the devil am I to do now?"

Two or three letters lay beside his plate; he flicked them apart with his shaking finger. "Bills—bills—bills!" he said. "All bills!"

Unopened, he chucked them one by one into the fire, but stopped at the last. "A lawyer's fist," he said, regarding the ominously legal-looking hand-writing. "Someone threatening proceedings again. Let 'em proceed!"

He was about to throw that communication also in the fire, but paused in the act, and laid it down by his plate again, putting another plate on the top of it to conceal it from his sight.

He took up the knife, old and worn and sharpened at the point, which lay by the loaf of bread, and looked at its edge.

"This is how poor old Fleming got out of the scrape," he said. "And Fleming wasn't in a worse hole than I am."

But he turned the knife upon the bread instead of his own throat, and having begun with an expression of distaste upon the salt fish, his appetite arrived with eating, and, that dish disposed of, he attacked the buttered eggs, and found himself in a fair way to make a good meal. For, in spite of his intemperate habits, he had an invariably good appetite—an almost indomitable cheerfulness also. The inability to take himself and his misfortunes seriously had been at the bottom of all his failures. With his family history and his temperament he was foreordained to disaster; but he met it smiling, with the courage which was more the outcome of indifference than of heroism.

"Which is the way to the workhouse, Polly?" he inquired of the little lodging-house servant who came to clear the table.

He had filled his pipe and had turned his chair to the fire. His blue eyes shone as brightly, his red hair was watered as carefully free of curl, his person was as neat and spruce and daintily cared for as if he had been the most immaculate of mothers' sons.

Polly, at her first place, and with an unbounded admiration and regard for the lodger who, if he did make a sight of work splashing about in his bath, was always free with his shillings and full of his fun, looked at the young man distrustfully.

"What you got to do wi' th' work'us?" Polly asked resentfully, and seized the bread under one arm and the remains of the haddock under the other.

"If folks have no money and don't want to starve, what do they do?" he asked, puffing at his pipe.

"They work," said Polly, laconically; pushed open the door with her foot, deposited the dishes in the yard-wide hall beyond, and returned for the rest of the breakfast-things.

"They work if they're lucky and born poor," he said. "But if they're like me they can't work, Polly, because they don't know how, and no one will give them the chance to learn. No. It'll have to be the workhouse, my good girl."

Upon which Polly snuffled loudly, and her tears fell—splash—upon the plates she was carrying away. It was not the first time that the workhouse had been threatened; the dread of her life was that the threat should be carried into effect. So she cried, and her poor little red hands shook as she shuffled the plates together.

"Here's a letter," she snuffled.

"Fling it on the fire, Polly."

"'Tain't opened. I 'ont, then. You should ope your letters."

"Open it for me, then."

So the little maid-of-all work opened, and, in obedience to his orders, she being a sixth-standard scholar, and not stumbling once at a hard word, read the letter.

And as she read, the young man sat upright in his chair, pulled the pipe from lips which had fallen open in astonishment, and fixed unblinking eyes of innocent blue upon the handmaiden.

For in legal phraseology, the sense of which, if not the words, was a sore stumbling-block to Polly, the letter set forth that by the death of a certain James Playford, legatee under the will of Mr Daniel Thrower's uncle, a sum of money had been released which now, according to the said will, was to be divided between the said uncle's nephews and nieces. Due deduction having been made for this and that, Mr Daniel Thrower's share was found to amount to the sum of £98, 17s. 6d., for which a cheque was herewith enclosed.

"Do you mean to say he's sent the money?" Mr Daniel Thrower demanded, in the accents of incredulity.

"There ain't no money—not a farden—only a bit o' paper," Polly said, with disappointment.

Dan seized the cheque from her hand. "All right!" he said; "I shan't go to that institution we spoke of just yet, Polly. We've got another chance, my girl."

Truth to say, he had had several in his life, but this seemed to him the happiest which had ever befallen. After each drunken outburst he made resolution that it should be the last, and remained a strictly temperate person till the madness seized him again. The resolution he made as he sat gazing at the cheque he held in his hand, being the last, was the one he meant to keep. Years ago an elder brother had gone out to New South Wales, had bought some land there, and had prospered. He was not a very sympathetic brother, and had not responded to the suggestion that the ungain-doing Dan should take himself, his bad fortune, his unsatisfactory habits, also to New South Wales to settle down beside him.

Dan was of opinion, however, that, once there, this brother would find a difficulty in getting rid of him. He thought with longing of that clean and healthy life, the escape from the slough into which his feet would always wander while he remained here. The means to escape he now held in his hand!

"Here I keep on sinking, sinking!" Dan said to himself, illustrating the process with a movement of the hand which held the cheque. "Bill—he's as hard as nails, but he'll hold me up. I shall begin over again. I shall be free of this infernal embroglio. I shall write my name on a clean page—"

He would not stop to repent; he would look out the first steamer that sailed; he would pay his debts—they were not, after all, many, for he had a constitutional objection to cheating people, and always paid when he could. He would say good-bye to the man for whose friendship's sake he had come here, and would shake the dust of the miserable little town where he had played the fool of late from his feet. It was three or four days, he remembered, since he had seen the friend of whom he thought; he would have news to take him now! So slipping the letter which contained the cheque into his pocket, he walked out into the April sunshine of the little High Street, and betook himself to Gunton's lodgings.

Gunton was the not altogether satisfactory assistant to the one doctor in the place. Going thus early, he would catch him before he started on his rounds.

No need to hurry, Dan! Before the good people of Hayford shall see again the young doctor flying round on his long legs to visit the pauper patients, or clattering in Doctor Owen's tall gig over the cobblestones of the High Street on his way to those invalids of least consideration entrusted to his care, the last trump shall sound.

He was not in the little sitting-room where Dan and he had smoked so many pipes together. The visitor was striding across the passage to the bedroom, also on the ground-floor, when the landlady issued therefrom; and the landlady was in tears.

"I have kep' these apartments respectable and comf'table, and not a week unlet, these seventeen year, come Michaelmas," she sobbed. "And never have I had a death in 'em before."

Dan recoiled before the word. "Death?" he said.

And she repeated the word. "Poor Mr Gunton, he have had one of his throats, and he was took worse yesterday morning. He kep' askin' for you, sir, and no one could say where you was; and now he have sent me to fetch you, whatever happen, and to say as he's a-dyin'!"

"It's one of his jokes," Dan said; but he had grown grey about the lips, and his mouth fell open.

He pushed open the bedroom door, half expecting to be greeted by a smothered laugh from Gunton, and a whispered account of the last trick he'd played the old woman.

But Gunton, poor fellow, who had laughed and played his foolish jests, and got into mischief industriously all through his short life, had laid his mirth aside to-day. He had done but indifferently well the few tasks allotted him, shirking them when he could; the business he had now on hand was a very serious one, and there was no slipping out of it. He had to die.

He told his friend so in so many words. "What's o'clock now?" he asked. "Eleven? By two I shall be dead."

Dan tried not to believe. "I'll go for the doctor—I'll fetch a nurse!" he said.

The other stayed him with his difficult speech. "Don't waste time. It's no good," he said. "I've seen men die like this. I know. Owen was here till ten minutes ago. I told him last night it was all up. You know what an old ass it is—he wouldn't listen. He listens now. He's wired for —" (naming a man locally celebrated in the profession). "He's driven, himself, to Fakenham for a nurse. I shall be dead before they get here. I told him so—the old ass! He's wired for my mother—she'll be too late. You can say I sent my love, Dan—"

All this in a hoarse, broken voice, interrupted by loud and painful breathing, and now and again by a short, rough cough.

"I didn't know you were seedy, old man! I'd have come at once," Dan said. "I've been on the spree again, for a day or so. It's the end. I'm not going to play the fool that fashion any more!"

"The end of my sprees!" poor Gunton said. "We've had one or two together, Dan. Don't look at me. I ain't pleasant to watch. Sorry. It won't be for long. Dan—my watch and studs, and a chain I never wore—they're"—he lifted a cold hand and tried to point to a little heap of trinkets lying on the drawers at the foot of the bed—"they're for you. Take them, will you? Take them now."

Dan nodded. "I'll take 'em, thank you, old man," he said, and sobbed suddenly. "Don't worry, Ted. Don't try to talk, dear old boy."

"I've got to. You know about Kitty. I was going to marry her next week. I took her away from the shop—made her give up her living. She's bought things to marry me. She can't pay for them. You—you—"

A struggle here, upon which Dan, in spite of himself, turned his back.

"I know," he said, brokenly. "I'll pay for them. I'll see to her. It'll be all right, Ted."

"No! My mother," the dying boy said; "tell her. She won't be pleased. Ask her to give Kitty a hundred pounds from me—with my love. Promise—promise."

"I promise," Dan said. "Anything—anything, dear old man. I know what you'll want done—don't, for God's sake, talk any more."

But for another hour of misery, of battling for breath, hideous to suffer and heart-breaking to witness, he would attempt to talk, irrationally at times, but now and again with a startling coherence. His mind ran on that gift of a hundred pounds. He sent message after message to the little shop-girl for whom, with the senseless prodigality of such youth, he had proposed to fling away his future. Again and again he adjured his friend to tell his mother what a good little girl Kitty was, how she had stuck to him and been a brick.

They said he was a clever fellow in his profession, the long-haired, long-legged young doctor, with his harum-scarum ways and his ready laugh. He had made a true diagnosis of his own case. Before doctors and nurses could be got to him he was dead.

"Don't look at me," was the last he said. "Pull the sheet over my face—don't look."

And so, with the thoughtfulness for others which had proclaimed him Gentleman in that inferior society where it had pleased him to move, he hid his suffering from the man who sat weeping like a woman beside him, and died.

It was Dan, his face blurred and swollen by crying, his usually darkened and subdued red hair proclaiming its curly nature in all the fierceness of its roseate hue—Dan, who at that moment would rather have been in any other place on earth—who received the bereaved mother, led her to the door of the death-chamber, and retired in miserable solitude to await the interview, to avoid which he would gladly have blown out his brains.

She came to him at last, a long, lean woman who had bent a stubborn back to many sorrows. A meek, unsubdued woman. The lankiness of limb, and the lankness of feature and hair, sufficiently pleasing in poor Ted, stretched forth at his long length yonder, were not such agreeable characteristics in the mother. Narrow face—narrow nature. In the thin features, contracted nostrils, close, small mouth, Dan might have read poor hope for Kitty.

"I have taken his jewellery," she said in her toneless voice. "I thought it best not to leave it about in a lodging-house. I miss a ring—a ring I gave him on his last birthday. Can you tell me where it is?"

She spread the watch, the chain, the sleeve-links, a certain pearl stud which Dan had noticed once or twice in his shirt when poor Gunton wore dress clothes, upon the table—all the poor, invaluable trifles which had lain on the drawers in that pathetic little heap bequeathed to the dead man's friend. "The ring is missing, you see," she said. She tied up the articles in a spare white handkerchief and slipped them into the pocket of her dress.

"Everything of his has become doubly precious to me," she said. "Perhaps you will be so good as to make inquiries about the ring."

Dan roused himself. Here was his opportunity. "I think the ring—" he began. "I think he gave the ring to Kitty, you know—the girl he was engaged to," he got out.

"Engaged?" the lady repeated. "My boy engaged—and without my knowledge!"

"We don't tell our mothers everything, I'm afraid," Dan said. He made a ghastly attempt to smile, to get back to his habitual easy manner which had forsaken him. "'Twouldn't be for our mothers' peace of mind—"

She interrupted him with cold dislike. "I know nothing of you and your mother," she said. "I know that there was perfect confidence between my son and me."

It was hard, after that, to tell her the story, but he told it, and saw her narrow face change from its frozen grieving to a still more frozen anger. She would not believe, or she affected not to believe, the story. A girl out of a little country shop to marry—her boy!

"You have no right to take away his character so, and he not here to defend himself!" she said. "He—I perceive that he has consorted with low company since he has been here; but he is a gentleman—my son, by birth and education."

"He was a gentleman," Dan said gently. Was—was? Ted was! Ted, who had been so alive, so "in it" in the jovial sense always—was! The word choked poor Dan, but he stumbled on, and told of the poor fellow's last charge to him, his last request to his mother.

Sometimes, in his confidential moments, Ted had spoken of this mother of his. "She is a good woman," he had said; "I suppose she never did, or said, or thought a wicked thing in her life."

She might be good, but she had now a heart as hard as the nether millstone. She did not choose to credit the story. She would not do her dear son's memory such an insult as to believe it. She looked with suspicion as well as dislike upon the poor friend with the rumpled red hair, with the fair skin, blurred and mottled, as such fair skins are wont to be, by his weeping. It was quite possible, she told herself in her miserable little wisdom, that he had made up the tale for his own ends. The hundred pounds was for himself, or at least he would share it. She would not believe; and presently she would hear no more.

"I must now really ask you to leave me alone," she said. "Your good feeling will show you that I have enough to bear."

"And you refuse to do this last thing poor Ted asked of you?" Dan said to her.

"I have no proof that he asked it," she answered.

And with that insult ringing in his ears, Dan went.

He pulled the door to upon him with a muttered oath on his lips; but he was not so enraged as another man would have been in his place. The "old girl" wasn't behaving well; but in Dan's experience, so many people did not behave well; and as it happened, the thing could be put right. If it had been yesterday, how helpless he would have been in the emergency! But old Playford's death had come just in the nick of time. As for himself and his chance—his last chance—well! He looked across at that other door behind which Ted lay. Ted and he had stuck together through ill report and good, had helped each other out of many a scrape, had had such good times!

Dan looked for a moment at the closed door, then stepped across the yard of matting and opened it.

Many a time he had run in without waiting for admission to his friend's lodgings, had pushed open the door to call a word to the young doctor, already gone to bed or not yet got up, perhaps. So, once more he opened the door far enough to admit his red head, and looked in. Ted was dead, he knew; but it takes time to reconcile us to the fact that the dead are also deaf, senseless, past grieving or comfort.

"It's all right, old man; don't you worry. I'll see to it," Dan said.

CARES OF A CURATE

"November 6th, 1901.

"... You were with me much down at H— in the spring, and saw many of the ins and outs of a certain affair then going on in which I was personally interested, and which took up a large portion of my time; and I think I owe it to you, Charles, to let you know how to all that foolishness there came a finish. This 'excellent bachelor' is not to be spoilt by matrimony. She wouldn't have me. And so on, and so on. I spare you all particulars, and you see that I am alive to tell the tale. It made things a little difficult at H—. I got away as soon as I could and met with another curacy in this place, and I write to you on the evening of my arrival. It looks a cheerful, pretty little spot, but I haven't shaken down yet, and thoughts of H—, and of last May when you were with me, keep turning up in my mind to-night.

"My vicar seems all right. I thought it very decent of him to meet me himself at the station. He apologised for having insisted on an answer to his written question—was I a confirmed bachelor? The ladies of the parish were in favour of a celibate curate, he said, and he himself did not want to be bothered by a man who would be getting married directly, and going away. I told him there would not be any fear of misdemeanour of that kind with me.

"He brought me on here—well no, he didn't, that was what I wished him to do. He took me to the vicarage and gave me tea. His daughter gave it, rather. You'd like the daughter. Not very young, and not pretending to be; filled with good sense, a practical, companionable sort of body. She, too, was good enough to approve my estate of confirmed bachelorhood. She said they had found things work so much pleasanter on these lines. The last three of her father's curates had been devoted to the single life. I asked, for the sake of conversation, what had become of them, and she told me, without the change of a muscle of her face, that they had married. The vicar awoke to the subject of our conversation here, and said that they had married his three other daughters.

"'Jessica is the only one left me now,' he said.

"'Jessica must always be left or what will become of you?' the sensible young woman said.

"A great many women would have felt it a little awkward, but she was quite unembarrassed. She very kindly put on her hat to show me the way to my rooms. Even came in, and sat talking for an hour. She said quite naturally that the best thing a woman got out of advancing years was the possibility of making of a man a friend. She is thirty-five, and isn't ashamed of the fact. Altogether a refreshing woman.

"My rooms are not like those at H—. Do you remember that evening in May when your sister had been on the river with the Hysopps, and she and Tom and the mother came in, and they brought Mary? The moon was on the water, and we would not have in the lamps, but sat and talked in that light. Well, there's no river here, and the moon doesn't shine, and there are one or two other things missing! But Mrs Bust, my landlady—what a name!—appears a decent sort, and to judge by my supper to-night, an excellent cook.

"By the way, every available jug and jar and glass is filled with chrysanthemums. No less than seven ladies, whose names she gave me, had brought up bunches during the day, Mrs Bust said.

"This really looks extremely kind of the people. I thought it such a pretty way of welcoming a stranger....

"26th November.

"I'm not in the least offended. Why should I be? I know, as you say, that lookers-on see most of the game, and I am sure that you are perfectly genuine in your advice. But I have had enough, thank you. It will last me my life. Besides, you are mistaken—she wouldn't. A girl like that with four hundred a year—I always knew the money was a bar—why should she? I've got no illusions about myself, as a rule. I was a fool ever to think it possible. Thank you—but don't say any more about it. I ask it as a favour. I have rolled a stone against that door, you understand. 'Want but a few things and complain of nothing' shall be my motto; and although at a certain time of my life I wanted a good deal, at least I won't complain.

"If only there were fewer women in the world! Fewer in B—, perhaps, would answer my purpose. The fact of my being a confirmed bachelor makes them feel safe with me, I suppose, but the fact is I can't stir for them, Charles; I stifle with them. I wish you'd run down and take some of the pressure off. I wish a few other good fellows would come and rescue me. Her mother said that Mary (the forbidden topic!) was not suited for a clergyman's wife, that she hated useful work. Perhaps that was why I liked her so much. She never bored me. These women—!

"They are as kind as angels. I'm going to run my pen through the above.

"I've got in a piano—you know my weakness for strumming? My landlady's daughter shares that weakness. I hear the piano begin before I reach the garden gate, I hear it shut with a bang as I come in at the door. Waltzes, played very quick, and galops with the loud pedal down and an impromptu bass. Her mother suggested to me that Cissy should come in and play to me in the evenings sometimes. I did not exactly jump at the offer, and Mrs Bust, to remove a possible objection in my mind, explained that of course she had not intended to leave her daughter alone with me; she herself could bring her sewing and chaperon her, she said.

"I am beginning to dread my meals because this good woman waits on me. I have begged to be allowed to pour out my own glass of beer and to reach my own salt-cellar. No use.

"Mrs Carter, an influential parishioner, living at a nice place called The Lawns (I haven't counted how many there are of them, but have noticed a few yards of grass-plot at the side of the house), said to me the other day that she believed I was a woman-hater. I had encountered fifteen of them at her house and was in a desperate mood. I said I was. I thought I was safe with Mrs Carter. I've met each one of that fifteen since, and she has in every case stopped to say to me—'Oh, I hear you're a woman-hater!' They all seemed to be mightily pleased. It put me in a stupid position. I managed to say something civil to each; but I have a bone to pick with Mrs Carter! She is always poking her fun at every one, and wants to know if I don't make an exception in favour of Jessica.

"Jessica!!

"She and I get on together, however. So we need; for she is an ardent worker in the parish, and morn and noon and dewy eve are she and I thrown together. Often, when I think to have an hour to myself for reading or writing, she comes to my room and sits over the fire with me, her petticoats carefully lifted, her feet on the fender—I am tempted to wish her at Jericho; but she is a good sort....

"5th December.

"Many thanks for your brilliant suggestion. Very thoughtful of you. Jessica is not in the least that kind of woman. She might have been married ten years ago if she had liked. She told me all about it. The last man who married the sister meant to have Jessica.

"I say, there's a tragedy, Charles! To feel as you do about the woman you want to marry, and to have to go through it with another!

"She's a splendid manager and organiser, and a devoted worker. She told me yesterday that if ever she did consent to marry it would have to be her father's curate; she would neither leave the parish nor her father, she said. A lot of women would have been embarrassed in saying that, and I can see the expression of your face as you read it. Spare your gibes. Jessica is miles above the ordinary tricks and wiles and falsities of women. You'd know it if you saw her. A stout, strong-looking young woman in thick boots and short skirts; a weather-beaten, serviceable being.

"It must have been for her sterling qualities those other men were in love with Jessica. All the same, dreadful, doubtless, to lose her.

"I note your news of H—. I have cut off all relations with that place. People there don't know where I am. Have forgotten that I exist, most likely. Do not trouble to send me any further information.

"Ah, my dear Charles! If I only might do my work for the next world after a manly fashion, as other men do the work of this! These women won't let me. They are in everything. They meddle and mar and make mischief. Half of the Fifteen (can you halve them?) are at loggerheads with the other half because of words I am reported to have said. They quarrel with each other, but, heaven help me! they won't quarrel with me. They make me perpetual presents, they ask me endless questions, they consult me in difficulties of their own ingenious making and always cropping up. Half of them have husbands they might go to, children to occupy their time. One is at least sixty—!

"A girl and her mother have been here to see me to-day. Mother indignant, girl in floods of tears. Some one of the Fifteen had said that the girl was 'running after' me. Me, with my thirty-eight years, my fortune of a hundred and fifty a year! Can't you see my blushes on the paper as I write it? Had her daughter by look, by word, by deed, done anything to deserve that cruel slander, the mother wanted to know? Then, was I not ashamed such things should be said? God knows I am ashamed, but what can I do? They are always saying such things one of another. How can I stop it?

"'You must not be so civil to them,' Jessica says.

"I assure her that without positive rudeness I can't be less civil than I am.

"'Then, be rude to them,' counsels Jessica.

"How can one man, standing alone, immersed in rummage sales, parish concerts, mothers' meetings, school teas, and other feminine functions, be rude to Fifteen women at once? Between you and me, I have tried it, in my desperation, in individual cases, and it has no effect. I have discovered you can't please a woman better than to bully her.

"'You must marry Jessica,' Mrs Carter says. 'Married to Jessica you will find yourself a mere man, a very ordinary person.'

"'I should want an extraordinary nerve to do it,' I was on the point of saying, but remembered in time how she had reported me to the Fifteen. The pulpit is becoming the only place where I can enjoy the luxury of free speech. Words spoken in any less public place are brought back to me distorted past recognition.

"Heigho! I am always grumbling. As a fact, people put themselves out in the most flattering manner to be kind to me; I suppose I am as comfortable here as I should be in any place after H—.

"Little Cissy Bust found out that I was fond of flowers. Since then she pulls off a chrysanthemum every morning from the plant in her mother's window, and lays it beside my plate. Sweet of the little thing, but I watch with dismay the blooms lessening on the maternal plant. The mother is a good sort, in her way, but as I've been working in it all day I don't care to be bothered with the tittle-tattle of the parish when I come home at night. She is always bringing me delicacies off her own table. I have to eat them, because she stops to see me do it....

"19th December.

"How many afternoon tea-cloths have I had given me since I came, Charles? Guess.

"Nine. I haven't the smallest use for one of them. I never get the chance of having tea at home in the afternoon, being always under the obligation to eat muffins in this lady's house or that. Jessica came in through wind and rain one day and said she'd like to have a cup. Here seemed my opportunity. I showed her the nine and facetiously asked her to choose; or should I spread them all at once? She always has too much in hand to stop to jest over trifles; she waved the tea-cloths aside, and seized her cup off Mrs Bust's tray, and went on talking shop. I don't want to decry Jessica. She's worth all the rest put together. While they gabble, she does things. If Mrs Carter (who hates the sight of her, by the way) and the rest of them would only let us alone!

"So the engagement at H— is broken off! It must be a blow to poor Holt, but I never thought him suited to her. Who is, I wonder? What a madness it was to think that she and I could pull together. Imagine that little teasing, irresponsible child in such a box as this, bored to death by these interminable women! For all her naughtiness and her folly she was wiser than I. But I am wiser now.

"Of course, if you hear of any fresh engagements or new freaks of the young lady, you will let me know at once.

"Mrs Bust was insolent about that cup of tea. I greatly hope Jessica did not notice the way she banged the tray down. She said afterwards that no single lady should come to a single gentleman's rooms, let alone take a meal with him. If there were other rooms to be had I would not put up with this creature. My dear Charles, I'm getting to be, in reality, what I've had the credit for being all along—a woman-hater.

"I go a good bit to Mrs Carter's. Her house is comfortable, and she is an amusing creature. Sees jokes, and cheers one up. She teases me about my beset condition, and tries to get me to say things. She calls me Job, and the Fifteen my comforters. Neither witty nor appropriate, but it pleases Mrs Carter. She says the least I can do is to give the nine donors of the nine tea-cloths tea. I frankly told her of the difficulty with Bust, who is inexorable on the matter of etiquette. It will be all right if she comes, Mrs Carter says. She is so set on it, I've had to give in. I've asked them. They're coming on Thursday.

"Oh, my dear old man, how my head aches!

"Mrs Carter keeps sending me up chickens, jellies, game, and things. She says I've shrunk three stone since I came. It's love, she says, and I shan't be all right till I'm married to Jessica.

"What rot women talk!

"Can this be true? She declares to me that the vicar told her in confidence he would soon be losing his daughter from his house, if not from his parish.

"You see the inference. There is not another even faintly eligible bachelor in the whole charming place. (Use your own epithet in place of the underlined word. I should rather like to hear you do it).

"I said, straight out, she had no business to repeat to me what, however silly, had been said in her private ear. She was quite unimpressed. 'In such a place as this what should we do if we did not repeat things?' she asked.

"She told me, as a huge joke, that her husband had overheard the servants saying she called me by my Christian name! Carter went to her for an explanation. No doubt she had chosen to call me 'Job,' or some nonsense of the kind, when the servants were in the room. She's delighted, and says Carter was quite annoyed.

"He's about the only Man in the woman-ridden place; after this I shall be ashamed to look him in the face.

"When Mrs Bust was taking away my supper to-night she requested me not in future to speak to her daughter as 'Cissy.' It was so very marked. I was not in the mood to receive the rebuff calmly, and she simmered down. Young girls got such strange ideas in their heads, she said. It was better not to be too familiar!

"Poor little Cissy, aged sixteen, and her flower on my plate! I've had a certain pleasure in that unfailing mark of a little girl's goodwill; but to receive a flower from Miss Bust! I shall hurl it into the coal-box in the morning....

"2nd January 1902.

"You harp a great deal on one string, old man. I know you mean it kindly, I know you'd like to see things put right for me in that quarter, but do believe I've had enough. I don't pretend—to you—it was a pleasant experience. I won't deny it was a nasty knock—but it's over, and Richard's himself again.

"You ask about the tea. Oh, well, there was no tea. At the last minute Mrs Bust refused to make tea for Mrs Carter. To the other nine she did not actively object—safety in numbers, I suppose—but Mrs Carter, it seems, had asked her during the progress of my last cold if she had neglected to air the sheets for my room. Such impertinence from any woman no lady could suffer, Mrs Bust informed me. Into her house Mrs Carter shall never set foot again. Seeing that I had laid in the cakes and sweeties and rubbish for the tea she suggested that she herself and Cissy should be of the company. In that case the most particular, she assured me, would have nothing to get hold of. I scrupled not to make plain to her that her plan did not commend itself to me.

"Mrs Carter is delighted, and tells the story, with additions, everywhere. She asked the nine to her own house and I had to show up. Carter was to have come home but of course he didn't. Small blame to him. By the way, he has become positively uncivil to me lately. In my hearing, the other night, he said something about the clergy 'for ever smothered with women's petticoats, and with their feet under better men's tables.' I have liked Carter hitherto, and shall have it out with him when I get the chance.

"You see, Charles, that girl fooled me thoroughly. I thought she liked me. You thought it yourself; you said so. I thought she meant me to know she liked. She is so young, so pretty, so rich in everything the world holds of value. If I had not fancied encouragement I never should have made the attempt. To come down such a crusher! Perhaps what you say is right. She may seem to think kindly of me now, she may even have spoken to your sister of the episode as you say; but let me put myself in the same place again and the same thing would happen. I'm not blaming her. God knows I don't blame her. I blame myself for being a blind ass. I hope she'll be happy, poor little girl. I want her to be. With all her irresponsibleness and her outside naughtiness and frivolity, her carelessness of men's feelings, her nonsense, and her teasing, pretty ways, I know that she is good at heart, sound, and sane and sweet. I want her to be happy!

"There is a girl among my Fifteen—she is quite young and has to be protected against herself. She has haunted me. When I got home she would be lurking in the dark of the road, when I went out I met her coming round the corner. Notes in her childish scrawl have fallen on me, thick as autumn leaves. I have had to see her mother at length. Mother, for my pains, told me roundly I was not a gentleman. I declare to you she abused me like a pickpocket, Charles.

"But this silly child had the excuse of youth. There is another of nearly three times her age to whom I had thought it safe to be civil. Well, it wasn't. She pursued me even within my own strong-hold, the pulpit. In a moment's weakness I had owned to her that I liked violets—pah! I am sick of the scent of them now. On Sunday morning I found a bunch of them, done up after a well-known fashion, with dried maiden-hair as a background, laid beside the pulpit cushion. I had good reason to know from whence it came. I said to her when she waylaid me on my homeward course that the woman who cleaned the church would have to be reprimanded. She had let fall a bunch of flowers from her frowsy dress upon the pulpit desk and had left them there. An unpardonable piece of negligence.

"'I thought you liked violets?' the foolish old woman said, looking ashamed; and I told her hardily that I loathed the sight of them and hoped never to look upon one again.

"This all seems only laughable to you. I can hear you snigger over it—and me! Laugh at me, but don't hate me as I do myself. A man nearing forty years of age, not particularly anything—either clever, or eloquent, or good-looking, or attractive. Don't I know it all? I can't write of it—

"And yet this one thing more I must tell you before I close.

"As I parted from the sensible, self-respecting, self-contained Jessica the other day—I protest to you my reliance on her womanly dignity and sturdy reasonableness has been to me as the shadow of a great rock in a weary land—I ran against her father, the old vicar. He put his hand on my shoulder, and looked at me with a kind of playful reproof in the face.

"'Ah, how long is this shilly-shallying to go on?' he asked.

"... I broke off there to see Mrs Carter. It has hitherto been a relief to see her. The only laughing I've done since I've been here has been with her. She did not laugh to-day. She came to me because she had no other friend, she said. She could not trust the gabbling womankind. Her husband had changed to her. He had become all at once unreasonable and unkind. He had told her that he did not trust her. He would no longer allow her to go to church, he had forbidden her to receive me again in his house.

"In utter bewilderment I could only ask her why. And then she burst into tears, and then—then there was another scene.

"Mrs Bust was no doubt listening at the door. At any rate she burst in upon us. I, for my part, was not sorry, but poor Mrs Carter—! Poor? Fool, idiot!

"She is forty years of age, her husband is a decent, honourable sort of fellow who worships her—

"That finishes the Carter friendship.

"If it were not for Jessica—good, matter-of-fact, reliable Jessica, welcome contrast to these hysterical, half-mad women, who laugh at and despise her—where should I be, Charles?...

"1st February.

"You have been a true friend to me and to her. I shall see you soon (D.V.), and then no doubt I shall say—nothing. But you will remember that I am grateful to you to the last drop of my heart's blood—and so is she.

"Now as for B.... The finish has come; it came to-day. Let us sing and give thanks with the best member that we have! All the same, the end has been a shock, and I wish it had come in some other way.

"She came in here at eleven this morning. You know who—Jessica. I thought she came to talk over last night's concert. It was a failure. The room was as empty as the church has been of late. Those—women (my cloth prohibits me from supplying the adjective, Charles. I leave it with satisfaction in your hands) with their gabble have robbed me of my last shred of character. I assure you I am regarded as a libertine in the place—a professional breaker of hearts, a Don Juan bragging of my conquests! Each of those Fifteen has her own tale to tell of her own wrongs and of my deceit. They hold indignation meetings in Mrs Carter's house. I shouldn't care the value of one of their hairpins, but one does not like to see the church empty; and it is not agreeable, having gone to the bother of getting up a concert, to sing to empty benches. It was not, however, to talk over the concert she had come.

"She had come to tell me she thought it would be better for us thoroughly to understand each other. I said I thought we had done so from the first. She told me she hoped so, but that we were going to speak out plainly now. She despised the underhand methods of other women, she said, and when she wanted to know a thing she went to the person capable of giving an answer and asked a direct question.

"Then she asked me, 'Did I mean to make her an offer of marriage?'

"In so many words she asked me, and never flinched.

"And I didn't flinch. I was so indignant, so outraged!

"'No!' I said.

"I hope I did not shout the word, but the room seemed to echo with it, somehow.

"'You mean that?' she asked; and I said that I meant it fervently.

"She got up and went to the door. There she waited, her hands in her coat-pockets, staring at the door. 'Of course you know that you have behaved disgracefully?' she said. 'I should never have trusted myself so much in your society but that I believed you to be an honourable man. I find you are not. If my father were younger he would punish you as you deserve. As it is—.'

"As it is, thank goodness, she went. Where's the good of bothering you with more of her invective?

"And I am going; to make room for another curate—another confirmed bachelor.

"She did not spare me of course. Among other agreeable things she said that I was a heartless Brute, and she hoped I should get what I deserved.

"I shall get a lot more than I deserve, between you and me, Charles. For, thanks to you and your pegging away, I wrote and asked little Mary once again if she would have me.

"And a letter has come from her this blessed morning to say that she will...."

MARY E. MANN – A CONCISE BIBLIOGRAPHY

The Parish of Hilby
The Eglamore Portraits
Rose at Honeypot
The Pattem Experiment
Olivia's Summer
A Lost Estate
The Parish Nurse
Gran'ma's Jane

Mrs Peter Howard
One Another's Burdens
Moonlight
The Mating of a Dove
The Fields of Dulditch
Among the Syringas
Susannah
The Cedar Star
A Sheaf of Corn
Mrs Day's Daughters
The Patten Experiment
Ben Pitcher's Elly (Short story)
Dora o' the Ringolets (Short story)
The Lost Housen (Short story)
Little Brother (Short story)